Bwembya's Mother

PATRICIA KASENGELE

A catalogue record for this book is available from the National Library of Australia

Publisher:
ASPG (Australian Self Publishing Group)
P.O. Box 159, Calwell, ACT Australia 2905
Email: publishaspg@gmail.com
http://www.inspiringpublishers.com

National Library of Australia Cataloguing-in-Publication entry

Author: Kasengele, Patricia

Title: **BWEMBYA'S MOTHER**/Patricia Kasengele

ISBN: 978-1-922920-25-6

Cover Picture: Picture taken by Patricia Kasengele August 2019 - Nelson Bay, NSW Australia

Disclaimer:
This book is written from my memories of my life to the best of my recollection.
It is also written using my diaries, copies of medical reports and files.

For Bwembya
Loving You Always
Mum

✦

Chapter 1

I never thought it would make a big difference in my life if I got married and had a child. I did not feel like I had to be married or have a child to fulfill my destiny. I was okay with the idea that I may not become a wife or a mother. I grew up around wonderful strong independent women who were married, not married, had children, did not have children and they seemed content. Women who made a difference to their families, their communities and to the world, women whose lives mattered. But I did get married and have children. My first-born child was called Bwembya. In our Bemba tradition, I then became known as Bana Bwembya, which means 'mother of Bwembya'. When I migrated to Australia, I found myself being called Bwembya's mother, a lot. At my son's childcare, schools, after school, vacation care, hospitals. I have been known as Bwembya's mother for thirty-five years. I learnt that having a child made a big difference in my life, just not in the way I would have imagined.

I was a quiet, shy, introverted young seventeen-year-old when I finished high school. I had dreams. Big dreams. I was going to be a lawyer and work at the International Court of Justice in The Hague. I was going to change the world or at least change people's lives. These dreams seemed like a lifetime away and quite different from the life I live now. I could never have imagined I would be where I am today. I thought that at this time in my life I would be living in a large house in Zambia, have a great stereo system, a high-flying job such as general manager of some non-government organisation after a stint in The Hague, and of course I'd be driving a Mercedes Benz. Simple achievable dreams!

I was born in a community clinic, in a small mining town called Mufulira in August 1960, the third child of six children in the Mfula family. My father, Jason, was a supervisor in charge of children and adult education for Africans at the Mufulira Copper Mines. Martha, my mum, was an instructor at a women's welfare centre. Both my parents had a teaching background. They were trailblazers. In 1965, Mum was one of the few Zambian women who could not only drive but had her own car, a little white mini cooper. Zambia was a British colony until October 1964.

Everywhere you looked there were remnants of colonial rule. The large sunlit bungalows, the tree-lined suburban streets, the cricket clubs, tennis clubs, golf clubs, cinemas, and public swimming pools. The streets were lined with huge Jacaranda trees. The bottom part of the tree trunks was painted white. One row of the stones lining the street was also painted white. Beneath these trees sat women selling food and drinks. Local barbers set up shop under the trees to cut the hair of men and boys. For many years, even when we moved to another town, my dad and my brothers got their hair cut under those trees.

Every morning, we woke up to the sound of a loud siren at six. The first siren signalled the start of the first shift of the day and the end of the night shift for the miners at the mine. There was a siren at midday and at six in the afternoon to signal the other change of shifts. As you drove through the small town, you would see men dressed in navy blue overalls and their different coloured hard hats going to and from the mines. In the air, there was a distinct strong smell of what the locals called 'senta'. The smell was like sulphur, and it came from the smelters in the mines.

I started school in January 1966. My uniform was a checked cotton green and white dress, with a white, round-edged collar, a green sweater, white socks, and brown leather shoes with a buckled strap across the front. I had a brown bookcase. My brothers, Reginald and Hector, had white shirts, green V-neck sweaters, grey shorts, grey knee-length socks with two green strips at the top and brown lace-up leather shoes. The boys had brown leather satchels on their backs.

Mum reminded us that we were in the first group of Black kids going to what was previously an all-white school. My brothers had been going to a non-white school and were now transferring to a new school. My parents were very anxious about what kind of a day we would have and whether we would come home safely. My older brother was told to look after me and he held my hand as we walked into the school grounds. I had a normal child's experience on their first day at school. I had no idea of the significance of this day for Black families like ours. I grew up with no memory of segregation between Black and white people.

I have a few distinct memories of early childhood. I remember being surprised to see a Black Santa when I was about five and how my brothers and I talked about it for days. His voice sounded like Dad's voice, but it was Santa, right? He had the red suit, the black boots, and the long white beard. And he did bring presents. He must have been Santa. I also remember the day my sister, Bwalya, was born the day before my fifth birthday. My dream of having a sister came true. I had been crossing my fingers all day when I was told Mum had gone to hospital to have a baby. I was the only girl stuck between the four boys. Reginald (Reggie) was eight years old, Hector (Heckie) seven years, I was five years old, Kenneth (Kenny) four years, and James three years old.

Near the end of 1966, we moved to Kitwe where my dad got a job as the liaison officer at Mindolo Ecumenical Centre. Mum also got a job teaching at the Women's Training Centre which was one of the programs at Mindolo. Dad was the director of Mindolo from 1971 to 1983. We lived at Mindolo from 1966 to 1983. Mindolo was a pan-African training centre founded in 1958. An interdenominational centre for people from different faiths and backgrounds providing programs such as women's leadership, youth leadership, agriculture, industry, and commerce. The campus is situated about seven kilometres from the city centre in Kitwe.

There were families from countries such as Zambia, Zimbabwe, Sudan, Sri Lanka, USA, Canada, England, Germany, Denmark, France, South Africa, Namibia, Botswana, Ethiopia, Kenya, Uganda, Sierra Leone, Malawi, Somalia, New Zealand, and Congo. We got to experience different customs and traditions from the families we lived with. We learnt to celebrate things like Guy Fawkes Night, Halloween, Thanksgiving. To eat foods like cowboy cookies, brownies, sloppy joes, Indian curries, and cottage pies. We were given a different view of the world, a broader, more enriched view.

The campus had tennis courts, a football field, a netball field, and a swimming pool. Often in the afternoons you could see a group of children walking around the campus involved in different activities. On hot days we would be at the pool at the top end of the campus, racing each other and causing a splash. We could be chasing butterflies with nets, catching tadpoles from the little ponds in front of the library, picking wildflowers from the grass area across the lake that looked like no man's land. The lake was near the middle of the campus with a small island in the middle. The lake provided many activities such as swimming, rowing boats, and fishing. There were potluck dinners by the lake, where each family brought a dish that was shared with everyone. Candles in brown bags were put on the water to light up the night. That was a spectacular sight. On Christmas eve, we had carols by candlelight. We sang carols and walked around the campus and ended up by the lake where tea and cakes were laid on tables outside the main dining room. At the little chapel near the back of the campus, there would be a nativity scene with men, women, and a baby in a manger. The children at Mindolo would sometimes put on Christmas plays with the help of a few creative parents.

Children were always in each other's houses. It was not unusual that if we asked Mum for a friend to sleep over, we would get a few knocks at the door in the evening and there would be mums or dads dropping off their kids in their pyjamas with their sleeping bags. 'Martha, we heard there was a sleepover happening here, so the kids wanted to come, too.' My mum with a genuine smile on her face would open the door and the kids would all pile into the living room where there would often be a fire. Mum never stressed. For dinner, we'd have whatever there was enough of to feed all the kids. Scrambled eggs, or baked beans on toast, soup, or hotdogs, followed by Milo or cocoa and biscuits or her fabulous scones. After dinner, one of our older cousins told us stories, usually ghost stories that would leave us screaming at shadows. Sometimes, my brother Heckie would hang glow-in-the-dark spiders and bats from the ceiling. He also had a black suit that had a glow-in-the-dark skeleton imprinted on the front. He would jump out of doorways to scare us silly.

There were families who did not live on campus who had great sleep-overs and pool parties. My brothers Reggie and Heckie would often be invited by one of these families, and I would be invited too, even though all the kids there were older than me. I think I was invited because most of the kids were boys, and there was only one girl in that age group. It was probably just to try and balance the numbers. The older kids all seemed very confident and self-assured. I would hang out with everyone by the pool, and they would be busy having races and trying to outdo each other. I could swim well, but I would sit quietly by the shallow end, at the edge of the pool with my feet dangling in the water. I was told to keep score, but my brother Heckie would notice me by the sidelines and get me involved in a game where I could keep up like tossing a beach ball to me or racing me, although he would always win - like really win, he'd swim two laps to my one.

We also had great times at home - especially when our parents were away. We did simple things like dancing in the rain. One rainy Saturday morning, I heard the rain on the tin roof that covered the veranda and looked outside through the glass sliding doors in the living room and saw that the big grey empty oil drum that stood outside was filling up with water. The drum was half under cover and half in the open. My sister and I looked at each other and ran into our room to change into our swimming costumes. I called out to the boys who were listening to music in their room, 'Hey, you guys, the drum is filling up. We are going out to play in the rain. Are you coming?' We often did this when it was raining. There'd be a flurry of movement as we all rushed to change into our swimming costumes.

In my blue and white stripped swimming costume, I ran onto the veranda to the edge where the roof stopped. Large cold drops of rain hit my warm brown skin and I screamed. 'Ahh!' The rain ran down from my head to my toes, and I was completely soaked in a couple of minutes. I heard screams all around me as my sister and brothers joined me. I splashed my sister with water from the drum. Soon we were all running around splashing each other and having a lot of fun. But all the fun would suddenly stop when we heard the crunch of wheels on the gravel at the side of the house. Our parents were back.

It was at Mindolo that I met one of my closest friends Beatrice. Our backyards were separated by a hedge which had a space between where our sugarcane grew, and their guava trees stood. We became inseparable for many years until her family moved to a farm in a regional area of Zambia. Beatrice and I remain close friends. We often talk about the wonderful childhood we had at Mindolo. Our children roll their eyes when they listen to us reminiscing. My girls particularly do this because when my husband Mwango and I took them to Mindolo, things were not as I had described them. The big lake, the numerous steps near the library, and the falls near the dam looked so much smaller than what I remember and had been describing for years. I did not feel so bad when we went to Chingola, where Mwango grew up, as things seemed to have shrunk there, too – especially the rugby and cricket fields, the big swimming pool, and the former big house where he grew up in.

My parents had an open, welcoming home. Our house was always filled with people. People who were related to us, who were friends, friends of friends, acquaintances, and strangers. We would be walking around campus and see a person with a suitcase walking down the long road from the main road to town and everyone would bet they were going to our house. Nine times out of ten they were. I found it peculiar that there would be people who were visiting their children in Kitwe but came to stay at our house. Dad would take them to visit their family at lunch time and pick them up after work. There was always one or two people who were not immediate family living with us. My parents took on young people and put them through school and sometimes college. I grew up in an environment surrounded by people.

When Mwango and I got married, we also had people coming to our house to visit, sleep over or live with us for short or extended periods. During our first year of marriage, we had a person we did not know knock at our door and stay overnight. We showed him the spare room, had dinner with him, watched TV until he said he was tired and needed to go to sleep. When he left the room, I turned to Mwango and said, 'Honey, who is that?'

He looked at me puzzled and said, 'I thought you knew who he was. I do not know that man. Isn't he one of your relatives?'

'No. I thought he was related to you', I replied.

We had an uneasy sleep that night. At breakfast during our conversation, the visitor mentioned Bana Mpundu (which means mother of twins). He was talking about Mwango's mum, who was Bana Mpundu. It was a relief to realise that he was not a stranger after all.

My parents were kind, respectful, and generous to people from all walks of life, wherever they were. I grew up learning to be kind and respectful to other people. I saw their acts of kindness, the way they lived their lives in service of other people. Despite the high positions my parents held at work or in the community, they remained humble people. My mum once met a Japanese man who seemed alone at a dinner they went to, and she invited him over for a meal to our house. A lifelong friendship started that day. He and my dad are still in contact. My dad was a giver. He would give away the last money in his wallet and then have no money for food. You had to live with my dad to understand.

On a visit to Zambia to attend a memorial for my mum at Chipili, the village where my dad lived, Mwango came into the bedroom after spending the day outside in the rotunda with Dad. 'Honey, your dad is a really interesting man. The whole day I have watched people coming to talk to him and get counsel. A lot of people asked for money for children's school fees, transport to go to a funeral, for food and other things. He gave all the money he had out of his wallet and then sent someone with a withdrawal slip to the bank in Mansa to get some money for someone who came after all the money ran out.'

During this trip to Chipili on a sunny bright morning in May 2016, I walked down a sandy winding path that seemed to be part of the wild bushy forest that surrounded the graveyard behind the church. It was the end of the rainy season in Zambia, and everything was green and fresh. It had been raining less than half an hour ago while we were inside the church. The rain was so heavy I thought we would all be soaked through as we left the church, and we had not brought our umbrellas – but it stopped as suddenly as it had started just before we sang the last hymn. I left the church before everyone else followed by my sister Bwalya and Mwango. Mwango held my hand as we negotiated the sandy rocky path to where there was a break in the trees. This area had been cleared of trees and there were six graves with room for another six. Other graves were scattered in between the tall leafy trees. You could make out the tombstones on the few graves that had them.

I looked around at the quiet peaceful trees that surrounded the clearing. The sunlight threw darts of light through the trees. Drops of water glistened on the wet leaves as sunlight reflected off them. I could feel the heat of the sun on my face and hear birds chirping in the distance. This was not like any graveyard I had been to before. I had not expected to feel at ease about being there. As we stood at the edge of the clearing, I heard the crowd of people who had been in the church coming down towards us. They were singing a hymn, but it was a hymn I did not know. It was cheerful, not mournful. I guess it was a memorial, not a funeral. A time to remember, not to cry.

Mum, you were so special, I thought as tears filled my eyes. I knew you were gone but being here where you lived most of your life made it real. You were always there for me. Listening to me when I talked to you. Providing counsel, wiping my forehead when I was sick. I smiled when I remembered how you rubbed Vicks or Tiger Balm on my face after a hot bath to help ease the massive headache I had when we were in Sydney. It was painful and made my eyes water, but it worked. Listening to people in church talk about what you meant to them surprised me. I learnt things I did not know about the work you had been doing in Chipili, the programs you championed for women, the impact you made, and how you were missed.

I closed my eyes to try to shut out the grief when I heard someone crying. No, not crying, wailing. Grief-stricken wailing. I opened my eyes and looked around to see who was wailing. There was a man standing on a rock a few metres away from where I stood. I could not tell how old he was. His clothes were almost black. Not just black in colour but black from not being washed. His hair was a huge tangle that looked like it had never seen a comb. He looked like a homeless person. Why was he calling out for my mum and wailing? Who was he? Everyone ignored him and stood a few metres away from him. He ignored everyone too and just continued to wail.

My cousin Mulenga saw me watching this man. I whispered, 'Who is he?' Mulenga answered, 'He is just some crazy person that Mum used to give food to when he would come begging. Mum would tell us to give him a towel, soap, a set of clean clothes and take him to the bathroom. Then when he had bathed and changed, she would give him some food to eat and some food to take with him when he left. Mum was the only person in the village who would even talk to him. Everybody else thinks he is crazy and chases him away if he comes near them.' I realised I was not the only person who would miss my mum.

We walked back to the house after the prayers, hymns, and laying of flowers on the grave. Mwango and I had travelled back to Zambia for the first anniversary of Mum's passing away. I had not been able to go to the funeral the year before because I had been too unwell to travel. The house seemed light and airy, like Mum was just in the other room. I had thought everything would look and feel different, but it did not. Everything was in its place.

The house was clean and exactly how Mum always had it, neat and tidy. The towels were laid out at the end of our beds with the windows flung wide open. I was home. Things had changed but things had stayed the same. Mum was in the house, even if she was not physically there. Mulenga had been helping her in the house as a housekeeper and continued to look after the house and maintain it in the way Mum had trained her to.

We were sitting in the living room after the memorial service, having lunch. The crowd from the church were enjoying the buffet laid out on the veranda. It had been a long day with hundreds of people attending the church service. I was amazed. I had expected a small family service, but my parents did not do things in small measures. Maybe that is where I get my tendency to make big things out of small things. There were four fine choirs in the church that almost seemed to be having a singing competition.

Mulenga walked into the room and handed me a red velvet jewellery box that had belonged to Mum. The box was quite old. Some of the fluff had rubbed and were bald spots on the lid. I took it, surprised but grateful to receive it. 'Mum gave this to me to give to you when the time came,' Mulenga said. I opened the box and the first thing I saw was a silver brooch with a large pink stone in the middle. I don't think the stone was anything special, but it gave a little glow that reflected on the silver around it, making it seem like there were more pink-coloured stones when there was just the one. A bit like my mum, I thought. A simple woman whose warmth radiated, spreading a glow to those around her.

The brooch was one of Mum's favourite brooches, but it was rarely out of the box. I thought of all the times as a little girl that

I had sat on the stool at the dressing table in my parents' room and Mum had let me look at and touch her jewellery. How I had wanted to grow up and put on her jewellery! Mum did not wear a lot of jewellery, except for earrings, which she wore all the time. I do not wear a lot of jewellery, but I always wear earrings. She would, however, wear jewellery on special occasions, just like I do. There was also a string of fine and delicate pearls in the jewellery box which I had not seen her wear for a long time. And there was a pair of teardrop pearl earrings and a brooch with five brown stones on it. I never thought I was like my mum, but the simple items in the jewellery box told a different story.

Like her, I have an understated simple elegance, and am comfortable in my skin. Or so I like to think. I like to think I inherited my beautiful mother's ability to wear a fur coat with a pair of Big W comfortable flat shoes, and at the same time to be able to dine with prime ministers. She believed in education for women and championed it her whole life. She was always learning something, even if it was only a new way of cooking. I learnt from her to be fiercely independent, although she told me once that I had taken it a bit too far. Far enough for it to be a detriment, she said. I like to be in charge of my life, to pay my own bills and buy my own cars and sell them when I felt like it. There was a time I had three cars in twelve months. I sold a car, bought a new car, was not happy with it, sold it and bought another car. Mwango just shook his head and laughed. My husband would have given me the world if I had asked for it, but I never did.

I tried to explain to my mum that I wanted to be able to live like I was alone, so that if I was ever alone, I would be alright. I had grown up seeing women being divorced or widowed and

I saw how the world could change in one breath. How one moment your life could be going very well, then suddenly it was not and you could be left in a financial mess. I knew my husband loved me a lot, but I also knew that just because he loved me did not mean things could not change. I have watched friends have an anniversary party where the husband got down on his knees and proclaimed undying love, but within a month their marriage was over.

My mum was a woman of faith but did not force it down anyone's throat. She carried her faith like a shield of armour – for protection, not for aggression. She believed in the power of prayer and passed that belief on to me. Having faith is not believing that what you want will happen, it is believing in what you cannot always see, that there is a bigger picture – and trusting that things happen for a reason. Over the years I have looked back at situations I thought should have gone one way and realised that if they had I would not have had the opportunities I had later.

Our parents loved us unconditionally and we grew up knowing that whatever we did they would love us. When we got bad grades or failed classes, it was never a big deal, it was just business as usual. Such patience and understanding. They did not spoil us but let us try to fly, even when we fell flat on our faces and bruised our egos. But despite their relaxed attitude they were strict on certain things: we had to make our beds when we were old enough to do so. We had to keep our room clean, take our plate to the kitchen after meals and do our chores, which increased as we got older. We had to be home for meals, go to school, be where we were supposed to be, and be respectful. If we misbehaved, we got punished or smacked. This was a normal part of our childhood. We just had to make sure we did not misbehave or get caught.

Punishments and spankings were not frequent, you had to be pushing your luck to get into that kind of trouble. Dad would just raise his voice. It sounded like the roar of a lion. He would start slow and loud and then get louder and louder. That usually stopped us in our tracks. In the evening, when we were all watching TV in the living room, Dad would not need to tell us to go to bed. He would slowly lift his hand to look at his watch and look up. We would all get up and leave the living room without a word. Mum usually gave a warning. The look. She would glance at you from the corner of her eye and if you did not change your behaviour, she would raise her eyebrow and finally turn her head to face you and nod her head while she closed her eyes. That was the final warning!

When my brother Heckie was in his teens, he took the family car for a joyride while my parents were away. He crashed the car, parked it back in the garage and put the keys back. When my parents noticed the large dent in the car, we were called to the living room and asked who had smashed the car. Hector answered, 'It was me, I thought you knew.' We all tensed up thinking he had gone too far this time. Dad got up and walked out of the room and never mentioned the smashed car again. This was not a one off. Hector crashed Mum's car years later in Canberra. My parents were more concerned that he was ok. It was just a car.

My dad spoilt me a little, just a little. Especially when I was very young. When I was about five years old, I got a special treat. It was early afternoon. Dad opened the car door to let me out. It was the first time I had gone to the office with him.

I would usually be having an afternoon nap after lunch, but on that day, Dad said I could go with him. My four brothers wanted to come with us, but Dad shook his head and said, 'Today is Patricia's turn to come with me on her own. You boys are staying at home.' Holding my hand, we walked through the long, wide glass doors that made a swooshing sound as they opened to let us in. A lady at a long table gave me a big smile and a little wave as she continued to talk on the phone. The room was big, with lots of soft comfortable-looking chairs and low wooden coffee tables. The floor was made of lots of wooden rectangles like the ones on the floor at home. There were pictures on the wall and flowers in vases near the windows. Dad gave the lady a little nod and we continued to walk down a long corridor.

He led me through a door and said, 'Here we are. This is my office.'

The dark green carpet was soft and spongy. Dad sat at his huge wooden desk in the corner of the room and started to talk to someone on the phone. I sat on the carpet near the front of the desk and put the bag with my toys on the floor next to me. I unpacked my toys and wriggled under the big wooden desk, pulling my dolls and tea set with me. I looked at the pair of shiny black leather men's shoes on the floor in front of me and placed the tea set between the shoes. I resisted the urge to touch the shiny shoes to see if there was any dust on them. I wanted to untie the shoelaces and see if I could tie them by myself, but I decided to just play with my toys.

I hummed softly to myself so as not to disturb the conversation and get the shushing I usually got when I talked and interrupted adult conversation. Mum usually just had to give me that look that needed no words. I continued to play with my toys and had a little tea party, ignoring everything going on around me, lost in my own little world. Much later, I heard the door open, and a voice saying, 'Jason, it is five o' clock, I am leaving now. Will there be anything I can do before I go?'

'No. Go ahead and go. I will be leaving shortly. Goodbye and see you tomorrow.' The black shoes moved, almost knocking over my tea set. A face appeared under the table and Dad said, 'Time to go home.'

From my dad I got to love music and taking long rides in the car. He liked to listen to different types of music. Local musicians and international musicians. He would be playing Kalindula, which is music that originated from the Luapula Province where he came from. He also listened to Jim Reeves, the Carpenters and to classical music. I remember him taking me and Beatrice to watch Miriam Makeba. I was not old enough to know who she was, but I loved going into the hotel, sitting at a table, having a meal, and listening to great music. It was only later when I was older and saw Miriam Makeba on the Cosby's that I understood that she was someone great, and how lucky we were to have seen her in concert. Miriam Makeba was a South African singer-songwriter who sang Afropop, jazz, and world music. She was also an actress, a civil rights activist, and a United Nations goodwill ambassador.

Dad liked to take drives in the car especially after a long day at work. He would pile us in the car, and we would drive to a little bakery in the middle of town in Kitwe or to a suburb called Parklands where there was a shopping centre. He would buy a few loaves of fresh bread and let us eat one loaf in the car. We would tear off the top of the loaf and pull out the soft white bread inside the crust and eat it. The car would be covered with breadcrumbs, but nobody seemed to care because we were having fun.

He taught us to be true to ourselves, to have a sense of pride and integrity. When I was in high school, I got myself a job at the library in Mindolo. I talked to the librarian and negotiated a job in the school holidays. Pay day came and all the library staff gathered to get their pay. Envelopes of money or cheques were handed out to everyone but me. The head librarian called me aside.

'Patricia, can I have a word with you?' I followed her into her office.

She turned to me and said, 'There is no pay packet for you because as you know, your father told me you would be working in a voluntary capacity. Thank you for your good work, you are doing a great job.'

At dinner that night, Dad explained. 'Patricia. I told the librarian not to pay you as it would not look good that the child of the director is getting paid to work at a place where her father is the boss. I think it is better that you just volunteer your time.'

I nodded and did not think about it anymore. I continued to work for nothing but the next holiday I went back to babysitting. There was a lot of babysitting available on campus as most of the families had young children, plus it was cash in hand.

When Dad was the high commissioner for Zambia to Australia from 1983 to 1991, he would sometimes send his driver home and drive himself to official dinners in Canberra if he thought it would be too long a day. I am sure he was one of the few High Commissioners who drove themselves to official functions. At home, which was the embassy residence, the grandkids knew that they had to take care of things in the house as they belonged to the Zambian government. I remember coming on holiday to Australia before we moved here permanently and there was a minor incident. My son, Bwembya, then three years old, knocked over an occasional table and the leg broke. My niece, Natasha, ran into the room where Mum and I were sitting, shouting, 'Grandma, Grandma, Bwembya has broken the government table.'

My biggest disappointment was when Nelson Mandela came to Australia. Mum was in Zambia on holiday. Dad was one of the dignitaries who had been invited to meet Nelson Mandela when he arrived. He was also invited to the official lunch. Since Mum was away, I was hoping to go in Mum's place, but Dad said, 'Sorry. The invitation is for me and my wife only. I cannot take someone who is not my wife.' I was crushed. I had stayed back in Canberra after the weekend, hoping I would be able to go.

Mum and Dad travelled through Africa and overseas a lot when we lived at Mindolo. Sometimes they would go together, but mostly they travelled separately. I really missed Mum when she was away as Dad did not quite fill Mum's shoes. When I was about six years old, I woke up feeling the hot sun on my face. The sun was coming through a small gap in the thick green curtains and shining a beam of light across the room. I rolled over and as I did so I felt a sharp pain in my tummy. My tummy hurt with each move I made as I slowly got myself out of bed. I could hear movement on the other side of the door. Doors banging, water running and feet making a dull thud on the wooden parquetry floor as someone ran up and down somewhere in the house.

I walked slowly up the corridor to the door of my parents' bedroom. I knocked a couple of times before I heard my dad say, 'Yes' in his loud, gruffy voice. I said, 'I am not feeling well', in a sad little voice. The door opened and my dad stood in the doorway looking down at me. He was still in his pyjamas and a checked dressing gown. 'What seems to be the problem,' he asked in a gentle voice.

'My tummy hurts,' I said and big tears started to roll down my face. I cried easily, Mum always said, like a river bursting its banks. Dad gently said, 'Where?'

'Here,' I said as I touched the place just below my belly button. Dad felt my head with the back of his hand, then wiped the tears on my face with the palm of his hand. His hand felt cool on my skin. He touched my tummy gently, giving it a little poke. 'Ouch!' I cried out.

'Let us go and get you something for that tummy,' he said as tears that were a gentle shower became a downpour. He took my hand and walked me down to the kitchen. The kitchen was on the other side of the house. Three corridors to get to the kitchen. The eight bedroomed house was shaped like an 'H' with the bedrooms on the first line of the H. My bedroom was the first bedroom at the top of the H. The line across consisted of the visitor's toilet, entryway into the house and the living room. On the other side of the H was the study, dining room, kitchen, and laundry. We walked into the kitchen where my four brothers Reggie, Heckie, Kenny, and James were sitting and eating cereal. They were already dressed in their uniforms and were mucking around as they ate their breakfast. The boys barely glanced my way as they continued to eat and taunt each other, racing to see who would finish their food first.

Dad let go of my hand, leaving me standing in the doorway and went to the fridge. He opened the fridge and took out a blue tin, put it on the counter and got a spoon out of the drawer next to the fridge. I looked at the tin. The tin said 'evaporated milk'. I was six and a half. I could read. I said nothing. Dad poured some evaporated milk onto the teaspoon and pointed the spoon to my mouth. I opened my mouth and drank the milk on the spoon. Mum never gave us evaporated milk when we had a sore tummy, she gave us that white chalky tasting medicine in a blue bottle that left your mouth feeling pasty. The evaporated milk made me feel a little bit sick. 'Alright, now go and brush your teeth and get ready for school.' I miss Mum, I thought as I walked to the bathroom. Mum would have let me stay at home until my tummy was better.

It was great that our parents travelled to different countries because we got lots of presents from different places. We got toys such as stackable babushka dolls and miniature electric toy cars that race on special tracks. My favourite presents were Dutch clogs, a cotton Mexican peasant blouse and a poncho. Bwalya and I had Scottish skirts from Scotland and from Kenya we got little slippers that had zebra leather at the top. On one of his trips, Dad brought a colour TV from overseas. No one else around us had a colour TV. We grew up feeling privileged, but Dad would always remind us we were not. We were fortunate, not privileged.

We had a house servant to clean and occasionally cook when there was no adult to cook. He could only cook roast chicken and roast potatoes, which we loved. When we were little, we had our beds made and our rooms cleaned. As we grew older, things changed. The girls who were in the house got to help cook the evening meal. We all had chores such as making our own beds and helping with the cleaning of the house on Sundays. Every evening there was a roster for clearing the table, washing the dishes, putting them away, soaking the dish towel in the sink and then mopping the kitchen floor. Girls had one night and boys the next.

The kitchen was where all the fun happened on evenings when there was nothing good on TV, or when we had guests. That was the place where Heckie taught us dance moves. We would move the kitchen table out of the way, and he would show us how to dance. The vinyl floor was easy to slide on and do quick turns to the Jackson Five music. We took dancing seriously. When we had a few songs choreographed we would go on a current affair show and dance on prime-time TV. My uncle had a friend who hosted a current affair show and we would call him when we wanted to dance, and he would organise a night for us to go on and dance during intermission. We were not shy about being on TV because we were used to putting on shows at Mindolo in front of people. We were always with other kids, so it was ok. We often took part in fashion parades at the Women's Training Centre once or twice a year, to show off the skills that the women had learnt in making clothes.

The steps outside the back door into the Kitchen were a favourite spot to sit on in the evenings. When there were dinners or music concerts in the main dining room for students and staff, we would sit on the back steps and listen to the music. Our house was the closest house to the dining room. Our friends would come from their houses and sit on the steps with us. We would have cocoa, Milo, or tea with some of Mum's scones or cakes. Mum taught cooking at the Women's Training Centre. There were always scones or cakes in the house. If we were lucky and it was summer, we would get soft drinks, though these were usually reserved for when we had guests and they were locked way in the pantry in the guest wing as we never knew when guests would drop by.

As we got older, we were allowed to go to what was called 'sessions'. Live bands such as the Boyfriends or the Witch would come and play in the dining hall or at the youth hall. If we were late getting back home, Mum would walk into the hall in her dressing gown and slippers, with curlers in her hair to get her kids. 'Kenny, James, Patricia, let's go! Where are the others?' Mum thought nothing of shouting our names through the crowd of dancing people. We were not annoyed or embarrassed, it was just the way it was. We knew we were lucky to be out having unsupervised fun when we were still children – except for the fact that most of the adults knew who we were and kept an eye on us. Mum had to make sure we got home safely and were tucked in our beds when she was ready to go to bed. We would still be dancing to the music as we walked home. Our house was so close to the dining room that we could hear the music from our beds. It was the sweetest way to go to sleep with a live band belting out 'Hey, Jude' by the Beatles.

In the back garden of our house, Mum had a vegetable garden where she grew spinach, carrots, sweet potatoes, pumpkins, onions, tomatoes, and other vegies. We would pull out carrots and sit at the edge of the bed eating them raw. Half-ripe tomatoes still tangy to taste were eaten straight from the vine. There were fruit trees lined around the oval-shaped garden. Guavas, avocados, mulberries, oranges, lemons, lime, grapefruits, mangoes, pomegranates, bananas, pawpaws, passion fruit, and tangerines. There was also a patch of sugar cane in one corner.

There was always some fruit in season that we could just pick to snack on in between meals. We loved to climb trees and sit there eating mangoes and guavas. Our clothes would have stains from the fruit, especially the mangoes and mulberries. Heckie loved to experiment and would have us making mulberry pies, jams, and ice cream flavoured with whatever fruit was in season. We made ice cream the old-fashioned way in an ice cream maker. All I remember is that you had to turn the handle and use lots of salt and ice. I was usually the one sitting on the top of the ice cream maker to hold it down while someone turned the handle.

We got to eat the fruit and vegetables, but we also learnt to be little farmers. We would go with mum to the garden, dig the soil and make garden beds, plant seeds, weed the garden beds, and harvest. Everyone had to participate with no exceptions. Although we would sometimes drag our feet, when we got there, we would often make everything a race and see who could finish first. We also took turns to water the garden during the evenings. There was a stationary water sprinkler that had to be moved every few minutes for all the plants in the garden to get watered. On hot nights we would run through the water to cool off. When the grass got wet, we would slide through it leaving a trail of muddy water and if we fell in, we would be covered in mud. That was ok as you just had to stand under the sprinkler to get all the mud off.

When Heckie was old enough to drive and my parents were not home, we would pile into the car, and he would do wheelies with Mum's white Datsun 2000 on the wet grass. All my brothers learnt to drive at a really young age. I got my driving licence when I was nineteen years old and on holiday from university.

I was taught to drive by one of my dad's drivers in his private time. I got my licence in two weeks. It was a tough two weeks. From the word go, I was driving the car. Dad's driver did not once get in the driver's seat. Mum's Datsun was a manual. I was taken out for driving lessons in the early morning and in the evening at peak hour. Peak hour! If the car stalled as it sometimes did when I was learning how to compress the clutch, I was calmly told to switch off the car and start again even if there were people hooting all around me.

'The car has stopped, what do I do?' I would shout.

'Switch the car off and start again.'

'Can you come and drive until we get out of this traffic?'

'Switch the car off and start again. Do not pay attention to anything outside this car. Let's go.' This was all said very calmly as he puffed the smoke from his cigarette out the open window.

From day one, I learnt parallel parking and reverse parking. I would go back and forth until I managed to park, even though it was painstakingly slow. My instructor would stand on the pavement, smoking a cigarette and shouting instructions through the open window. All I heard was, 'Come slowly, turn the wheel to the left'.

'Stop, go back out and start again,'

'Come.'

'Turn.'

'Turn the wheel back to the right.'

'Straighten the steering.'

'Stop.'

At the end of the day, he took me to a park where there were empty oil drums stacked with car tyres in two rows. I had to reverse six metres and go back and forth until I got it right and came out the other side. We stayed there till it was dark and I had managed to come out the other side. The car bumped the drums a lot but did not damage the car. The only driving on the road was driving to and from the driving lessons into the city centre for the parallel parking and across to the other side of Kitwe where the drums were set up and then back home. On two Saturdays we were out the whole day with me parallel parking and reverse parking while my instructor smoked his cigarettes and drank his bottles of coke. We went home for lunch, had a one-hour break, and went out again till dark.

Two weeks after we started the lessons, I was able to drive through the drums with ease and could parallel park like a pro. 'I think you are ready now. I have booked your test for Thursday at lunch time. You will need to bring some money to pay for the test and the licence.'

'Really, you think I am ready?'

'You are ready. Now start the car and let's drive home like you are driving for the test. Use roads that have an intersection with hills to practice stopping and turning at the top of a hill.'

I went for my test and breezed through it.

The police officer who gave me the test was shocked.

'Young lady. How long have you been driving?'

'Two weeks,' I answered.

'What? No one can learn to parallel park and reverse park in two weeks. You must be one of those people who drive around without licences for years illegally.' 'No,' I laughed, 'I have never driven before this, but my teacher was very strict and made me practice a lot.'

'Still, two weeks, no way,' the police officer said. I knew my instructor was proud of me as he had a silly smirk on his face as he said, 'Ok, people with a licence, get in the car and drive us home.'

I walked to the car and took off the L plates. I could not wait to see the look on my brothers' faces when I told them, because they didn't know I was having driving lessons. In fact, only Mum knew as she had to pay for them. Three weeks ago, Dad was leaving for a trip overseas, and I was on holiday from university, so I asked him if his driver could teach me to drive while I was on holiday. He agreed, but as long as Mum let me use her car for the lessons.

I could not believe I was now going home with a driver's licence. My brothers were upset.

'There is no way you could have gotten a driver's licence; you can't even drive.' 'How come Dad let the driver teach you how to drive?'

'You can't get a licence after two weeks. That is impossible.'

'You must have bribed the police.' They knew I could not have bribed the police. Where would I get the money? Not from our parents, that's for sure. They could not figure it out, so they asked the driver.

'Patricia is an exceptionally good driver,' he said, 'I have never seen a woman who can parallel park as well as she can. I was extremely impressed.' Coming from a man who did not say much, this was high praise. They knew the driver was not the kind of person to take any nonsense from anyone and he would not have let me get away with cheating. They could not figure it out so I told them I would take them for a ride, and they could see for themselves. I got the keys from Mum and drove the boys into town. It felt strange as I was usually in the backseat and there I was, driving the troops. The boys had all been driving for years, but none of them had even thought of getting a driver's licence. After that, I was allowed to drive most family cars. My uncles and aunties would let me drive their cars and would sometimes send me on errands like dropping my cousins off at school or taking them to after-school activities. For a long time, my brothers kept insisting I had bribed the police. I must admit I did feel a little smug for a while, especially when Mum and Dad handed the keys to me as my brothers stood there.

Mum had a fenced-off area of the garden that had a hen house with chickens, ducks, rabbits, and pigeons. There was a pigeon house on the top of the hen house. One of our chores was to open the hen house in the morning so the chickens and ducks could run around the enclosure, and to open the rabbit hatch so the rabbits could come out and run around. We'd also opened the pigeon house so the pigeons could go out and fly around or join the chickens in the enclosure. In the evening just before the sun set, we had to put all the birds and animals back into their enclosures. Every afternoon at sundown you would hear the noise of different animals as they were being herded into their enclosures. I was not particularly good at dealing with animals, so I kept out of the way most of the time. My cousin Mulenga had no such issues. She could catch a chicken, kill it, pluck the feathers off the chicken and have it cooked on the table within a couple of hours.

My parents raised happy, well-adjusted children. But they did not do it alone. We were raised by all the adults at Mindolo. We were carefree and roamed the campus safely all day or night. There were no fences between the houses. Some houses had hedges around them, but none had them all the way round. The campus was a gated community with guards at the main entrance to check who came in and out. Everyone inside knew who we were, who our parents were and where we lived.

There was an American lady who lived next door to us called Mrs Mules. Her house had a thatched roof and was painted white. She had many cats that would sit on the windowsill outside my window and make noises all night and scare the hell out of me. I had a corner bedroom, so there would be cats on both windows. When I opened my curtains, I would see lots of little eyes looking back at me. Mrs Mules was an older lady with white hair that looked like it had a rinse in it. She had a cottage in the bush near a place called Rodwins that was situated on the road between Kitwe and Mufulira, about half an hour from Mindolo. There was a lake surrounded by trees and a picnic spot with barbeque facilities and a paddling pool. It had a foofie slide, which was a pulley system attached to a cable suspended over the lake. Most of the time we fell into the lake before we got the other side. There were also canoes available for hire.

When we went to Rodwins we went as a family, or with the other families, and spent the day there having fun with adults cooking on the barbeque. Mrs Mules and another American lady would go to the cottage for weekends. When I was about eight or nine, they would take me with them. The cottage was made from stone with a thatched roof. There was a wading pool made of stone and concrete that I would spend all day in while the two ladies lay in the sun, had cups of tea with cake and read books. I would lie in the cool water and float with my arms and legs spread out feeling the sun on my face or play with my dolls on a mat beside the pool. I enjoyed having the attention and it more than made up for the scary nights with the cats outside my window.

Beatrice and I did a lot of things together. We went to Girl Guides, music class and ballet class and we even got to meet the president of Zambia. On that special day in 1966 we wore matching cotton dresses with a stiff petticoat inside, white shoes and socks, and our hair was straightened and curled. Our hair was straightened with a hot comb that was heated on the stove. You could hear the hair sizzle as the comb went through. The hair was curled using short pieces of insulated copper wire which was very uncomfortable, but the result was lovely curly hair. We presented the President with flowers. We had been practicing for days to curtsey and walk. The President came to unveil the Dag Hammarskjold Memorial at Mindolo. Dag Hammarskjold was the second Secretary General of the United Nations who was killed in a plane accident while flying to Ndola in Zambia in 1961.

I had to become independent when I went to boarding school at the age of thirteen. I went to a Catholic school in Lusaka, the capital city of Zambia. I did not know many people there and so I had to make new friends. It took me a little while to get used to waking up early in the morning and having a cold shower. I learnt to have quick showers. Step in front of the shower, wet my face clothe and lather it with soap. Scrub my body quickly and step into the cold water to rinse off the soap. I learnt to spend my day in queues when I was not in class. Queue to get in the shower, queue to get into the chapel for morning mass or prayers, queue to get into the dining room, queue to get into class, queue at the tuckshop or anywhere else that we had to be on the school grounds. I learnt to do chores I would not have imagined doing. Like scrubbing floors, scrubbing toilets, sweeping dormitories, polishing floors, and working in the canteen. I learnt to speak when I was spoken to, to be seen and not be heard. I made a few good friends and I loved learning.

However, I was unwell with rheumatic fever during my last two years of high school. I spent a lot of time in bed and there was a period in form four (year eleven), when I spent a few months in hospital and at home on bed rest. I was in a private hospital, so it was great. The food was good, my room was great, and the nurses were wonderful. Heckie came to visit me at the hospital almost every day after school and would go home with Mum when she came for afternoon visitation. I was away from school for a few months and when I went back to school for form five (year twelve), the headmistress advised my dad that they would like me to repeat form four as I had missed so much. Dad asked me what I wanted to do. I decided I wanted to finish school with my classmates. I recall the day the results of the Cambridge High School Certificate came out. The phone rang one evening. The red phone. There were two phone lines in the house. The normal grey phone and the red phone. We were allowed to use the grey phone but not the red phone. Dad answered the red phone in the bedroom. We used to call the red phones the hotline. We were all sitting in the living room engrossed in a movie when we heard a loud yell coming from the bedroom. Dad rushed out of the bedroom into the living room and ran straight to me and gave me a big hug and a kiss on the cheek. I was surprised, he was not usually so demonstrative and loud.

'That was your uncle Mark on the phone,' he said. 'He went to check your form five results. You passed with flying colours. You got a division one.' Dad was stunned, I was stunned, and everyone was stunned.

I had been so unwell in form five, I was in bed half the time. I was just hoping to pass all my subjects and that was all. To get a division one was unimaginable. I always thought I was an average student, but I was beginning to rethink that. Maybe I was almost as smart as Heckie was, maybe not. Heckie was supposed to be the smarty-pants in the family. He hardly ever studied and spent his life mucking around but he somehow seemed to land on his feet. He was an all-rounder who could do a lot of things well. Like play tennis, swim, and play soccer.

✦

Chapter 2

I completed high school in 1977 and went to a university in Lusaka from 1978 to 1981. University was different from boarding school. There were boys everywhere. It was an adjustment attending class with the opposite sex. My friends at university were different from my friends at school. They were confident, self-assured, and stylish. I had to learn to find my feet in a different environment. This was not a gated campus anymore. There were no adults to watch you everywhere you went. I did what I do best. I observed. I would sit in what was called the mingling area, where the canteen and student centre were situated and I watched, listened, and learnt.

The campus was a concrete jungle of buildings of different sizes and heights. There seemed to be people around at all hours of the day. Students didn't seem to be getting a lot of sleep. Music played from rooms in the residences till well into the night. As you walked around the residences, there were people hanging out of windows smoking, talking, and just watching the parade of students going about their business. There was lots of fun to be had if you had the money or the connections to go to movies, restaurants, discos, and parties. My mum opened a bank account for me when I went to university so I would always have money, and not have to rely on anyone. When I was on campus, I always had money to buy what I wanted and did not have to depend on anyone to buy my drinks or pay for taxies if the situation arose. She taught me to always have some money tucked away in my wallet for emergencies. My friends and I had money and connections to people who knew where all the fun was. We knew people who managed cinemas, owned clubs, and discos. At the end of the week, we hung out of our windows and watched the world go by as we waited for the sun to go down and for the fun to begin.

I left university in 1981 after being excluded from law school and had a gap year. I spent the year preparing to go to Bennett College in the United States. I wrote my TEFOL and SAT exams, which were required to get into an American college or university. During the gap year, I worked for a commercial bank in Lusaka, which was across the road from the bank where Mwango was working. Mwango and I started dating at the end of 1981 just as I started work at the commercial bank. During my gap year, I lived with Beatrice in a suburb called Kabwata. A very medium-to-low socio-economic working-class suburb.

On the day I moved into the little one-bedroom flat, a friend of mine picked me up from the bus stop and drove me to my new home. We walked round the corner through a space in the wire fence that was meant to have a gate, but it did not. The path was uneven dried scorched earth that looked like concrete. It was dry and unforgiving. Outside the fence about a hundred metres away was a tavern. It was two in the afternoon and already the music was blaring through the neighbourhood. There were lots of people walking up and down the road at the side of the tavern and crossing the road to the local market, which was full of brightly clothed people, food, and goods.

We walked out of the sun into the shaded area of a building. I looked up at the tall block of flats that was shutting out the sun. We were in an alley way that led to a dead end. There were two doors on the left in this alley. This was where I was going to live, a basement flat tucked away in a corner. I opened the door, and my friend carried my big brown cardboard suitcase into the flat. 'This is it,' he said. I had never been here before, but he looked like he had. He gave me a smart salute and walked out the door, saying, 'See you!' as he turned the corner. I stood in the dim entrance and looked around. To my left was a kitchen. The kitchen was tiny with a little window that opened at the top of the wall on the right-hand side of the door. The window was near the ceiling, like the small ventilation windows you find in bathrooms. You would have to stand on a chair to be able to see outside, which was good as our flat was at ground level.

I looked around the beautifully decorated living room and bedroom. It was neat and tidy; everything was in its place as I knew it would be. Any place that Beatrice lived in was neat and tidy. I had known her since we were six years old and that is who she was, everything in its place. We were now twenty-one, out in the big grown-up world. We had jobs that paid us money and all the things we needed. A big black-and-white TV, a music system, and a fully furnished place to live. We had a lot of fun in that little flat. Not the kind of fun I was expecting moving away from home. The freedom to stay out late and go on dates with dashing young men, or maybe not-so-dashing young men. No, not that kind of fun.

I got to make friends with a group of lovely young women, with whom I could talk, laugh, and cry. Most Saturday afternoons a group of our close girlfriends would come to the flat and we would go into the kitchen and cook. The room would be filled with lovely smells of food, especially the dried little white bait fish called kapenta. During our time in the flat, Beatrice and I liked to cook kapenta. We bought the little fish at the big busy market across the road. To cook the kapenta, we would first soak it in a pot of boiling water for a few minutes until the fish went a little soft and flexible. We'd then drain the water and place the fish on a paper towel or newspaper to soak up the moisture. We'd fry a white onion that was cut up into strips in a frying pan, add chopped tomatoes, then the kapenta. When the fish was almost cooked, we added a dash of salt, pepper, and a little curry powder for seasoning. Our Saturday afternoon ritual was to watch cartoons on TV and for snacks, eat kapenta.

When Mwango and I started dating, I was twenty-one and just coming out of a relationship. I was not looking for romance. In fact, I shied away from any attachments. Mwango was twenty-three and just recovering from a terrible car accident in which he was injured and his long-term girlfriend was killed. He was not looking for a relationship. Beatrice was the catalyst to our getting together. I knew Mwango as an acquaintance whom I had said hello to when our paths had crossed at university, but that was it. I knew some members of Mwango's family, especially his cousin and his aunt who were in my class in high school.

Not long after I started working at the bank, we were informed that there would be an end-of-year dinner dance. I was still feeling vulnerable and not interested in men, period, but had to have a date for the end-of-year function. Beatrice and I had bumped into Mwango a few times that month and I had introduced her to him. Beatrice thought Mwango was cute, and she suggested I take him to the dinner dance. She hounded me for weeks on end and finally I decided I would ask him. I walked up to the bank across the road and went up to a lady at the reception. 'Excuse me, could I please see Mr Mwango Kasengele?' I said.

'Who should I say is requesting to see him,' she asked.

'If you could let him know it is Patricia Mfula.'

'Thank you.'

The receptionist picked up the phone and called Mwango's office. 'Good morning, Mr Kasengele, there is a Patricia Mfula here to see you.'

I waited for a few minutes, and then I saw Mwango coming through a door off the reception area. My heart was beating fast, and I was thinking 'What am I doing here?' As Mwango walked towards me he had a smile on his face. He was wearing a well-cut suit in pine needle green and a cream shirt that looked like it was silk. It had a slight shine to it; it was very subtle like a dress Mum had in her wardrobe that was silk. The tie was maroon with tiny flecks of cream through it. I had never really looked at him before; Beatrice was right, he was kind of cute. Especially that twinkle in his eye, and the half grin on his face like he was going to burst into laughter.

I had not dressed to impress. I had not even decided I was going to see Mwango until I got to work. Beatrice and I were always well dressed, so I was looking fine. It was who we were. I said hello to Mwango and told him about the dinner dance at work and asked if he would like to go with me. He said, 'I will think about it and let you know.' I wanted the floor to swallow me as I said goodbye and walked back to work. Maybe I should have dressed to impress or maybe I should have just called him on the phone, that way there would have been less embarrassment. Thanks, Beatrice.

Two weeks went by, and I had not heard from him. The function was that weekend. What was I going to do?

'Beatrice, I am so embarrassed. I guess I will have to go to the dinner dance alone.' Beatrice being Beatrice just ignored me and told me to go and remind him. Two days later, I walked into the bank and faced Mwango again. He spoke before I had the chance to say anything. 'Hello. Sorry, I did not get back to you. Of course, I will go to the dinner dance with you. What time is it and where?'

'It's at six thirty on Saturday at the Woodpeckers Inn in Woodlands,' I answered.

'That is ok. I will pick you up at six o'clock on Saturday,' said Mwango. I told him the address where I lived, and we arranged the pickup.

Saturday came and I was standing outside with Beatrice, agitated. It was twenty-five past six in the evening. He was late. I was dressed in a peach-coloured cap-sleeved silk top, fitted at the waist, with tiny buttons down the front. A plain black skirt with slits down the sides from the knee down. Black high-heeled sandals with pencil thin heels that I could barely walk in but that looked like they belonged on a catwalk. Beatrice had helped me get ready. I looked at her and said, 'You know that this is embarrassing. I guess he is not coming. Why did I agree to your crazy ideas? I feel so stupid.'

As I finished saying this, a flustered anxious-looking Mwango came round the corner. 'Sorry, I am so late. The cab is just around the corner. Hi, Beatrice,' he said, 'How are you? Patricia, you look great. Shall we go?'

We arrived at the venue and the manager from the bank where I worked was greeting everyone at the door. He knew my dad through their business networks. He had given me a lecture when I first started working at the bank about the importance of education, work, and careers. He told me that this job was a stop-gap and he expected me to get a degree and not to get comfortable in the job. I shyly introduced Mwango to him. He fired a few questions at Mwango who answered to his satisfaction apparently as he told us to stand there and called a waiter. He asked the waiter to put one table away from the long configuration of tables that formed one table in the middle of the room. This table was put in a corner with candles and a bottle of champagne.

The manager led us to the table, sat with us, and talked to Mwango for a while before he went to welcome everyone and start the night off. I was left sitting with Mwango who I did not really know anything about. I thought that when he came with me, we would sit at tables with everyone else and he would be fine as he knew most of the young people I worked with at the bank. I was wrong. I was sitting opposite him in a dimly lit corner with a bottle of champagne and candles.

All my workmates were looking at us and obviously talking about us. I felt embarrassed again. I hoped he did not feel like I had set this all up. He started talking to me about my brother. He and my brother Heckie apparently were good friends. Soon he had me laughing out loud as he told stories of my brothers' antics at youth service military camp when they finished school, and how he clowned around. We talked for hours until it was time to go home. I forgot to be shy. We did not leave the table the whole time and did not talk to anyone else that night till we were outside looking for a cab to go home.

We dated casually until we went to a Valentine's ball in February. We had a long talk as we walked home through quiet leafy suburbs. After the dinner dance in Ridgeway, instead of taking a cab we were so busy talking, we just walked and walked. Mwango said to me, 'Patricia. I do not love you. I will not say I love you until I do.' I later came to realise that this was typical of Mwango. 'I love spending time with you,' he continued, 'so if you want to keep dating me, I would love that. I would not have ever thought of dating you as you are Heckie's little sister, but I really like you.' I told him how I felt, how I was not ready for a relationship, but I liked spending time with him, and we could just wait and see what happened. The courtship had officially begun.

Anyone who knows the suburb Kabwata knows that it is always busy. There are people everywhere at all hours of the night. After a night out, Mwango would walk me home. He lived in Kabwata, too, on the other side of the suburb with his cousin Joshua in another block of flats. I had met Ba Joshua (as we call older people in Zambia) a couple of times but always from a distance. One Saturday, we were getting ready to go out and Mwango wanted to go back home to pick up his jacket. We walked over to their flat, up the flights of stairs and into the flat. As we walked into the living room, we found Ba Joshua sitting in the living room watching TV. He greeted us and I went over to shake his hand and give a little curtsey as is tradition when greeting adults older than you.

Ba Joshua looked serious and imposing. Like an older uncle, not a cousin. I sat down in a chair as close to the door as possible. Mwango went into his room to get his jacket. Ba Joshua turned to me and asked me some questions about who I was and what I did. He then said, 'Ba mayo, could you please cook me some food before you go'. I looked up at Mwango who was walking into the room from the bedroom. He looked back at me with a smirk on his face. Ba Joshua walked into the kitchen, and I followed him. He opened the cupboard and took out some dried fish in a plastic bag. He took some vegetables out of the fridge and showed me where the mealie meal was. He then walked back to the living room.

I looked at the dried fish and the vegetables on the table then at the clock on the wall. It was about seven in the evening. Dried fish? Really? I had never cooked dried fish before, but I had seen my mum and Mulenga cook it lots of times. It usually took a few hours to cook. Like half the day. He was not joking. I heard Ba Joshua and Mwango start talking in the living room and put on some music. I guess I had better start cooking. I soaked the fish in boiling water for ten minutes to help it cook faster, prepared the green pumpkin leaves, and got the porridge for the nshima ready. Nshima is prepared by mixing mealie meal and boiled water and stirred until it is thick. You let it cook on low for a minimum of fifteen minutes then add more mealie meal until it is hard enough not to fall off a spoon if you turn it over.

I was determined to make a memorable meal, better than what Mulenga made. I added a bit of tomato paste to the fish, which you do not normally do to give it a bit of taste. The fish came out thoroughly cooked even though I only had a few hours to cook it. Soaking the fish had helped. The food was great. Ba Joshua was extremely impressed and told me so. Mwango was impressed. I was impressed. I smelt like dried fish, but I was very happy. We did not go out that night. We stayed and listened to jazz music with Ba Joshua. I was introduced to jazz. It was not bad at all, especially the jazz that had lyrics to it.

✦

Chapter 3

My parents believed in their children having a good education. My brother Reggie went to a university in Kansas, USA, and my brother Hector went to college in Texas, USA. In 1982, I went to Bennett College in Greensboro, North Carolina. Bennett College is a private women's liberal arts college that was founded in the late 1800s. I flew to Greensboro via London and New York. I was met at the airport by a driver from the college in an older style stretch limousine that belonged to the college. It was the end of August and still a little warm. I arrived at the campus and was escorted to the dormitory where I stayed during my first year. The building was in the style of the era it was built in the 1900s but was very well maintained. Large bedrooms were shared by two students. I shared a room with a freshman called Maria who was eighteen. I had just turned twenty-two and felt ancient.

The campus was incredibly beautiful with a lot of tall trees and greenery as is typical of many colleges and universities in North Carolina. Autumn was my favourite time of the year when the leaves on the trees changed to yellow, orange, red, and brown. The ground was covered in leaves as fall set in. I loved to wear boots and kick the leaves as we made our way across the open spaces. We had leaf fights where we would pick up handfuls of leaves and throw them at each other, often on our way to class, where we arrived late and breathless from the exercise.

I arrived at college a few weeks before autumn began. I loved the weather – until winter came. I had been to England on holiday, but it had been in spring, so I had no idea what cold weather was until I came to North Carolina and experienced my first winter. The campus looked lovely covered in snow. We were often late for class as we were busy throwing snowballs at each other and arrived in the class with wet overcoats. Thankfully, the classrooms were heated.

When I arrived at Bennett College the semester had already commenced. Registration was long over. I was taken to the administration building to get registered by the international student adviser. I had studied law at the university in Zambia and assumed I could continue to do so. It took a few explanations before I understood that if I were to study law, I would have to start from scratch. American law is different from British law on which the Zambian syllabus was based. Suddenly, the excitement of coming to America faded. I would have to take up a four-year prelaw degree then go to law school to get a degree that I would not be able to use in Zambia. That was not an option. It was decided that I would take a variety of courses in that first year then decide on a major in the second year. In the first year, I took courses such as English, biology, maths, philosophy, business communication, psychology, human development, social welfare, economics, behavioural science, social services, and research.

At the end of the second semester, the head of the department of social work approached me about pursuing social work, as I had excelled in both social work and psychology. I consequently decided on a degree majoring in social work with psychology as a minor. During my senior year, I had placements in different places such as a hospital, a school for gifted children, a community college, and a preschool. I was sent on a placement to a childcare centre. This centre was a pre-school for children with special needs. On the first day, I was overwhelmed. By the end of the day, I learnt that the children were just kids who needed a little more help than most. It was my very first encounter with children with disabilities, and it ignited an interest in the disability field.

I was busy with schoolwork, but I also tried to have a little fun when I was not studying and writing assignments. During the first few weeks of my arrival in Greensboro, Sharon (a girl from my dorm at Bennett College) and I had gone shopping downtown. You could get a bus, but it was walking distance, probably a mere six kilometres away. Sharon was a quiet, lovely natured girl with glasses. We were walking back to campus as it was a lovely warm day. A brown Toyota Corolla stopped in front of us, and two young men got out and started to talk to us. They were students at University of North Carolina Greensboro (UNCG). The young man driving the car was Nigerian and the passenger, an African-American. They asked us who we were and where we were going. Could they give us a ride back to campus? They seemed harmless. Sharon said yes. I thought she was from there so she should know if that was ok. We were driven back to campus, and all seemed well. When we got to campus, they asked us to go out to dinner with them. Sharon said yes and they organised to pick us up. I was surprised as we had just met them, but Sharon seemed fine with the idea, so it probably was.

Later that evening, we got ready to go out. I looked at Sharon and she had transformed herself into someone quite different from her usual wallflower-looking self. The hair was teased and curled. She had makeup on! The guys arrived at eight in the evening on the dot. We got in the car and drove for what seemed a long time to the other side of town where UNCG was. We arrived at a complex with expensive-looking townhouses or condos as they were known there. We parked and went into one of the condos. This condo belonged to one of their friends. He was an older fellow from Nigeria. The place had four levels. We went down to the basement, which looked like a club. It even had a mirror ball hanging on the ceiling. He had a big reel-to-reel music system. The room was dim with strobing lights. I was impressed that students live like that. We listened to music and danced a bit. We had some food delivered and all seemed all right, as there were five of us. There wasn't a lot of talking going on as the music was loud. Around midnight, we were ready to go home because we had a curfew at Bennett. The guys said we should go for a quick cup of coffee at their apartment before we left.

The apartment, a few doors down, was smaller than the one we had been in. It had only two levels but was spacious and beautifully decorated. We walked in and sat in the living room. Cigarettes came out and the three of them started to smoke. I declined. I know the smell of pot; it smells the same whether you are in Zambia or America. Within a couple of minutes, Sharon and Mike disappeared behind one of the doors leading off the living room. Gilbert walked upstairs to what looked like a loft area and lay on a bed.

'Come on up', he said.

'No, thank you', I said. 'I must get back before curfew. I will see you guys later. Tell Sharon I have gone.' I walked out of the apartment and out into the parking lot. I walked around the complex until I found a pay phone. I looked in my purse. I only had twenty dollars and some coins. Would twenty be enough for a cab back to Bennett? Then I remembered the secret stash. How my mum had taught me to always have some money tucked away in my wallet for emergencies. I searched the little pocket at the back of the purse and there was a fifty-dollar note. I walked to the front of the apartment block, wrote down the address of the complex, walked back to the pay phone and called a cab. Thank you, Mum.

I enjoyed my time at Bennett and made a few close friends. The best thing was that Chileshe, a relative and one of my best friends, was in Richmond, Virginia. We talked on the phone almost every day. We spent a lot of time back and forth between Richmond and Greensboro, spending most holidays together. Having a Bennett College education was one of the best gifts my parents gave to me. I met some wonderful teachers, advisors, and students. I met some strong powerful women through Bennett College. The college sponsored a social-cultural history of Black women. A three-day event that featured keynote speakers like Margaret Alexander Walker (poet and writer) and Paula Giddings (editor of *Essence Magazine*).

It was at Bennett College that I learnt to trust and believe in myself, to reinforce my belief that I was somebody special. Well, every Bennett Belle was told she was special. During my first year at Bennett, I was asked to sing for visitors at our open day in our dormitory. I was always singing to myself, and someone must have dobbed me in. I dressed carefully and my roommate helped me to style my hair. My dress was of a deep purple colour with faint large light grey flowers. The dress was a cocktail, below-the-knee dress. To finish off the look, I wore light grey stockings and matching court shoes.

I walked up to the top of the steps leading to the sunken living room area opposite the front door. There, a medium-sized room was full of people seated or standing by the walls. I did not feel nervous or anxious. We were always singing in the kitchen at home. I could do this. I stayed at the top of the stairs as I was introduced. I moved from the side of the open space to the middle. Everyone stopped talking. There was silence. There was no music to cue me in. This was it. I started singing softly, getting louder as I sang the song, 'One day in your life'. I looked around me. No one was laughing. They were smiling and looking at me. I thought I sounded ok as my voice reached out into the quiet room. Not loud and forceful but calm and with feeling. I imagined my brother Heckie singing this Michael Jackson song in the kitchen at home, with a broom as a microphone and my sister and I dancing behind him, his backup singers. There was no need for music, I could hear the music in my head. My feet were tapping to the music ever so slightly out of sight in my shoes. I followed the music as it rose and fell in my head, until the last beat of the song. When I finished the song, everybody clapped and whistled. I sang another song by Michael Jackson, titled, 'We've got forever'. There was a standing ovation. I was surprised. I was singing in the land of great singers and people were clapping? I had heard the calibre of singers from the fine arts building when I walked across the lawn to class. I had heard the choir singing in the chapel on Thursdays. That was singing. Maybe my voice was different and that is what they liked. I gave a little bow and quickly ran to my room.

Mwango and I were engaged on my birthday in August 1984. He came to Greensboro to visit me and surprised me with a marriage proposal. I was surprised! Not that he wanted to marry me, but because I was not expecting a proposal that day. It was my birthday; I was just happy he was there to share it with me. The day I was leaving Zambia to go to Greensboro in 1982, Mwango sent a letter to be delivered to me by hand at the international airport departure lounge. I had flown in from Kitwe that evening and was in transit to London. Aunty Janet and Uncle Linus had come to the Airport in Lusaka to see me off. While we were sitting there, a protocol officer brought a letter to me from Mwango.

'Excuse me. Are you Miss Mfula?' I looked up.

'Yes, I am,' I answered.

'I was asked to bring a letter to you from Mr Kasengele.' He handed me the medium-sized khaki envelope and left.

I put the thick envelope into my bag, feeling impatient to get on the plane so I could read my letter. It was my first letter from Mwango. I had butterflies in my stomach. A few weeks before over the phone, he had said that when I went to America we should probably just break up as a long-distance relationship would not work for him. I had gone back to Kitwe to live with my parents for the last few months before I left for the US, to sort paperwork and prepare for the trip. I was glad that this conversation was over the phone so he could not see the tears that started rolling down my face. They were not a gentle shower; they were a silent downpour. I could not believe he would say such a thing. But I also knew how brutally honest he could be.

I have never been able to decide if this was a good thing or a bad thing. Because sometimes we do not always want to hear the truth. I cried for a few minutes. Long enough to make my eyes puffy. I wiped my tears, washed my face, and went into the kitchen to help Mulenga make dinner.

Obviously, uncle and aunty heard the protocol officer ask if I was Miss Mfula and that the letter was from Mr Kasengele. They did not miss a beat. Aunty Janet said, 'You have to make sure you work hard and get good grades. Your parents have given you a chance to go to America to get a degree. No playing around.' Uncle Linus did not totally agree. 'Yes, you need to study hard, but also have a good time. You get few chances to see the world and have great experiences. I would have liked to go to San Francisco to see the Golden Gate Bridge. I would love to live in San Francisco if I had the chance. Make good use of your time over there, don't just study.'

'How can you tell Patricia to go and have fun? She is going to school,' Aunty reprimanded uncle. I found myself laughing out loud at them and promised I would try to do both. Within a few minutes there was a boarding call and I left them with lots of hugs, before I tore myself away, walked through the gate, and up the stairs into the aircraft.

I sat in my seat, put on my seatbelt, and read the fifteen-page letter before we had even taken off. I read the letter over and over all the way to Greensboro. In the letter, Mwango said that he was missing me, and I had not even gone yet. He had decided that I was the person he wanted to marry. That he loved me and wanted to spend the rest of his life with me. In the envelope were two cassette tapes. Tapes with jazz music on them. Most of the songs were without lyrics. I would listen to the tapes while I studied or wrote assignments. I got to know every song on the tapes very well. Particularly a song by Earl Klugh titled 'I Never Thought I'd Leave You'.

Getting engaged on my birthday was a wonderful gesture. In Greensboro, we did what all young people do when they are in love. Walked around holding hands, sat on the couch holding hands, drove the car with one hand while holding hands. We called Mum and Dad and informed them of the good news. They wished us well. In April as I was planning to return to Zambia, I got a letter from my dad. He was on his way to Zambia. Mwango and I are both from families that are relatively modern but still value traditions. We discussed Dad being in Zambia when I arrived and what a great opportunity for him to formally ask for my hand in marriage. Mwango started talking to his side of the family in preparation for this.

I received a well-rounded education that made me confident and self-assured. I learnt that it was ok to dream big and have high aspirations. I felt ready to go out into the world and make a difference. In April 1985, I completed my senior year at Bennett College and returned to Zambia with a Bachelor of Arts Degree in Social Work and a minor in Psychology. I received the Social Work Departmental Award. A certificate of merit for distinction in social work. I flew back to Zambia and arrived in Lusaka with a lot of excitement. Happy to see Mwango and my dad who I had not seen in three years.

One evening a week after I arrived in Lusaka, Uncle Linus, with whom I was staying, called me into the living room. In the living room were my dad, his four brothers and Aunty Janet. 'Patricia, sit down', Uncle Linus said. 'We would like to have a word with you'. I sat down in a chair near the doorway. 'I have received a phone call from a representative of Mwango Kasengele that they would like to come and have a meeting with us regarding you and the young man. We need to formally ask you a few questions', he said. 'Do you know who Mwango Kasengele is?'

'Yes, I do', I answered.

'Is he someone you are interested in getting married to?'

'Yes, he is', I replied.

'Ok. That is all we wanted to know. The representatives will be coming on Tuesday evening, so make sure you are here. You may go', said Uncle Linus. I got up and left the room, relieved that it was so easy.

On the Tuesday evening, I was in the kitchen with my cousin Elise. We heard cars arriving and people being welcomed into the house. I heard my name being called. I walked into the living room and sat in the only chair that was not occupied. A dining room chair placed at the side of the room near the kitchen. I bowed my head to acknowledge the adults in the room, like a well-brought-up child should do, and looked down at my hands. 'Patricia, we have asked you here today because we have visitors here on behalf of Mr Mwango Kasengele. Do you know Mr Mwango Kasengele?' asked Uncle Linus.

'Yes, I do', I answered politely looking up at my uncle as I spoke.

'They would like to know if you are at all interested in getting married to this young man.'

'Yes, I am', I replied, looking down at my hands as I spoke.

'Thank you, Mayo, (which means Mum) you may now go.'

I got up and walked backwards out of the room until I reached the dining room where I turned and went into the kitchen.

When the guests left, I was called back into the living room where my dad, uncles and my Aunty Janet were sitting, enjoying refreshments. Uncle Linus had opened some bottles of wine and Dad who does not drink was having a Fanta. On the coffee table was an enamel bowl with money in it. Local currency Kwacha notes. When the plate of money is accepted by the family of the prospective bride, it means the groom's side of the family are allowed to come and start negotiations. My dad was happy he was here to witness the first stage of the rituals. He drank his Fanta as if it was champagne. I enjoyed a large cup of tea. There were a few more visits of the representatives to make a formal offer and discuss the impending marriage, including the bride price. We were now formally engaged. We were married at the end of August 1985 at the Cathedral of the Holy Cross in Lusaka, Zambia, Africa.

On the wedding day, I woke up early after only a few hours' sleep. The night before the house had been filled with people who had come for the wedding from other parts of the country, as well as from other countries. Aunty Janet and Uncle Linus's house was a sprawling five-bedroom single-level house set in the middle of a large block of beautifully manicured lawns. I sat with my maternal and paternal aunts and talked until way past midnight. We talked about family and life, and shared stories about things that had happened in the past. My mum who had come from Australia to attend the wedding had gone to bed early in one of the bedrooms assigned to her. I was lucky that my cousin Elise and I got to sleep in our own beds with no other guests squeezed into our already crowded bedroom. The room was filled with boxes of material from my Aunty Janet's business, and my eight large suitcases that I had brought with me from the United States a few months before.

The preparations for the wedding went smoothly. In true Zambian style, Mwango and I did not really have too much to do with the planning. There was a committee set up with members from Mwango's family and from my family to handle the organisation. Before I came back to Zambia, I thought I would have some control over my wedding especially since my parents were in Australia, but I was wrong.

I had bought myself a dress to wear. It was a cream satin cocktail-length dress with spaghetti straps and tiny pleats right around the bottom. This was complemented by a beautiful white lace long-sleeved straight top that went over the satin dress, stopping just above the pleats, and a cute little hat with a tiny veil matching the dress perfectly. I never got to wear that dress at the wedding, but I did end up wearing it at the evening party that followed the reception.

My dad bought the dress I wore to my wedding. It was a big fluffy dress like the ones I never wanted to wear. The type of wedding dresses I thought I hated. Mum brought three dresses with her from Australia that Dad had purchased for me. The wedding dress and two below-the-knee layered chiffon cocktail dresses. He had gone shopping without telling anyone and bought me the three dresses and two for Mum. My brother Heckie was a fashion designer and was hoping he would be choosing my dress as he knew my taste and could improve on it. Mum was not too impressed that Dad had chosen her dresses, but he did her proud, and when I put on the wedding dress I was surprised to feel like a princess.

The dress was a beautiful A-line, square neckline, floor-length organza on taffeta dress. The bodice of the dress was covered with lace material, which extended to the high collar at the back and to the long-puffed sleeves that tapered at the elbows and fitted tight to the wrists. At the bottom of the dress there were four layers of gathered lace. At the back of the dress, the same gathered lace went down in gentle layers from the waist to the floor. My mum's dress was a sleeveless powder blue dress of taffeta and chiffon. A chiffon long-sleeved waist-length matching jacket completed the outfit. While Dad provided the dresses, Mum made our wedding cake, a three-tiered heart-shaped fruitcake which she carried, carefully wrapped and boxed, all the way from Australia on the seat next to her.

The preparations went smoothly unless you count the fact that my uncle Linus, who was giving me away, was late coming out of the house. I was in the car waiting for him impatiently. The priest had warned us that he had another wedding after our wedding, and that he would be leaving the church ten minutes after the wedding was supposed to start if we were not there. There was no leeway for traditional bride lateness, not on his time.

Uncle Linus dressed in a dark suit with a white shirt, walked out of the house still tying his tie and got in the car. The Mercedes we were driven to the church in lost its balloons as we sped to get to the church, but we made it with a couple of minutes to spare.

The bridal party was waiting at the entrance of the church. Uncle Linus stood next to me, and I could feel my heart beating a little bit faster than normal. I tried to see through the veil into the church, but it was difficult to see anything, then the organ started playing the wedding march. The sound was loud and beautiful. The matron of honour held the front of my veil and pushed it gently back from my face. The rule at the cathedral was that no bride was to enter the church with her veil down. I had to walk down the aisle and be seen by everyone in the church. The matron, dressed in a cream cocktail-length dress, walked into the church followed by the page boy and the flower girl. The page boy was in a black suit, white shirt, and a black bow tie. The flower girl had a white dress made to mimic the style of my dress. Uncle took my hand and walked me slowly into the church. The three bridesmaids who wore powder-blue cocktail-length dresses walked in after us.

I focused on walking slowly without tripping on my dress. Halfway down the aisle, I fixed my eyes on Mwango who had turned to look at us walking towards him. He looked nervous but had a slight smile, a half-grin on his face. He looked his usual handsome self. He was wearing a black Pierre Cardin suit, a white wing-tipped shirt, a black bow tie, and he had a white carnation in the lapel of his suit. I was impressed. But I would not have expected anything less. He always dressed well. The man had style. The three best men wore light grey suits, white shirts, and black bow ties with red carnations in their lapels. I smiled back at Mwango and saw him visibly relax. I was glad the veil was off my face, and I could see his reaction. Uncle Linus took my hand and placed it in Mwango's hand. His hand was soft and warm. We looked into each other's eyes and the priest started the wedding ceremony.

'Dearly beloved, we are gathered here today to witness the marriage of Mwango and Patricia.'

Everything after that seemed surreal except for the feel of Mwango's strong and encouraging hand in mine. We promised to love each other till death do us part. And we did.

✦

Chapter 4

The week after the wedding, we went to Ndola. Mwango had been transferred to the branch in Ndola. Ndola is about three hours by car from Lusaka and about an hour from Kitwe. Our new home was a two-bedroom ground-floor unit in a gated company-owned residential block of flats. We settled into life in Ndola, and were soon part of Ndola's affluent society, attending fabulous cocktail and dinner parties. The little black dresses I had started to wear while at Bennett College came in handy. The casual corner outfits Chileshe and I collected while I was in Greensboro were out on display. Our shopping sprees usually lasted a whole day. The colour coordination and mix-and-match combinations were things we learnt from reading *Essence* magazine. We had similar taste and loved clothes.

Not everything went quite so smoothly. Pregnancy made me a little more sensitive than normal. Mwango and I went for lunch at an Indian restaurant in Ndola with one of our best men. We had been to this restaurant a few times and loved the food. We ordered lunch and were waiting for the food when our friend said,

'So how is married life?' And as he did so, he hit Mwango on the shoulder playfully.

'It's great, except my wife can't cook,' answered Mwango. I looked at him in disbelief and started to cry.

'How can you say that?' I said.

'Honey, I am only joking,' he replied with a horrified look on his face.

People around us had stopped eating and were staring at our table.

'I am sorry,' he said, 'I did not mean that. I am just kidding.'

He took my hand, but I was unable to stop the tears. I knew from the look he gave me that he was telling the truth. He reached into the pocket of his trousers and took out a clean handkerchief. He always had two clean, crisp handkerchiefs, one in each pocket and he gently dabbed my tears dry and held my hand. I pulled myself together.

'I know you were,' I said, 'but don't make jokes like that.' He did not learn from that experience and from time to time would cause me to tear up, but as I grew older, I didn't cry, I would just call him out on it. 'That is not funny at all, Honey.' I also got to know that when he had a little smirk on his face he was just joking, and I would ignore him.

In April 1986, after a difficult pregnancy our son Bwembya was born. The pregnancy and the birth were not what you would classify textbook experiences. The doctor walked into the room in the labour ward where I had been lying in active labour for over eight hours. It was after five in the morning. I focussed and looked at him in the bright light that filled the room but did not recognize him. I had not seen him before. He was apparently the doctor on duty. I had heard the nurses discussing paging the doctor on duty as I tried to catch my breath in between contractions.

He came in looking like someone woke him up from a deep sleep. I lay there quietly as he gently touched my stomach and pushed and poked. He did not say a word. All I heard were few grunts here, a few grunts there and the noise of some sort of a machine starting. No one told me what was going on. I felt a strange sensation like something was being sucked out of me. I could not see what was happening beyond the sheet covering the lower part of my body. The doctor looked up. He was holding something in his hands and then he laid a slime-covered little body on my chest and left the room without a word to me.

I watched the baby as his little arms and legs moved up and down, his skin covered in a grey paste-like substance, eyes tightly closed. He did not cry. I did not cry. There were no bells or whistles. But something stirred inside me, something strong and powerful. It felt like a bonding of souls, like I knew him from before, something familiar, as if we shared something that no one else knew. No sounds. No words. Harmony. I was secretively relieved he was a boy. We had been calling this baby 'him' from the moment we knew I was pregnant. But just because we thought it was a boy did not mean it was going to be a boy. We named the baby Bwembya (pronounced Bwem bia).

Bwembya was the name Mwango and I decided we would name our first child when we got engaged. We thought the name had a nice ring to it. It was a unisex name, and so Bwembya it was. We became Bashi Bwembya and Bana Bwembya, which means 'father of Bwembya' and 'mother of Bwembya'. I felt like I had achieved something. Perhaps it was because I had survived childbirth without drugs, although I did have a helping hand from the sleep-deprived doctor. My mom probably never knew that I had a vacuum extraction, it never came up in conversation. Everyone just sent congratulations. I had produced a son. Great.

Life with a little baby was not all we imagined it would be. At ten days old, the baby was spiking high fevers and crying continuously. My sister-in-law advised us to take him to the local children's hospital. The large imposing group of buildings stood on the top of a hill. It looked grand and majestic despite the paint peeling away at the edges. We drove up the long driveway to where there was a parking lot. The car stopped and Mwango got out and opened the door to the backseat where I was seated, carefully holding our son who was almost two weeks old.

I eased myself out of the car carefully, trying not to rouse the baby from his fretful sleep on my shoulder. Bwembya had cried non-stop for a few days, had a temperature, and was very grumpy. This was our first child, and I was not sure what was wrong with him and why he kept crying and feeling so hot. I rocked him back and forth as I was getting out of the car and fortunately, he whinged but continued sleeping fretfully. His forehead felt hot against my cheek as I pulled him closer so he could feel my skin-on-skin contact, as that seemed to help calm him down for the short periods he slept.

My sister-in-law got out of the front passenger seat and pointed to the entrance of the hospital. The hospital looked clean enough on the outside. A few bougainvillea plants grew out of the red, hard earth that looked as dry as rock. There was no grass to be seen from where we were standing, just red earth and concrete. The windowpanes and the doors were painted white in contrast to the green walls. There were a few broken windows that were boarded up with some cardboard. We followed my sister-in-law along the concrete footpath and up a set of stairs that led to a door labelled 'Admissions'.

We were greeted by an admissions officer in white shirt and navy-blue trousers. He was seated at a desk opposite the door near the wall at the back of the room. On either side of the desk were long, wooden benches with a few women and children seated. Some women were holding cards with numbers on them. The room was painted white with the floors a red patchy colour, the patchy colour you see when red polish is rubbed into concrete floors. It was sparsely furnished, but the admissions desk had a grey desk fan and a rotary dial telephone. The window behind the desk was wide open, letting in a cool gentle breeze. Pale green washed-out cotton curtains flapped in the breeze in the windows. The administration officer asked us if we had been here before and the name of the child. My sister-in-law did not answer but instead asked to see the matron as she was expecting us. To tell her the Kasengeles were here. The officer sat up straight, picked up the phone and called the matron.

It was the first time I stepped into a hospital to an admissions or emergency department with my son. The hospital was something you could not imagine unless you had lived in a Third World country and had had the experience of visiting public hospitals in the 1980s. Babies slept in clean but sometimes stained well-worn linen. Water dripped from broken taps and sick kids cried around you. I was shocked out of my pretty little cosy world. If my baby had not been so sick, I would have been out of there and made the effort to drive to Kitwe to the hospital where he was born. But he was too sick to drive to a better hospital. I spent three days in hospital with the baby.

There was a mother's shelter, which consisted of a long dormitory-like room with no furniture in it. Most of the windows in the room were broken, letting in a cool breeze. There were no threadbare faded curtains there, just a room with a bare concrete floor with a few badly stained dirty mattresses. You had to bring your own linen and beddings. Most of the women just wrapped their African print material around them and slept on the floor. I took one look and there was no way I was going to stay in there. Fortunately for me, Bwembya got a little room to himself and one of the kind nurses found me an old cot mattress that was placed next to the cot and that is where I slept. My husband brought some linen from home, and I was all set to sleep. When the lights were dimmed, a thousand cockroaches appeared from nowhere. There was not much sleep that night.

Despite all this, the staff were wonderful with all the children. I was grateful to them. My son got great care and when his temperature went back to normal, we were discharged. However, when we left the hospital with him, he was still unwell. Mwango and I paced up and down the house for days trying to soothe him. He would only stop crying if he were held in certain positions and if you rocked him gently as you walked up and down. Gone were our peaceful nights. 'Welcome to the club,' said some more experienced parents, 'this is the way things are when you have a child.'

Bwembya was not breast-fed. I could not breastfeed him. It was not from lack of trying. The nurses at the hospital tried and my mother-in-law tried to make him drink breastmilk. The nurses tried feeding him from a dropper, on a spoon, in a cup, in a bottle, but one taste and he would let out a howl and turn the other way. We did not have special feeding clinics to help mothers adjust or babies adjust, this was a Third World country. So S26 formula it was.

Being bottle-fed made it easy for anyone to look after Bwembya. When we went to bed, we took a tray with the baby's formula, a flask of hot water and clean bottles with cooled water in them, so we could quickly mix the formula and feed him. Mwango was a very hands-on father, which is unusual in Zambian society. The cot was on Mwango's side of the bed. It had one side that you could slide down so that the base of the cot and the bed were level. I offered to swap sides with Mwango so I could be near the baby, but he did not see why I had to be the one next to the baby. So, the cot stayed on his side of the bed near the window away from the door. Often, Mwango would jump up at the slightest sound to feed and change Bwembya, and I would sit up and watch him.

One day in the third week, when I was changing his nappy, I noticed a lump that seemed to blow up like a balloon just below his tummy on one side. Fortunately for us, a close childhood friend of Mwango's, a doctor, happened to be there when I was changing Bwembya's nappy. He quickly diagnosed him as having an inguinal hernia and referred him to a specialist in the hospital where Bwembya was born. Within a couple of days, he had an operation and things settled down to normal again. Three months later, the same thing happened and Bwembya ended up with a hernia operation on the other side of his groin.

Apparently, we were told by a few well-meaning elders, Bwembya was getting sick because of his name. One opinion was that because he was not named after a person, he had not inherited a spirit. To counteract this opinion (just in case we were wrong), we gave him a middle name, after Mwango's father. The other opinion was that we should expect trouble, because after all Bwembya in Bemba (our language), means a whip, so we were being whipped. The name Bwembya was such a mouthful that he became known as simply 'B'. Things settled down well after our teething pains.

In September 1986, Mwango was accepted into a master's degree program at a university in Edinburgh, Scotland. As my parents had lived in Canberra for three years, they thought it would be a good opportunity for Bwembya and I to visit Canberra, so they could see their grandchild before I went to Scotland. Mwango left for Scotland and Bwembya and I went on our first visit to Australia. My parents lived in O'Malley in Canberra, with my older brother Heckie, my younger brothers Kenny and James, as well as my sister Bwalya. Reggie, the oldest in the family, was in Zambia.

It was my first time in Australia. My dad met me at the airport in Sydney late one evening. With little fuss and fanfare, we cleared customs, got in the car and drove to Canberra. We arrived in Canberra in the early hours of the morning. Everyone was still awake waiting for us to get back home. Mum had a light dinner and tea with scones waiting. I was home. Bwalya, the boys, and I talked till the sun came up.

I stayed in Canberra for about three months. Bwembya was growing bigger slowly and was a lovable chubby, easy-going baby. My sister and her friends fell in love with him, and I had no lack of babysitters. While we were in Canberra, Bwembya was in a fashion parade at the TAFE where my brother Hector was studying fashion design. Hector had designed a beautiful fluffy cream sheepskin baby carrier. One of his fellow students carried Bwembya in it at the fashion show. Bwembya revelled in all this and there was not a peep out of him on or off the stage despite the loud music and flashing lights. I also modelled some of my brother's suits that day, but I found the loud music a little over the top. Hector, Bwembya and I all had a lot of fun on stage, and only arrived home in the early hours of the morning. The poor baby was fast asleep in the car seat.

In November, we got news that Mwango's father had passed away in Zambia after a long illness. The plan had been that Mwango would come to Australia for Christmas then we would go back to Scotland together. However, within a few days, Bwembya and I proceeded to Scotland to join Mwango so that I could be with him following his father's death. I walked through the airport to the arrival area pushing Bwembya's pram. As I was moving forward, I saw a man standing in front of me with his knees bent and his arms outstretched. He had a thick grey jacket and a big smile on his face. It took me half a minute to realise it was Mwango. In the three months he had been in Scotland, he had put on enough weight for me not to recognise him right away. I told him this and he laughed out loud. He had been staying in a house organised by the university where meals were provided. He was not used to all the big breakfasts and all the potatoes he had to eat.

✦

Chapter 5

Edinburgh is a beautiful city. I have many fond memories of spending lots of quality time with Bwembya as we tried to cope with living in such a cold climate with a baby. I remember the first time it snowed. It was a cold brisk Sunday afternoon. Mwango was studying, so I decided to take Bwembya out for a walk into the town centre. I had only been out a short time when it started to snow. Within five minutes it was snowing so hard the wheels of the pram were getting stuck in the snow. So much for dreaming of a white Christmas, I thought, as the pram refused to budge. Bwembya sat in the pram amazed at this white stuff that was falling into his pram. Being a Sunday there were very few buses, luckily a taxi happened to be passing by, so I hailed it, picked up the pram, unceremoniously plonked it into the taxi and headed for home. I had seen all the snow I needed when I lived in Greensboro. When you have had to scrape ice off a windscreen in the mornings and drive through slush to get to school, snow was not a novelty.

I loved living in Edinburgh. If it was not for the cold weather, I would live there permanently. The people were friendly, there was always someone to help me lift the pram on and off buses, or with heavy bags. Our first flat was at Haddon's court. There were four flats with two flats on each level. We lived on the second level. In the flat opposite us lived an older lady who used to beg me to leave Bwembya with her whenever I went out shopping. The minute she heard my door open, she would rush out and say, 'You're not taking that wee one out into the cold, my dear, are you?' So, I would leave Bwembya with her and go and run my errands. We did not have very long conversations as her Scottish accent was very difficult to understand but as time passed, I learnt to understand people.

Even from an early age, Bwembya had the charm to make strangers stop in the street and smile or talk to him. On a visit to London there was an incident with a half a litre glass feeding bottle. This bottle was a 'Nuk' brand which my brother Hector convinced me to buy one night at a late-night chemist in Canberra. I was balancing the pram as I went up a steep escalator in a London underground train station, almost at the top, when a little hand stretched out and hurled the empty Nuk bottle backwards. A young man with pink hair, earrings, and more mascara than I would dare use, caught the bottle with one flick of a hand. When I got to the top, I wondered whether to rush off as I looked back and saw three leather clad guys slowly coming up to meet me. The one with the bottle held it out to me and one of the other two said very politely, 'Would you like a hand?' Two of them picked up the pram, one at each end and proceeded up a long set of stairs leading out onto the street. I rushed up after them to ensure they did not take off with my baby. I heard cooing voices as they talked to him on the way up. At the entrance to the underground station, they bid us a warm, 'Tara love' and off they went. That is one of the stories about the bottle that ended on a positive note, other incidents were not so pleasant.

One night, Bwembya was lying in bed drinking his bottle, when as soon as it was empty, he threw it, but that time it landed on the other side of the room, in my face. I let out a painful scream that sent Mwango rushing into the room from the living room where he was studying. He had a good laugh about it. 'Honey, he is only a baby.' The black eye I had the next day was not very funny to me. This 'Nuk' bottle was around for a long time until one night when Bwembya was about fourteen months old, he threw it at the wall as usual and it broke into tiny pieces. I was not sorry to see it go.

In February 1987, Mum decided to pay us a visit from Australia, to come and do some shopping and pick up Bwembya. I had decided I would like to study some management courses and Mum wanted to spend some time with him. She flew over for a few weeks and went back with him to Canberra where he spent seven months. Over the few weeks Mum stayed with us, we enjoyed shopping and some mother and daughter time. She also cooked us finger-licking food and we ate like royalty. Over the years she specialised in cooking and excelled at it. She can sniff a mistake a mile away if you put too much of something in a dish. The chef at the house in Canberra was always nervous when Mum went to check what food had been prepared. We would all sit there thinking how delicious the food was and Mum would come out and say, you put too much of this and that in, or you let the whatever it was stay too long on the heat that it's become rubbery.

My husband was always extremely happy when my mother came to stay. They got along like a house on fire, and she treated him like a king. I was the sorry one, as he expected the standards for the cooking and the home maintenance to continue after she had left. When he walked into the house, a tray was waiting with a snack. His dinner was served in a different way, because as Mum said, it was all in the presentation. I had thought of serving him mashed potatoes and sausages on a tray with a red rose but resisted the temptation.

I went to London with Mum on the train and saw her and Bwembya off to Australia after organising his passport at the embassy. I was comfortable handing over Bwembya to my mother without a second thought. While he was in Australia, Bwembya frequently attended university with his godmother, my young sister Bwalya when Mum was busy (she was a high commissioner's wife, after all), or he was with my brothers. Even Dad took time to look after Bwembya, although this mostly entailed taking him to the shops or for a ride in the car. A long ride. Dad still loved his long rides.

Meanwhile, I went to a college in Edinburgh and studied some management and computer courses. I also managed to do some part-time youth work with a local regional council working with kids by the docks. I learnt to play snooker with the teenagers – and learnt a few choice swear words. I began to acquire a street education. I put away my Calvin Klein jeans and put on some acid-wash jeans with sneakers and I could walk down a seedy street and not be afraid. I would get a 'Hello, Miss' from kids smoking in corners and hanging around shops. I became part of the landscape.

Mwango and I were like ships that passed each other in the night. He was busy going to school during the day and studying and writing his thesis when he was not in class. I would spend the day typing the work he had done the night before onto a floppy disc. I could use the computer and he could not. On some evenings, I worked in an Indian restaurant and then in an Italian restaurant while Mwango studied at home, but on weekends we tried to spend a little time together. We visited castles, had picnics on hilltops overlooking the town, watched the military tattoo, and hung out with the few friends we made.

During the six months Bwembya was in Australia, I missed him a lot. Heckie sent me a video of Bwembya's christening and first birthday. I missed the milestones. The video showed Bwembya learning to walk, his christening at the church Mum and Dad attended in Manuka, and his first birthday. He was also saying his first word, 'mum, mum, mum'. My sister Bwalya had been training him to call her mum. She would come into view of the camera and call Bwembya, and he would hobble over to her calling her mum. There was a big grin on her face as she stared into the video camera.

Bwalya was not a Bennett Belle. She went to a university in Canberra, and I am sure she had a few choice words pass through her gorgeous head, on the days our loving mum quietly opened her bedroom door (after Aunty Bwalya had crawled into bed a few hours earlier from a late night out), and Mum quietly placed Bwembya on the bed. You see, Mum would sometimes be running late for some morning tea with other high commissioners' wives or one of her friends would call her and tell her there is a sale at one of her favourite shops. She could not miss a good sale.

My gorgeous sister would roll over in her sleep dreaming of some handsome prince she met at the club to be woken by a terrible smell which could not be coming from the prince in her dream. Little fingers poking her eyes and her nose, that could not be her prince, could it? Then there would be the wet sloppy kisses on her face, sometimes a little drool. That was certainly not prince charming. She would open one eye, look through the haze of sleep, and see a little prince sitting there grinning at her. At those moments, I am not so sure my sister wanted to hear how all aunties are mothers to their sister's children, but I know she would lovingly change his nappy, give him a bottle and the two of them would then sleep until Mum came back with some nice treat for them, as she always did.

Mwango travelled to Australia in July that year and came back with Bwembya in August. I could not believe it when Bwembya came back, he had grown so big and had started saying a few words such as mum, light, hector, head, nose. We settled right into parenthood again, and we also had a few sleepless nights with the dreadful ear infections. The rest of our time in Edinburgh was very busy. I finished typing Mwango's thesis and he got ready to complete his masters.

Bwembya and I returned to Zambia in October and Mwango stayed behind for a month to finish presenting his MSc thesis. When we got back to Zambia, things started to change. Bwembya stopped talking and was generally a different little boy. I took him to a doctor who blamed this on his travelling so much from country to country that he was confused with the language difference.

Mwango returned to Zambia and went straight back to work at the bank. Bwembya started going to day-care a few mornings a week and I began looking for a job. In February 1988, I got a job with a pension fund as a pensions officer. I loved the job which involved working with pensioners who were receiving benefits from the fund. I learnt a lot of things on the job such as how artificial limbs were made, what they were made of and who made them. I got to network and negotiate with companies and health facilities that were involved in the process. I bought coffins, went to funerals, bought chemicals for prosthetics, and sometimes food and resources for pensioners. I helped pensioners access their pensions, receive lump sums, and developed business plans for small business ventures. I also helped them submit their plans and set up businesses.

I got to drive a shift-stick old Land Rover that I used when all the other pool cars were unavailable. The first car I learnt to drive in was a manual, so it was easy enough for me to adjust to driving a Land Rover. I enjoyed running around in the old car going into compounds and suburbs that had untarred roads with deep potholes.

The first time I drove it, some of the staff stood in the doorway and watched. A few of them had tried to talk me out of driving that dusty old car, but I was determined to go out on my visit. I was not about to wait until one of the other pool cars were available. In my light blue linen suit and patent black heels, I put my foot on the step under the door and swung my body smoothly into the car. I closed the door, started the car, pressed the clutch, and bunny-hopped for a few meters until I got control of it. The staff in the doorway clapped as I turned out of the company car park into the main road and off I went. In Zambia, I was not called Patricia at work, I was Mrs Kasengele. Those were the days of typing pools and switch boards. Staff lived in company houses and company buses were available to take staff to and from work.

Mum came to Zambia in January 1988 with my sister, Bwalya, and my brother, Heckie. They both found jobs and settled in Luanshya, a small mining town about forty-five minutes away from Ndola. Bwalya was a teacher for a private school, and Hector was a fashion designer for an international company that made men's clothing, mainly suits. Their arrival was wonderful for Mwango and I. Mwango and Heckie got to go out to watch rugby and drink Cointreau, their favourite drink at the time. When Reggie came over, he would go and watch rugby, too, but he was more of a whiskey drinking man. Mwango was a whiskey drinking man when Reggie was around.

Mum stayed with us for a short time and went to Chipili to check on their house and see her family. I was happy to have my sister around. Bwalya, Mwenya (Heckie's fiancée), and I would sometimes accompany the boys to watch rugby, but we really went to people-watch, eat barbequed meat, socialise and just plain gossip. Not malicious gossip, catching up gossip, the good kind. When we were not at the rugby club, Bwalya and I were at the hairdressers or stayed home watching videos. There was a video club at a private house across the road where we were members. We would also occasionally go to the public market to buy cheaper fruits and vegetables.

One Saturday, we parked the car, a white Toyota Corona, and walked into the market. We were stopped by a young man carrying lots of jewellery. 'Come on Ba sister, buy yourself a new watch.'

I turned to him and said, 'I have no money to buy jewellery, my friend.'

'Sister, that is a lie. Look at the car you are driving. You must be loaded. Would you prefer I steal from you, or you buy something from me?'

He did look like he could snatch my purse right there and then and there would be nothing I could do about it. I looked him in the eye and said, 'It is because of that car that I am broke, and I have to come to this market to buy food.'

He laughed out loud and said, 'You have really answered me there. You are right, it is a possibility. I will let you go. Have a good day.' He walked off, laughing. I had learnt to talk the language that people around me understood, that would keep me safe.

In May 1988, my two brothers Heckie and Reggie both got married within three weeks of each other. Dad came for the weddings and returned to Australia shortly afterwards. Mum was still in Zambia. Bwembya was generally hyperactive, so I spent ninety per cent of the afternoon at Heckie's wedding reception outside with him. He was being too disruptive inside and people wanted to be able to hear the speeches. I did not mind too much sitting outside on the step with Bwembya. I had picked up a plate of food, sat outside, and he ended up with icing from a cake all over his face and clothes. We had our own little tea party outside. Three weeks later, I missed Reggie's wedding. The day before the wedding, Hector, his wife Mwenya, and their two-year-old daughter Natasha, were involved in a car accident. Mwenya and Natasha were injured in the accident, so Mum and I spent the next day at the hospital looking for them.

Life seemed ideal at the time. We both had great jobs, and a nice home filled with all the lovely things we had shipped from Scotland. There was also a maid to clean the house, and a nanny to look after Bwembya. Mwango took me out for lunch or dinner at least once a month and my brothers and my sister were around a lot. However, that ideal life did not last too long. In 1988 the teacher at Bwembya's childcare first picked up that something was wrong with Bwembya. She said she thought Bwembya had a problem with his hearing and needed to have it checked out.

I told Mwango, who flipped and said the teacher had to be out of her mind, there was nothing wrong with our child.

One day, I walked in from work and Bwembya was watching a music video in the living room. I was standing right near him and called out his name a few times, but he did not seem to hear me. He happened to look in my direction, saw me, the biggest grin spread over his face, and he ran to me with his arms stretched out. The penny dropped. He had not heard me. All the clues had been right in front of me, and I had not seen them. I should have known. Despite initial opposition from Mwango who thought I was overreacting, I arranged to see a hearing specialist at the hospital where Bwembya was born.

The specialist said he could not test Bwembya properly as the instruments they had were for adults, mainly miners who had lost their hearing in the mines because of the noise from the machines underground. Bwembya would not be able to give him a response to questions as to what sounds he could hear. He said he had a lot of wax in his ears and that could be the problem, so we got some eardrops to melt the wax, but that did not solve it. Our perfect little world was not so perfect, after all, we might have a child with a hearing problem. That was unthinkable.

In September 1988, I found out I was expecting our second child. As with my first pregnancy, I was extremely sick. Mum was still around and just about to head back to Australia, but with my history of traumatic pregnancy, she decided to take Bwembya back with her. I was too sick to argue about anything and so Bwembya went off to Australia once again. In March 1989, my sister Bwalya, and my niece Natasha, Heckie's three-year-old daughter, also travelled to Australia. Mum and Dad wanted

Natasha to live with them so that Bwembya could have another child in the house.

After a problematic pregnancy with what was diagnosed as an irritable uterus, our daughter Bupe was born a month early in April 1989, three days after Bwembya's birthday. Bupe was not the name we had planned for our child if she was a girl, but I was so sick during my pregnancy that when Dad heard I had a baby, he sent a message that she was to be called Bupe because she was a gift. Bupe means gift in Bemba. Bupe was tiny but strong enough not to need any specialist care. Mwango was still a doting father but not as hands-on with Bupe. He did not get up in the middle of the night to change and feed her, but he liked to hold her and have her sleeping on his shoulder a lot. Life was easier as Bupe was breastfed and bottle-fed. If I had to go out for dinner or a movie, she was fine having a bottle of formula.

My parents had planned for us to visit Australia as soon as the baby was born so Mwango, Bupe, and I travelled to Australia when Bupe was three weeks old for what we thought was a much-needed break. We arrived in Canberra at one in the morning after a thirteen-hour flight and a three-hour drive. Dad woke Bwembya up and brought him into the living room. He looked much bigger than he was and weighed a ton for a three-year-old. He was solidly built but not fat. I must admit I was a little alarmed because he seemed so much bigger than I thought he should be. It must have been mother's intuition, I was just uncomfortable with him being almost too healthy, but I did not mention this to anyone. He was still a handsome, gorgeous little boy. It felt good to be a family again and to see my Bwembya after so many months.

✦

Chapter 6

The room we were sitting in was cool despite it being a hot humid day outside. It was the formal living room of the Zambian High Commissioner's house where my parents lived. I was impressed. The house was a sprawling two-level house in the quiet leafy suburb of O'Malley. It was set on top of a hill, the last house on the street. The gardens were perfectly manicured and seemed to come alive in the early mornings with all sorts of animals. There were rabbits nibbling at flowers and kangaroos eating the larger plants. Mum was not impressed. She ran outside with a broom to chase the culprits out of her garden, laughing as she almost slipped on the dew on the grass. The front garden was a hive of activity every morning.

Lunch was a jolly affair with lots of noise and lots of food. Sunday was the cook's day off, so Mum had cooked lunch. Mum always made food that left you feeling like you had never eaten anything better. The meal was simple. The roast chicken was cooked to perfection, crisp and tasty and there was a variety of salads. I loved the Waldorf salad that had apples in it. The green apples gave it a tartness that complemented the dressing in the salad. Desert was Mum's famous apple crumble, or apple grumble as she jokingly named it, with ice-cream or cream.

After lunch, my parents called Mwango and I to the formal living room for a chat. We had only been in Australia for a day. Dad sat there calmly and told us that they had made an appointment with doctors in Sydney at the children's hospital for Monday, as there seemed to be a problem with Bwembya's health. I looked at my dad and then at my mum not really understanding what was going on. I was still very jet-lagged and had to ask Dad to repeat what he had just said. He said that one of the doctors they had taken Bwembya to see when he was sick had said there was something wrong with him, but he needed to send him to a specialist in Sydney to confirm what it was. Dad said that that was why he had wanted us to come to Australia for genetic testing. We did not think too much about it. I thought maybe it was diabetes or something genetic like that, as diabetes ran in my dad's family.

On the Monday morning, Dad, Mwango, Bwembya, Bupe and I drove to Sydney. We arrived at the children's hospital in Camperdown for the early morning appointment at half past eight and went straight to the day ward where Bwembya was admitted. Following the intake procedure, we met the genetic specialist for the first time. It was early May 1989. We did not know how often we were going to see him over the next few years, and what a prominent role he was going to play in our child's life. A team of doctors and geneticists spent most of the morning telling us what they suspected was wrong with Bwembya.

Mucopolysaccharide seemed a very long complicated name for a disease my little boy probably had. Bwembya most likely had MPS type II, known as Hunter Syndrome, in which the individual lacked an enzyme called iduronate sulphatase.

MPS type II caused varying degrees of physical disability and sometimes intellectual disability. It was the only MPS type that affected predominantly males. Not much sank in that day at the hospital, except that Bwembya's life expectancy was limited. I was shattered. It could not be, not this little three-year-old boy who was so full of life. I could not cry. I could not react, I just tried to take everything in, to understand.

Bwembya and I had our hair plucked. It hurt a lot. Each of about 100 individual hairs had to have a bulb (root) at the bottom. The bulb of the hair was to be grown in the lab and the results of the test would take a few months. I had to grin and put up with the pain. Mwango held Bwembya, as clumps of hair were pulled from his head, so that it was easier and quicker for him than removing one hair at a time. I felt each tug and pull in my heart as he twisted and cried in pain. We had got on the plane three days before thinking we were going on holiday, and to see our son, but we only had one day to enjoy it before the bombshell hit that turned our whole world upside down.

It was an awfully long day, but I kept calm. I used to cry at the drop of a hat, now I faced a crisis and could not shed a tear. I focused all my energy, making sure my children and husband were ok. When we had finished everything, we had come to do at the hospital it was early evening. We drove to the airport and picked up my sister-in-law Fidelia (Reggie's wife) and her son who was three months old.

The drive back to Canberra was uncomfortably quiet. My sister-in-law looked at all of us perplexed. To ensure she did not think we were not thrilled to have her here, I whispered what had happened that day. While we were in the car a song played on the radio that almost broke me. Whenever I hear that song,

I remember that long silent heavy drive. The song was, 'Where do broken hearts go' by Whitney Houston. We got home had something to eat, put a tired Bwembya to bed, and then finally went to our rooms downstairs. That was when I cried my heart out and Mwango and I just held each other and let it all out for about two minutes. We never asked why. We realised this was the way things were, and we had to just deal with it.

Over the next three weeks we had lots of deep discussions with Mum and Dad. We thought about what our future could be with emphasis on what would be in the best interests of Bwembya. We decided to move to Australia, so we could understand this disease and learn what we needed to do to give him the best life possible. Mwango started looking for a job and had a couple of interviews while we were in Canberra then we went back to Zambia and began the process of dismantling our lives. We were going to start again in a new country with no clear idea about where we were going, or how we were going to get there.

Chapter 7

arrived in Australia with Bupe on a visitor's visa in September 1989. Mwango, who had been offered a two-year contract with an Australian bank, stayed in Zambia to sort out our visas. I came ahead to be with Bwembya. I learnt that he sometimes swallowed food whole without chewing, that the worm-like things in his stool were spaghetti and not worms and that the round little things were grapes swallowed whole, and there was no need to panic. I learnt that he did not like to be hugged too closely and that he was as prickly as a pear. He would only let you hug him if he was not feeling well. I learnt that putting him in the car and going for a long drive was the best way to get him to sleep. I also learnt that I had to always have the child lock on the car door and that he could wind down windows.

Bwembya was an overactive three-year-old with a will of his own. If any door was left open, he would race out into the road as fast as his little legs could carry him. As fast as a tornado, my mum used to say. Fortunately, O'Malley was a quiet suburb with not many cars on the streets. Most people in our street knew who Jason and Martha's grandchild was and would catch him and bring him home. I felt like I had to have eyes in the back of my head considering how quickly he could vanish.

It was fortunate that there were lots of adults in the house, so we always had someone looking out for the kids or taking them out.

One day, I decided to take the kids out for a treat on my own to Woden Mall. We got out of the car and walked into David Jones. I stopped to strap Bupe into the pram but when I looked up, Bwembya was gone. Natasha looked at me and said, 'He went that way,' pointing towards the doors through to all the shops. We raced up and down the shops but could not see him. I went up to the information desk and asked them to announce that a little three-year-old was missing. Fortunately, as we were walking up and down the mall, we came across two older ladies leading Bwembya along. They knew who he was. He was 'Martha's grandson'. They knew Mum from Mothers' Union at the Anglican Church.

Mothers' Union is an Anglican organisation that spreads over 84 countries and is highly active in Africa. Mum joined Mothers Union when she was in Zambia and had been an active member most of her adult lifetime. In Zambia, members of the organisation wore a uniform that consisted of a navy-blue skirt, white shirt or t-shirt and a white head scarf as optional. The women are involved in providing encouragement, strength, and support to women and their families. They work with and help the underprivileged. Mum joined the Mothers' Union in Australia and continued to be an active member during her time there. I grew up thinking I was going to be in the Mothers' Union one day. When the time was right, I was going to put on the blue and white uniform and join the union and my mum working for the church. I never did. My life has been full of many things, except Mothers' Union.

Bwembya attended a special school three days a week and a 'normal' day care two mornings a week. I slowly started taking over the responsibility and care of the kids from Mum. I would get Bwembya and Natasha up in the morning, get them ready for school, and put them into the car ready to start the day. Natasha attended a preschool in Narrabundah. I started to look at Bwembya's hyperactivity and general behaviour. I paid attention to the ingredients, especially additives in food, when I went shopping. I reduced the amount of sugar he was getting, including from fruit and juices. We substituted plain muesli bars for the chocolate-coated variety, and Poppers with pure juice for those with additives. Within a few months I saw a calmer, less hyperactive little boy. A normal boisterous little boy.

Mwango arrived in Australia on the first day of December. A week later, Mwango, Bupe, and I moved to Sydney where he started work. We stayed in the city at the Park Hotel Apartments for two months. It was exciting being in the middle of a busy city like Sydney but a few days before Christmas, Bwembya was admitted to the hospital with the flu and so I went to Canberra to be with him and help Mum. I spent the days comforting, singing, and rocking a sick little boy. I would put him on my back with a chitenge, which is a piece of African fabric about two metres long. This way I could be close to him, rock him, walk around, and do other things such as read a book or watch telly. He came out of the hospital on Christmas eve and spent Christmas with us and after Christmas we went back to Sydney. Mwango went to work during the week, and I went exploring and house hunting. My brothers Kenny and James drove to Sydney over the weekends and showed us around the city.

House hunting in Sydney was interesting. I had no idea where to look. I would get on a train and ride until I came to an area I liked. When the train rolled into Campsie, and I saw people from different countries, I got out and went to the first real estate office I came across. I was shown a few houses and put a deposit on a house on Beamish Street. I think my sister and my brothers were a little shell-shocked when they came to visit me from Canberra. Campsie is a far cry from O'Malley. I had no idea where Campsie was in relation to other suburbs, or where it was in relation to the centre of the city. But it looked multicultural, so Campsie it was. The brick house I chose had three bedrooms, a white picket fence and a big backyard. It was a short distance to the shops and the train station.

In February 1990, I started working for an organisation for people with intellectual disabilities for eight hours a week in the evening as a social educator. It provided services for people with an intellectual disability living in the community. Working in the evening meant I was home late as I had to travel on public transport to Schofields, Merrylands, and Emerton. A few nights I found Mwango pacing up and down the front yard anxiously waiting for me, but a few weeks into my job, Mum offered us her little red Toyota Corolla. We agreed on condition that we paid her for it when we were in a better position financially. The little red car was a life saver. I would be home in an hour instead of two to three hours with platform changes at different train stations. I had no trouble driving around Sydney. I had driven in Washington and New York in the US, so Sydney was no big deal. The little car meant we could drive to Canberra every second weekend. It was freedom!

One afternoon when we were in Canberra, Mum and I went to buy groceries at Woolworths. They had some lovely cotton nightdresses for girls. I bought one each for Natasha and Bupe. We went home and after the kids had their bath, the girls put on their new nightdresses. We were sitting down having dinner and Bwembya started to cry. His eyes filled up and tears ran down his face. Everyone was concerned.

'Bwembya, what is the matter?'

'Bwembya why are you crying?'

He just cried silently, looking at the girls. It then hit me: 'Mum, we did not buy Bwembya pyjamas.'

'The girls got new nighties and he got nothing.'

I got up and beckoned Bwalya. We went straight to Woolworths and got Bwembya a new pair of pyjamas. As soon as we walked into the living room and Bwembya saw the pyjamas, a big smile covered his face and the tears stopped. I was learning fast what my son's needs were without him saying a word.

In the first week of April, I started a part-time job at an organisation for people with spinal injuries in Homebush as a personal aid. To be honest, I thought personal aid was to be a personal assistant. I really thought I was going for a job as an assistant (secretary) to a manager or something. Anyway, I got the job and did not regret it. I did not tell many people exactly what I did, even my husband, my parents, my sister, my brothers, people like that. They would have thought I was better off waiting for the right job. But it was a job, and I did it well and enjoyed it.

I enjoyed the job because I guess I love helping people have the best quality of life they can have. The work was humbling because I was just doing a job, but this was other people's lives, a part of their everyday they could not leave at work.

They needed me to help them do things we take for granted like getting out of the car, using the phone, sitting properly in a chair, eating, and going to the bathroom with a little dignity. They were wonderful people with big spirits who embraced me and made me feel like I mattered.

We settled into our Campsie house and enjoyed the eighth months we lived there. The house had good-size bedrooms and a fenced-off back garden. In April, Bwembya and Natasha came over in the school holidays. Bwembya had finally come to live with us and did not return to Canberra at the end of the holidays. My sister Bwalya and I enjoyed many hours of fun, too, bargain-shopping in the little hidden clothes shops on Beamish Street and the surrounding streets. I started going to the children's hospital at Camperdown with Bwembya for appointments with different people. There was so much drama involved on trips to the hospital. Bwembya had never been on public transport in Australia, let alone a train. He thought it was a big adventure and tried to pull the emergency lever on the train, hop off at every train stop and race through the carriages. From Campsie to Camperdown involved a train and a bus trip and by the time I got to Camperdown I was all sweaty and puffed out.

At Camperdown, we saw all manner of specialist like ear, nose and throat (ENT) doctors, cardiologists, neurologists, dentists, occupational therapists, physiotherapists, speech therapists, geneticists, and social workers. We received a lot of information and advice, most of which was useful. One of the doctors recommended a general practitioner in Campsie who became our GP for many years.

I did not always take the advice I was given. I occasionally took a different route. Before the start of the second school term, a recommendation was made for Bwembya to attend a school near Parramatta. We arrived at the school for our appointment at nine thirty in the morning and following a tour of the school it was suggested that Bwembya spend a couple of hours in one of the classes. He was placed in a hearing-impaired class. I sat at the back of the classroom observing. Bwembya was doing his own thing, playing with toys and half-taking part in what was happening with the rest of the class and looking up at the teacher from time to time. On our way out, one of the teaching staff called me to the side and whispered to me, 'I believe that Bwembya can hear. You should get him tested again. This would not be the right school for him.'

'What do you mean?' I said to her.

'It seems like he must be able to hear some things, judging by his reactions to some instructions,' she said. I thought about what she said and agreed that sometimes even without the hearing aids, Bwembya reacted to things around him.

A week after our visit, we had an appointment with a counsellor. When we arrived, the counsellor pointed to a couple of chairs opposite where she was sitting. I lifted Bwembya up and sat him in a chair then sat down next to him.

'Good morning, Patricia. Good morning, B.'

'Good morning,' I said back to her.

She opened a white folder marked Bwembya Kasengele along the side.

'How did the visit to the school go?'

'It went fine,' I answered.

'Great. Did you manage to get him enrolled into the school?'

'No, I did not.'

She looked up at me and smiled.

'Do you need any help with that? I can call the principal and organise everything with the department of education.'

I looked back at her and smiled, not sure how I was going to explain what I had to say. I did not want to get the staff member at the school into any trouble or appear ungrateful.

'I have decided I would prefer Bwembya went to another school other than that school.' She looked shocked.

'What do you mean? That is the best school for a child with Bwembya's needs in Sydney. They help children who have a hearing impairment and problem with speech like Bwembya has. Their teaching methods are one of the best in Sydney. We have recommended a lot of children to that program and following Bwembya's assessment we all felt that that would be the best school for him. Is it the distance? Do you need assistance with transport or housing? There are different services we can tap into to help.'

I looked into her eyes as she was talking. My heart was racing. I did not believe I was going to say this.

'I will not take my child to that school as I feel that it is not an appropriate school for him.'

She looked at me like I had suddenly gone crazy.

'Mrs Kasengele, this school is our recommendation and if you disagree with our expert recommendation then you are quite free to find your own appropriate educational facility.'

I got up and stood Bwembya up beside me. Holding his hand and picking up my handbag I turned to her and said, 'Thank you very much for all your patience and support. I will work with the Department of Education directly to find Bwembya a school near where we live that is appropriate for him.'

To find Bwembya a school near where we lived, I looked in the phone book for schools in the area. I made a lot of phone calls and visited a few schools. I was able to interview the staff at schools and get Bwembya set up in a school within a few weeks and I got Bwembya's reports from his school in Canberra. He started kindergarten after his fourth birthday at a school in Strathfield. I would drop him off at school and pick him up at the end of the day on my way from work. After a few weeks, the school bus would pick him up and drop him off at home.

In April, shortly after I started work in Homebush but before I got my first pay, we were at home on a Sunday when Mwango said to me, 'Honey, I will not be able to go to work until Wednesday.'

'Why not,' I asked.

'I have no money for the train to get to work until pay day on Wednesday,' he said.

I had used all the money we had in our bank account to buy groceries and just managed to get everything the kids needed. I had five dollars left on me which was not enough to give my husband to catch a train to work. The doorbell rang. It was my dad.

'Hello, everyone. I was in Sydney to drop someone off at the airport. I thought I should pop in and see how you all are.'

Dad stayed for a couple of hours, had some lunch, and played with the kids. At the end of the visit, we were standing by the car saying our goodbyes when Dad turned to me and said, 'By the way, I still have Bwembya's last month's allowance,' and gave it to me. Bwembya had been getting an allowance of $50 from my parents. We saw Dad off and walked back to the house.

At the front door, Mwango turned to me and said, 'I can't believe this. I can go to work tomorrow.'

'I didn't want to ask Dad for money. I couldn't,' I said to him.

'I thought of asking him, but it did not feel right to me, too,' said Mwango.

I never told my dad this story, but I told the girls so that they do not think that we were always comfortable. We were migrants starting from scratch. We had family and we had jobs, but we had some difficult times, too. I told them stories like when I had to pretend not to want to eat anything but plain rice so that there was enough food for the kids and enough money to buy nappies for two children and school supplies for Bwembya. Or about counting the number of slices of bread to make sure that everyone had breakfast and bread for school lunch. My parents would have given us money. My siblings would have given us money. But Mwango and I wanted to do this on our own if we could.

During a routine specialist visit at the children's hospital, Bwembya had a hearing test and it was decided that he had glue ear and required grommets. Grommets are tiny tubes that are inserted into the eardrum to help drain fluid from the ear. Bwembya had been prescribed hearing aids, which my parents had bought for him, but we had a really hard time getting him to wear them. He would throw them into pot plants, dust bins, under furniture, anywhere but leave them in his ears.

One Saturday in Canberra, my brother James, and his girlfriend Shaunagh decided to take Bwembya and Natasha out on a cultural experience to the National Gallery. They packed all the things they needed including snacks and juice for the children. Natasha, smiling with no front teeth and Bwembya with his cheeky grin. They went through the gallery looking at the paintings. Halfway through Shaunagh turned around to James and said, 'Where are his hearing aids? They are not in his ears.'

'Bwembya, where are your hearing aids?'

Bwembya looked up and just smiled.

'Natasha, do you have any idea where Bwembya's hearing aids are?'

Natasha stood there and said, 'No'. They looked everywhere, in the car, in the cafeteria, nothing. They told the people in the gallery they had lost hearing aids. An hour later, they had just about given up and were ready to go home when Shaunagh said, 'No, no, hang on. This child was our responsibility, I am not going back to your mum's place to say we have lost his hearing aids.' So, they stood there wondering where the hearing aids could be, and finally, one of them mentioned the bins. They started looking in the bins, and sure enough, there were the hearing aids.

In the middle of the year, Bwembya had an operation and got his first set of grommets. The difference the grommets made was unbelievable. We could give him instructions and he would obey. The tantrums almost totally disappeared. The sometimes prickly, cranky child became a happy, smiley kid. One day, I found him sitting on the toilet humming away. Bwembya had used the toilet on his own (without the toilet timing) for the first time. There was a kid the doctors told us would be unlikely to be toilet trained just proving them wrong. I thought my heart was going to burst with joy. I ran into the living room where Mwango and Bwalya were sitting. 'Honey! Honey!' I screamed.

'What is it?' Mwango stood up, alarmed.

'Bwembya has gone to the toilet and done a poo on his own in the toilet.'

Mwango and Bwalya rushed into the toilet and came out screaming with delight. We sounded like a mad house. We behaved like we had won the lotto. It was momentous. No more training pants and nappies. Bwalya went and got a bottle of champagne from her box of wines. We called Dad and Kenny in Canberra and they too started to celebrate and opened a bottle of champagne. I had a few sips of champagne. This was big because I did not drink at the time and my dad was a teetotaler, he had his cup of tea. 'To Bwembya. Hip, hip, hurray!'

At the end of April, Mum, Dad, and Natasha left for Zambia. Natasha was finally going back to her parents, and her little brother who was born in January that year. Mum and Dad were going home for a few weeks' leave. In June Heckie, and Mwenya had a bad car accident. Mwenya broke her spine and was paralysed from the neck down. Natasha had hardly had time to bond with her mother before the accident. We were all concerned and prayed that Mwenya would be alright. She was in hospital for about nine months.

I finished work in Homebush at the end of July as my hours with my other job increased from eight hours a week to sixteen hours a week. I had applied to what seemed like hundreds of jobs over those first eight months, and the main reason provided for not giving me a job was because I had no Australian experience. I kept looking, churning out applications, and sending them. I had a job and that was alright for now, especially that the job was in the evening, and I had a car that would take me to work and home safely – but I wanted a job that was nine to five.

Chapter 8

We had been in Sydney for six months and had a small group of friends. Mwango reconnected with a Zambian friend whom he had met in Sydney while he was in Australia picking up Bwembya in 1986 but one of the first friends Mwango made was a young man from South Africa. He was a lawyer and they met in the city at lunch time and became incredibly good friends. Through him we met Rusty and Joy who also became great friends of the family. Within a year, they moved within walking distance to us in Bexley. We also met a few other friends from different parts of the world. We spent a lot of time at barbeques and picnics with our newfound friends and life started to settle into a pattern.

Every second weekend and during holidays we went to Canberra to visit my parents. The weekends in Canberra were great. We would leave Sydney after work and get to Canberra in the evening in time for a late dinner and go to bed in the early hours of the morning. The kids always woke up early so I would get up to give them breakfast and watch cartoons with them. Mum would be up early, too, followed by Dad and then the rest of the adults. We spent most of the time by the pool in summer or playing tennis in the tennis courts in the backyard. The pool was a covered indoor pool so even in winter we would hang around the pool area. Dad and I both loved to eat 'tute', which is the bemba word for cassava. Mum would start a fire in a brazier and Dad and I would roast cassava by the pool. We would eat the cassava with roasted peanuts.

Early in August, Bwalya got a job in Sydney, and she came to live with us until the end of October when she found a unit in Mosman. At the end of August, we moved to a three-bedroom house on Preddy's Road in Bexley. The house was a white weather board house with a big garden and a white picket fence. The front yard was just lawn with some calla lilies growing on the left side of the house under the bedroom window. The lilies had long stalks and big white flowers that I loved to put in vases in the house. The front yard was big enough for a game of cricket or soccer. The backyard was of a good size, too. There were gates at the side of the house separating the front yard and the backyard. This was a welcome feature as the kids could play in the backyard in an enclosed area. The back of the house had a covered veranda where we spent a lot of time watching the kids play on the lawn with their bicycles, skateboards, trampoline, and a little wading pool.

Because of the move, Bwembya was out of the school region for his current school so I had to find a school in our local area. I loved the school and Bwembya's teacher, so I was not happy to be moving schools. I was the treasurer for the P and C association for the school and had a good rapport with the staff. I decided to leave him there for a while and transported him to school myself on my way to work. As the school bus could no longer take him home, I had to arrange afterschool care for him for about half an hour each day. This proved difficult to do, so I got a transfer for Bwembya to a school in Arncliffe. On the day

I met the principal, she told me she understood I was not very happy to be moving Bwembya's school but that their school was just as nice and had a very good reputation. She said she was sure Bwembya would enjoy this school just as much as he had enjoyed his old school, and he did.

In September, I applied for a full-time position as a training officer working with an organisation for people with intellectual disabilities. I got the job and started working in Ryde on a big campus that had a sheltered workshop, community participation programs, and a residential service. My job involved designing and implementing programs, staff training, conducting individual vocational and residential assessments, hands-on vocational and social skills training, report writing and research, as well as liaison with staff, parents, and carers. I felt like I had arrived at a job that was rewarding and fulfilling. I loved everything about it.

Bwembya was enjoying his new school and I was incredibly happy with it. For the second time in one year, I thought a school was the best in Sydney. I joined the school's P and C association and became the secretary and then the treasurer.

I had started full-time work, so I had to organise after-school care for Bwembya. This was one of my earliest challenges. I made a few calls, asked at the school if there was an after-school service he could access, but without success. I must have been the only mother of a special needs child living in the St George area who needed after-school care. I called a helpline who referred me on and on. Then I called every after-school care in the area and explained my dilemma. They all said they did not have the resources or the trained staff to care for a child with special needs. Then one of the after-school centres referred me to a community organisation who ran an after-school care in a church hall in Kogarah. They offered to give Bwembya a trial if I was willing to assist staff with Bwembya's needs. After a few trials and with assistance from the staff at school, Bwembya settled in.

The rest of year passed uneventfully although Bwembya had a lot of ear infections and high temperatures, so I spent a lot of time in the GP's office. When I was not at work I was at home with the kids, or going shopping, to the markets, the park or to church. We spent Christmas in Canberra with the family. Mum was still in Zambia from the time my parents had gone on holiday earlier in the year. It was a hot summer, so the kids enjoyed spending a lot of time in the pool

In March 1991, I was woken up by someone touching me. It was the middle of the night, and the room was dark with only a little light filtering in through the door that led to the living room. Our bedroom was at the back of the house. There were two doors into the bedroom. One door led into the living room and the other door led into the area at the back of the house to the laundry and back door. We used to leave the door to the living room open, so that we could hear the kids who were in one of the two bedrooms in front of the house. Bupe liked to run into our bedroom at night and stand next to my bed when she woke up at night. I had assumed it would be her. I looked up but there was nobody there. Someone was talking to me but there was no one there. Was I still asleep and dreaming? The voice sounded like my sister-in-law Mwenya in Zambia. She was talking about how I should look after Natasha and what kind of care she needed. It scared the life out of me.

'Honey,' I shouted.

Mwango woke up immediately. 'What is the matter?' He switched on the bedside lamp and looked at me. I was shaking and wondering what had just happened.

'I don't know if I was dreaming but I was sure Mwenya was just here talking to me about Tasha.'

'You must have been dreaming,' Mwango said, putting his arms around my shoulders. 'Go to sleep it was just a dream.'

It did not feel like a dream to me. It felt very real. A few hours later, I got a phone call just as I walked into the office at work from Dad. Mwenya, who had been in hospital since the car accident last June, had passed away a few hours ago.

When I rang Mwango to tell him the news, he said, 'So maybe you were not dreaming.' My dad left for Zambia the next day to attend the funeral. Mum was still in Zambia at the time.

In April, Bwembya turned five. On his birthday, Bwembya and I took a trip to the south coast. The school was taking part in an excursion for kids from different schools in Sydney and Bwembya was one of the few students chosen from his school because it was his birthday. But I woke up that day feeling unwell. Every muscle in my body was aching and my head was hurting. I wanted Bwembya to enjoy his birthday and the excursion, so I got up, took some medication, and got ready. We left home early in the morning. Mwango dropped us off at the school. There was a line of vintage cars lined up outside the school and the birthday boy got to pick which car he rode in. In an open-topped car, seated in the back like royalty, we were driven to Bankstown airport. I am sure that the weather was lovely, but I was cold, miserable, and wrapped up for the day. The wind was blowing as I climbed up the narrow stairs into the aircraft, guiding Bwembya in front of me, while carrying his backpack and my handbag.

The plane was one of those vintage planes, solid enough I am sure, but throughout the flight, I felt like we were going to lose a wing or a propeller or an engine. Bwembya was not at all bothered by the flight and seemed to be enjoying it all. Because I had a stuffy nose, my ears were popping, and I was extremely uncomfortable. I was very grateful when we landed safely. It was a shaky rattling landing but a safe one just the same. I have never been so glad to see the ground. We were driven in buses from the airport to a farm in Moruya. The organisers of the day took one look at me and showed me a room with a bed. I put my stuff in there and went on a few hayrides with the birthday boy. There was a big birthday cake with candles on it for Bwembya. We sang 'happy birthday' and cut the cake. I had some cake and a cup of tea and passed out on the comfortable bed in the back room, until I was woken up for the trip back home. Bwembya had a lovely day and enjoyed himself.

In June 1991, I left my job in Ryde and got a job with a disability service in Burwood as a branch coordinator because it was closer to home. I was responsible for the day-to-day running of the centre. This included developing and establishing programs, supervision of training staff, occupational health and safety, equipment maintenance, record keeping, supervising operations in the workshop, and training of adults with an intellectual disability.

In November, I was appointed general manager of the organisation and occupied that position from November 1991 to August 1997. I was responsible for the overall management of the organisation which included a community access program, an employment training centre, a mobile car detailing service, an early intervention program and a residential group home for people with disabilities. I loved that job. The people I worked with were warm, supportive, and nurturing. It was the most family friendly workplace I had ever worked in. People gave more than a hundred per cent to the job and to their friends. If I was in a meeting or running late at some training, staff in their own time would volunteer to pick up the kids and take them home with them until I picked them up. These wonderful people became like family.

Mwango and I were both in full-time work and the kids were in school and childcare. Early in the year, Bupe started going to a childcare centre in Campsie. I would drop her off and pick her up on my way to work. She was a loveable, quiet two-year-old who loved to curl up and have someone read to her. In the holidays, the kids spent time with Mum in Canberra. She was back from Zambia and Natasha had come back with Mum after the death of her mother. Having my mum around during those first few years we were in Australia was a blessing. When Bwembya had to go into hospital for tests, Mum flew down from Canberra to be with me. She would stay a few days and we would do some fun things like go to the markets at Redfern with the kids. Bwembya usually went tearing down the aisle thinking this was a big play area for hide and seek.

We spent a lot of time outdoors. We would often take the kids on picnics with Rusty and Joy to the botanical gardens or the beach. Their children Sam and Kiara were the same ages as Bwembya and Bupe. We were all very good friends and were in and out of each other's houses. Joy and I went to the pool to swim laps early in the morning in summer. We also played tennis in the evenings at some courts round the corner. Most weekends were spent having barbeques at each other's houses.

The end of 1991 was Christmas party time. Every year at work we had a big bash to which staff and their families were invited. The kids had a ball, and Bwembya loved the dancing and loud noise. Everyone was excited and made a lot of noise singing along to the music. They yelled and stomped to old disco favourites and of course to the well-loved 'Grease' music which Bwembya was crazy about.

Mum and Dad went back to Zambia at the end of 1991. My dad had been in Australia for eight years and was recalled. He was retiring to Chipili where both my parents were from. We all went to the airport to see them off. A few days later, Bwembya went into hospital to get his umbilical hernia repaired. Hospital had almost become a part of our day-to-day lives. I felt like I lived there. I cannot count how many times in the early years I sat on my own in the waiting room while Bwembya was having some minor surgery. I felt so alone and so apprehensive, although I never let on. It was my life, my child, my responsibility. It was just the way things were. I never questioned, never asked for someone to come with me or told anyone how I felt at those times, but I was so relieved each time the doctor or nurse came out and said everything was fine and I could go into the recovery ward.

At the end of the year, I had to find vacation care for Bwembya. After ringing around to everyone I could, I organised with some organisation, I cannot recall who, to provide a worker to be with Bwembya when he was at a vacation centre in Penshurst. There was a lot of negotiation involved and it all took some fine tuning as the worker could only start at ten in the morning and I had to be at work at half past eight in Burwood. We worked it out that I dropped him off at the church hall where he went for afterschool care, then the worker would pick him up at ten and take him to Penshurst for the day and bring him back to the church in the afternoon, where I picked him up after work. But this meant I was paying two sets of vacation care fees. That couldn't be helped, it was more important that Bwembya was being looked after. This arrangement only happened for a couple of holidays as the centre in Penshurst eventually agreed to take him without a carer as he fitted in so well and was no trouble.

Bwembya's vacation care was sorted, but I still had to sort out Bupe's holiday care. Bupe's childcare was closed for three weeks after Christmas. I had the week before and the week after Christmas as annual leave. Fortunately, one of the staff at the daycare had offered to look after Bupe at her home if we could drop her off and pick her up. We were willing to pay but she would not have it, so we got her a present instead. Mwango would leave with a very sleepy Bupe still in her pyjamas at half past six in the morning, drive from Bexley to Ryde where she lived and drop Bupe off, then drive to Meadowbank train station and hop on a train to work. He would retrace his steps on his way home and be home at around seven in the evening. It was a long day for a little girl, but she was in good hands.

As my parents were no longer in Canberra, we had Christmas at our place. This became a new tradition in which we had Christmas at home with the family. There were lots of presents for the kids to open from all their aunty and uncles and us. Bwalya and I cooked a lovely meal that would have had Mum smiling. We had been taught well. A turkey, rolled pork with herb stuffing, ham, roast potatoes, rice with saffron spices, carrots, a green salad, mince pies, Christmas pudding, gingerbread, a gingerbread house for the kids, vanilla ice cream, custard, and to put a little Zambian tradition in the picture like Mum used to do, we had a whole big mango each. We were all so full that we went outside on the back veranda and lounged on the outdoor furniture having cool drinks for a couple of hours.

The next year, 1992, started off quietly with the usual round of medical appointments. Bwembya had stiffness in his joints, problems with hearing due to glue ear, an enlarged liver and spleen, limited speech, and a mild developmental delay. He had an appointment in the first week in January with a physiotherapist at the Children's Hospital. I was incredibly lucky to have my sister Bwalya in Sydney and my friend Joy living nearby because it meant a lot of shopping trips to Hurstville. Bwalya worked in the city and on Thursday night she would catch the train to Bexley, we would have dinner then leave the kids with Mwango and the three of us would hit the shops. I was still young, energetic, and thought nothing of driving Bwalya home to Mosman after late-night shopping. We had money to spend, so we shopped.

Bwembya was having a good time at school. He had a birthday party and went to the Easter show with the school and came home with lots of show bags. His home life got better when Bwalya and Natasha arrived from Zambia the day before his sixth birthday party. Bwalya had gone to Zambia on holiday for a couple of weeks. Heckie had signed over legal custody for Natasha to Mwango and me until he got himself organised and got a job. He had lost his job shortly after his wife died. Bwembya and Natasha had spent a lot of time together, so we thought it would be better for her to be in a stable environment until Heckie was able to sort himself out. Natasha, who was my goddaughter, became part of our family. She started year one at a catholic school, which was around the corner in the next street from where I worked. This worked very well as I would put Bwembya on his school bus, drop Bupe off at childcare, and Tasha would go to work with me, then I would walk her across to school at half past eight in the morning and pick her up at half past three in the afternoon. I had no shortage of people to offer to walk her to school from the staff who often came in early to work or pick her up at the end of the day if I was busy.

The year passed slowly but was full of activity and relative calm in the big scheme of things. The kids and I spent a lot of time at the pool in summer. I taught the girls how to swim. I started off using floaties and kick boards and then used the good old-fashioned tactic of dropping them in the pool. I'd stand there shouting instructions for them to move their arms and legs, or to slow it down or speed it up. They did not drown – and they learnt to swim. When they could stay afloat and swim six metres, I enrolled them in swimming lessons. The girls had a busy life with swimming lessons, tennis, piano lessons, and brownies. Bwembya and I spent a lot of time in different places waiting for them either in the car or taking walks.

I spent a lot of time at P and C meetings and school functions such as selling tickets at car boot sales, helping at school fetes, the usual things mothers get involved in when fundraising for different schools.

For Bwembya, the year was a continuous round of medical and specialist appointments, but we made sure he had a full life and went wherever we went. He continued growing and developing new skills, like learning how to blow his nose. When he had a cold, I used to put a bit of pepper on the tip of his nose to make him sneeze, as he had not learnt how to blow his nose.

The things we take for granted he could not do automatically. It took a few weeks of demonstration and encouragement but finally he got it.

I was fortunate to be able to have a few babysitters I could use when we went out in the evenings. The family across the road had two daughters who would babysit for us in the evenings. When I first saw the girls, they were standing across the road watching our kids play. Then one day they came over and asked what was wrong with Bwembya as he reminded them of their cousin who had MPS. We got talking and I knew who they were talking about as I had joined the MPS society at that time and was on the committee running the society. I got to know their cousin and his parents very well as he was near Bwembya's age and had Hunter Syndrome (MPS II) like him. They were perfect babysitters as they understood a little about MPS.

At the beginning of the year, my brother James and his girlfriend Shaunagh came to live with us for a few weeks. She would pick up the kids from childcare and after school if she finished work early. On days when Shaunagh had an early shift, I would come home to a cooked meal and bathed kids, so I could put my feet up. I don't know how many books she would read to Bupe in one night. I would be lying in bed in my room next to the living room and hear Bupe going 'more' when Shaunagh finished one book. Both James and Shaunagh loved my little troop and spent a lot of time with them, giving Mwango and I much needed time out.

We had a lot of fun as a family. As a couple, Mwango and I tried to make time for each other. I even went to rugby league games to watch St George play. They usually lost. I had to give Mwango top marks for loyalty. He was convinced every year that

St George was going to win. It took a long time but finally they did win. I bought him a St George DVD gift set for Christmas that year. I would make time to meet him in the city for lunch, even if it meant that I would take a picnic lunch that we could have in Hyde Park. We would go out with friends for dinner usually in Newtown to Indian, Thai, and Italian restaurants. We even went out to nightclubs for a little bit of dancing. But mostly the two of us went out for dinner or to concerts.

In July, we went away for a weekend to the Blue Mountains for 'Christmas in July". Bwalya came to babysit the kids for the weekend. It was a golf tournament weekend with Mwango's team at work. Mwango played golf a lot. I had never played golf but that weekend I did. As I stepped on to the turf, I asked Mwango what I was supposed to do, and he gave me a few tips about how to swing the golf club and to make sure I followed through. It was all in the follow through, he repeated. I played golf for the very first time and won a golf trophy for nearest to the pin. It is the only trophy I have won for a sport. I had ribbons and medals from swimming and track when I was in primary school but no trophies. I did gloat a little and feel on top of the world. Mwango had been playing golf for years and had not won a trophy.

The highlight of 1992 for the family was that in October, James and Shaunagh announced they were engaged and were getting married in May the following year. We had been waiting for so long that when they told us we said we thought it was about time. My exact words were 'about *bloody* time'. Shaunagh burst out laughing. Her mum had said almost the same thing. They had been dating for about six years. We had been waiting for them to catch up to what the rest of us thought. Mwango drove James to Dubbo to ask Shaunagh's dad for her hand in marriage.

We kept some of the Zambian traditions going even if it was just a few.

In the middle of November, I collapsed at work, and it took three months to work out it was my thyroid that was causing the problem. I went on eighteen months of oral intervention, then had radioactive iodine to stop the thyroid functioning, and then onto thyroid replacement therapy. At last, I had a name to what had been making me feel chronically tired for a few years. I had assumed my feeling tired was normal for a person looking after three young children.

✦

Chapter 9

The year 1993 started off with Bwembya sick with an earache and a throat infection. Bupe was three years old and had started going to a kindergarten near home. This was the year I decided to enrol Bwembya who was six and Natasha who was six and a half in tennis lessons. The kids had half-hour sessions. It was a good try, but I had not yet grasped the implications of this MPS thing. Natasha had no problem and loved it. Bwembya loved it, too. He raced around the court with the teacher chasing him. When the teacher hit the ball at him, he caught it alright, but he caught the ball with his hand instead of hitting it with the racket. He would run around the court bouncing the ball up and down and have a great time. The teacher had no idea what to do. Bwembya thought it was all a big joke, so the tennis lessons trial for him was short lived.

At this stage in our lives, MPS was just a big word and we had no real understanding of what the impact and side effects were. A lot of the information was just incomprehensible jargon to us. The disease was terminal, that we understood, but the rest we could not take in at first. All we knew was that there was an end date soon. We thought we could just live in the now and let the future take care of itself. If we faced an obstacle we just turned around and used a different route or went with the flow.

At the end of April, Mum came to Australia to attend James and Shaunagh's wedding. The wedding was in Dubbo. Kenny was one of the best men and the girls were flower girls. My sister Bwalya read one of the readings. Not wanting to be left out of the fun, Bwembya went and perched on the banister at the front of the church. He then took Kenny's top hat, put it on and joined the best men on their bench. The wedding was a blend of Western and African culture. The boys wore tuxedos but had a sash made of a bright-coloured West African material called *kente*. My sister and I wore Nigerian lace outfits. Mum and the other African ladies at the wedding wore outfits made from African material.

The Zambian ladies at the wedding sang a bemba song in church that Mum taught us. In English, the song translated to: *This man should not live alone. We give you this woman to help you with your work. And to the woman, we give you to this man to share your life together, in good time and in hard times.* Well, something like that. The wedding reception was held at my sister-in-law's parents' house in a big white marquee on the lawn at the back of the property. We had a wonderful time eating great food and dancing till the early hours of the morning.

My life was busy. I worked full time, served on the MPS committee, the school P & C, and I taught Sunday school at the church in Bexley. I also started a small business management course and a post-graduate certificate in personal management. In addition to all that, I kept the house clean and cooked great meals. Nothing worked without a routine. Assorted sandwiches were made on Sunday night for the week ahead, and frozen. The kids chose what they wanted in the evening for the next day and it was put in the fridge overnight. I would wake up at six in the morning, bathed, got breakfast ready, woke the kids up, brushed their teeth, washed their faces, and got them dressed for the day. While they had breakfast, I got dressed, made the beds, and tidied the rooms.

After breakfast, we would wait for the school bus to pick up Bwembya, put him on the bus, then drop the girls off at school and go to work. After work I would pick them all up from their respective places. If there were activities, I would take them and wait for them. Swimming lessons, brownies, piano, or tennis. On Thursday, we went to the library and did the grocery shopping. Friday was relaxing day. The kids got to choose their videos at the video club, and they had a choice of what to have for dinner. We usually made things at home like pizza, hamburgers, hotdogs, or meat pies. If I was too tired to cook, I would usually buy chicken and chips from Red Rooster, which was at the end of our street.

On weekends, the kids woke up early and watched cartoons. When they were little, I would wake up early with them and doze on the couch. I would give them Nutri Grain cereal with no milk, which they would eat while they watched TV. Mwango would wake up later and if he got up on time would make them his famous breakfast of eggs, baked beans, bacon, and toast. Bwalya and Kenny usually came during the day and spent the afternoon with us. The boys would barbeque on the Weber and the day would finish off on a good note. Sunday was always church time in the morning. The kids went to Sunday school, and I taught Sunday school.

While routines worked fine for most things in our life, there were areas where I made sure things were not too routine. Bwembya was used to a structured environment at home and at school, but I decided that for my child to have a normal life he had to learn to be able to function without routine. I had seen in the few years he had been with us how routine ruled our lives and the drama it caused if I made even a small change to it. He would get cranky and throw a tantrum. He'd race up and down, stomping his feet and making a lot of noise while biting his right thumb. Being randomly confronted with tantrums I decided something had to change. Bwembya was usually such a pleasant, delightful kid, so I had to find a way to manage his reactions.

I decided I would disrupt our routine so much that change became normal – and it worked. I would vary what we did after school, like go to the library instead of going straight home. I varied where we shopped, went to different supermarkets and shopped on different days, sometimes after work or in the evening. I routinely changed who picked him up from after school or from vacation care. It became okay for his Uncle James, Uncle Kenny, Aunty Shaunagh, or one of our babysitters to pick him up from school. We went and visited different people on weekends and did not rush home for bedtime or bath time. Sometimes the kids would have a bath in the morning instead of in the evening at the same time every day. I made it normal for things to be out of routine, so he did not get fazed by change, and it made a big difference to our lives.

I addressed the issue of him getting his message understood. He had periodical hearing checks and got a set of grommets every year till he was about ten years old. Once the grommets were implanted, he seemed to settle a bit more. I also found that explaining to Bwembya what we were doing next if it was out of routine worked. I would shout over my shoulder, 'We have to stop at Woollies to get some bread, guys, so we all have to go, and we won't be long.' We had children with different needs and vulnerabilities. We treated them the same as much as possible and we expected everyone around us to do the same. If someone wanted to take one child, they took all three, unless it was a birthday party or activity for a particular group of kids.

We bought the kids bikes one Christmas. Bwembya never rode his but other children who came to visit had a lot of fun riding it. However, he did have a lot of fun pushing it up and down while he ran alongside it or watching the wheels turn when it was upside down. Even with the training wheels on, he never felt quite comfortable riding it. He rode his little red and yellow tricycle for a long time. When I picked him up at school some days, he would be riding round the cycle track at school on one of the large three-wheeler bikes, his little greenish blue bicycle helmet on his head, which made his head look bigger than it already was. Some days I would see a teacher running behind him holding a bike with training wheels steady while he paddled away.

We moved to Canonbury grove in Bexley North in June 1994, the day after my brother Heckie died. On the Thursday evening we received a call from my sister-in-law Fidelia that Heckie was very sick in hospital in Kitwe and that she and my brother Reggie were driving down to see him. I had taken the day off work, picked up the keys for the house at the real estate agents and started to move stuff all day long. In the evening, Kenny and James had come to help continue the move. About seven in the evening, I decided to check how Heckie was by phoning Zambia while we were at the new house. I called my sister-in-law's place of work. I was told 'Mrs Mfula has gone to her brother-in-law's funeral.' I told the others and we thought there must be some mistake, someone would have called, it was unthinkable.

I started calling everyone I could think of. None of the close family members were at home or at work but I finally got through to one of my dad's close friends. The person who answered the phone said something like, 'I am sorry he is not here; he has gone with Mr Mfula to Chipili to take the body of Mr Mfula's son for the burial there.' That is how I found out my brother had died. Heckie had died from cerebral malaria. He was thirty-five years old. I can't describe how the first death in my immediate family felt like, especially having to tell Natasha her dad had died. I had to tell a little girl who had lost her mother three years previously, that her father had also died.

I held my grief in check because of Natasha. When she came back to Australia after her mother died, I had to sit down and explain about death and dying. Mum asked me to have a talk with her as she was asking questions. No-one had explained to her at her level, what death was all about. She was only five when her mother died. I remember using examples in nature to explain death; how everything dies eventually. The circle of life. This time I did not need to use examples, she knew exactly what had happened and clung to me for days, watching me like a hawk in case I disappeared in a puff of smoke.

We were all absolutely devastated but somehow muddled through this difficult time. Bwalya was living with us because she was just getting ready to return to Zambia to live and had given up her apartment to stay with us the last few months before she left. James left for Zambia within a few days and Bwalya a week later. I was unable to travel as I was waiting for our immigration papers to be processed. Neither Kenny nor I were able to go for the funeral. It took a lot to hold it together. When I needed to cry, I went off for a drive or to Joy's place where I had a good cry and a cup of tea. Then in September, Mwango's mum died in a car accident but he managed to get a bridging visa and went to Zambia for the funeral. We had two major deaths in a few short months.

Our lives carried on with some minor mishaps, such as when lead was discovered in the soil at Bwembya's school, and he was one of the kids affected. It was all over the news for weeks. We had people come to our house to check for lead poison in our carpets, soil, and house to make sure Bwembya had not got the lead poison from our home. He was put on a special diet and monitored for a while. Other than that, he was becoming more independent and starting to do things on his own without the girls. I got him onto a Sunday recreational outing program with a disability program in the St George area. The bus would pick him up at ten in the morning and drop him off in the afternoon around three. He loved the outings and was out like a shot when he heard the bus driver hoot in the driveway.

The family went to church on Sundays, and we had a group of friends that we had lunch with, went on outings to the beach or to the cricket with, particularly with Paul and Jackie. They had a house on the coast, and we would often go there for a few weeks in the holidays or at long weekends. These holidays were fun for the kids as we just relaxed and took long walks along the beach. Bwembya was still able to walk long distances, but he and I spent most of the day on the beach under a beach umbrella while the girls and Mwango swam. We got a taste of the beach life and after this we went to the coast two or three times a year, sometimes up to the Central Coast, North Coast and at other times down to the South Coast.

The kids and I had a full life and like most mothers do, I spent a lot of time with them. The girls were involved in different activities like the swimming squad at the local pool. Bwembya and I would swim in the little pool while we waited, or we would go to the shops to do the groceries. Bwembya loved the pool at Bexley North. Our house was on a hill overlooking the pool, so to get to the pool we had to go down the hill that sloped right to the pool. As soon as we got out of the house, he would race down to the pool with us running after him so he would not get run over. He was fast in his little flip-flops, swimmers, and hat. He had a funny way of running with his adorable little knock knees and his flip-flops making a funny loud clap-like noise when he ran. We preferred to walk, or should I say run to the pool twice a week, to get some exercise.

Swimming was a good activity for all of us. Bwembya would not get out of the pool until the girls, and I were literally out the gates, then he would dash after us dripping wet. So, we were all fit and bronzed (as bronzed as brown people can get). We loved the pool, and all the staff knew us very well because we were locals. But things changed when Bwembya was about seven years old. We went to the pool one Saturday afternoon and the girls had their swim squad training. Bwembya headed to the little pool as usual and stuck his foot in, but he looked like he felt it was too cold and went and sat back down at the table where we'd left our bags. I called him over thinking he was playing a game, picked him up and put him in the water, but he cried out and dashed out and sat down.

While I was standing there looking at him and wondering what was going on, I saw him start shaking and drop to the ground. I jumped out of the pool quickly. I knew a fit when

I saw one, having worked with people who had epilepsy. In fact, I knew exactly what it was, a grand mal seizure (that means a big one). I laid him flat on the ground and made sure his airways were open, then turned him onto his side, covered him with a towel, and shouted instructions to the staff at the pool to call an ambulance. Thank God for the senior first aid training that was a requirement at work. By the time the ambulance came, Bwembya had stopped fitting and was dazed.

I went in the ambulance to St George hospital with him and one of the pool staff drove my car to the hospital with the girls in it. We usually went to the Children's Hospital at Camperdown, which had just moved to Westmead. Because we had no mobile phones back then, I phoned home and left a message for Mwango on the answering machine, and he came to the hospital a few hours later and took the girls home.

Bwembya and I stayed at the hospital for a few days while they ran some tests. It was the one and only fit he ever had but it made me buy one of those big brick mobile phones and a bigger handbag to fit it in. It was shortly after this incident that Bwembya was diagnosed with cardiomyopathy, and he started taking medication for his heart. He was started on half a Lasix tablet. I was concerned when the medication prescribed for Bwembya was a tablet because until then he had never taken tablets, his medicine had always been in liquid form. I assumed there was going to be a problem, but to my surprise, he took the tablet and just chewed it and swallowed it like he had done it before.

Bwembya was growing up slowly and there were no more cracked mirrors in the dentist office. Whenever we went for a check-up, the dentist would usually have two or three mirrors cracked while he was trying to look at Bwembya's teeth, as Bwembya hated anything in his mouth, so he would just clamp down on the little mirrors or spatulas. He would stay in the chair under protest for the shortest time possible, half the time the dentist would have to compromise by examining his teeth while he stood ready to bolt through the door.

Bwembya was starting to be less introverted and was taking more of an interest in what was going on around him. It seemed like when the ear infections decreased and grommets were not needed anymore, his hearing and his comprehension improved. He could go to Sunday school and participate as part of the group. His attention span increased and his ability to interact improved. He paid more attention to what was going on around him and he could sit and watch a video from beginning to end without wandering off. He could also sit in the car with me while I waited for the girls at some activity or another without wanting to climb out of the window or open the door and run down the road. He was my big little boy.

In October 1995, on Natasha's tenth birthday, James and Shaunagh had a baby girl called Malaika. We were all delighted, our Sydney family was growing. In November, Mum and Dad came to visit from Zambia for six weeks and spent Christmas with us. During their stay Bwembya, had carpel tunnel operations on both wrists. Most people would have a difficult time having an operation on just one wrist, but it did not seem to bother him much. He had his grandma to look after him and he was happy. He also had a high pain threshold.

As always it was nice to have Mum around. She moved into Bwembya's room with him after his operation so she could watch him, and I could go to bed without having to be up to check on him so often. Just being able to relax and not be alert all the time was good. Having Dad around was wonderful too because he took the girls to school and picked them up at the end of the day and could also take them to their swimming lessons.

At the end of the year, I realised that we had so many appointments at the children's hospital in Westmead that it did not make sense to be travelling so far so often. So, in the New Year we started looking for a place near the hospital and eventually moved to Baulkham Hills. This move was carried out with some reluctance as we all loved our schools, friends, church, and activities. But as always, Bwembya's best interests were a big factor in the decisions we made.

Bwembya was determined to do what he wanted when he wanted to. When he was about eight years old, he had plaster of Paris put on his legs to lengthen the muscles at the back of his ankles that were constricted and causing him to walk on tiptoe. Calipers were tried but he outgrew them very quickly. Then night splints were tried, but he took them off as soon as he got under the sheets, so plaster it was. I was in the kitchen cooking one afternoon and I happened to glance out of the window and there was Bwembya on the trampoline. Plastered legs and all, jumping away with no support. When I say I had no words, I literally mean I had no words. The girls were in the house watching TV. He had pulled the little round trampoline next to the big trampoline to get up on to it and then managed to stand up on the trampoline and jump up and down.

That was my son: a child who cut himself in the shower when he slipped and fell but carried on standing inside the shower while blood ran down his back. As a result of which he had to have about eight stitches, all without a whinge. He was also a child who would turn the hot water tap higher till he almost burned himself when I was momentarily distracted. And he was tidy and liked to put everything I used back in its place. When I came home from work and knew I had to go out soon I would leave my handbag and shoes in the living room and then when I went to get them everything would be gone, only to turn up neatly packed where they belonged.

He was a child who would go around wearing shoes too big for him and hum along peacefully in his own little world, or wear his gumboots season to season, come rain or shine. He would wear socks with his sandals if his feet felt a little cold. As a result, I would hide his sandals during winter. Sometimes I hid them so well that come summer I'd forget where I had put them. He was the child to whom I sang tenderly at bedtime, and who'd continue to hum himself to sleep except when the hum became loud enough to wake the whole house. Then he would laugh and chuckle to jokes only he could understand.

Chapter 10

We moved to Baulkham Hills in April 1996. The house was a four-bedroom single-level brick house. It had a swimming pool and a built-in outdoor barbeque which delighted Mwango. He was not too happy about the pool, but I kept my end of the deal. If I wanted a pool, then I had to be responsible for it. It was a reasonable arrangement as he was away so often, and his precious time home could not be spent cleaning the pool. There was also a mobile pool service in the area which would test the water and deliver chemicals. We were good to go.

Our move meant that the girls and Bwembya moved school. The girls started school at a catholic school in Baulkham Hills and Bwembya went to the Hills School in Northmead. I was sceptical of this new school. Again, the school proved me wrong. The principal and the staff were wonderful. Each school seemed to give Bwembya a little more than the last school. The change in my son in the first two years at the Hills was remarkable. The staff tapped into his potential and put him in a class that brought out the best in him. In his last few years of school, Bwembya was in a class with kids with sight impairment, but they were teenagers with all the normal teenager likes and dislikes.

This was the school that got him into the pool again, it took a few months of a gently, gentle approach but he eventually got in. After the drama at Bexley, he did not want to go near a pool again. Our house in Baulkham Hills had a pool and he would stand as far away from the pool as possible when people were outside. When no one was near he would go to the side of the pool and flick the water. The pool was a semi-in-ground pool. The second year we were at Moona Avenue he wanted a small plastic pool for Christmas. We knew this because when we asked him what he wanted for Christmas, he cut out a picture of the pool at school and brought it home and kept showing us. So that year he got a pool for Christmas and had a wonderful time lying in it while the girls swam in the big pool, but he still dashed out of the little pool every time someone came near him.

We settled into a new routine in our new neighbourhood. Again, before and after school for Bwembya became an issue. The before and after-school (OOSH) where the girls went at Baulkham Heights agreed to give Bwembya a try because Natasha and Bupe were there and would be able to let them know what Bwembya wanted if they could not understand him. Then there was an issue with school bus picking up and dropping Bwembya off. The driver could not leave the bus with other kids in it so we worked it out for the driver to hoot and one of the staff at the OOSH would take Bwembya out to the bus in the morning and get him off the bus in the afternoon. The ladies at the OOSH were wonderful. After a while, Bwembya was just one of the kids there. Baulkham Hills Council ran a vacation care program at Baulkham Heights during the holidays and the kids all attended the program.

The kids treated Bwembya like he was a movie star or something. We would be in Newtown parking the car to look at a map and a group of young ladies would tap on the window shouting and waving at Bwembya, 'Hi B, hi B!' We would roll down the window and they would introduce themselves. 'We did some community service at the Hills School.' The excitement was interesting to see, particularly as Bwembya would glance at them and literally smile and ignore them. I used to wonder what he was thinking; it was probably 'Here come my fan club.'

The kids and I spent a lot of time together during this period as Mwango had taken a position with the bank that involved travelling all over Australia and overseas. He left early on Monday morning and returned Friday night. If he was across the country, he would be gone for two to three weeks and overseas sometimes five weeks. So, my life was busy. The girls started guides at Crestwood, but I held off other activities for over a year as I was doing so many things at once. I was still on the MPS committee, the Hills School Council, working full time and virtually a single mum.

Once again, I had to develop a routine that worked for me and the kids. Bwembya needed help to do everything like brush his teeth, wash his face, brush his hair and get dressed. MPS causes stiffness in the connective tissue and Bwembya was stiff mainly in the shoulders, which meant he was not able to lift his arms high enough to pull anything over his head or above his shoulders. He was also stiff in his wrists and hands, so he had difficulty with a lot of fine motor activities like tie shoelaces, do up buttons, etc. But being Bwembya, he did all the little bits he could by himself then came to me for help with what he couldn't do. When he was dressed, we would all have breakfast, and be out the door to before-school care.

After work, I would pick everybody up at Baulkham Heights, go home, cook while the kids did homework or played outside, or swam in the pool in summer. One night a week the girls went to girl guides at different times as they were in different groups, so it meant going out three times the same night. Guides did not last for more than a year because Bwembya decided he was tired and was not going to go out three times in one night, and this clearly was not negotiable with him. It was probably one of the few times I had to concede defeat as I usually worked my way around things, but I was only one person and even though the Guide Hall was around the corner I could not leave Bwembya in the house alone or send the girls out alone. They were very disappointed, but they understood and did not want to see a cranky little boy every time we had to go out.

Bwembya started being involved in more activities on his own. He started off with a Saturday club at a school in Epping. We would drop him off in the morning at ten and pick him up at around three in the afternoon. The group went on outings every second Saturday. He was with the Saturday program for a year, then he joined the Junior Activity Group (JAG) in Telopea. We were not so sure he got much out of Saturday club as the kids in that program had mostly moderate to severe disabilities, but JAG was a different story. He was once again racing to get out of the car when we got to Telopea. He loved the program and to put the icing on the cake some of his classmates were in the group. He would start to pack his lunch on the Saturdays that JAG was on (it was on fortnightly in school term) and be out by the car with his bag before we were ready to go. From JAG, he progressed to peer support, which is for the older age group, but they met at Rooty Hill.

This was the year Bwembya first went away to Camp Breakaway for a week with some of the kids from his school. He had a ball, judging by the talk with the staff and the pictures taken at the camp. He came back happy and healthy. Camp Breakaway is a purpose-built holiday camp for people with disabilities. It is on the Central Coast at San Remo in New South Wales. The camp has cabins set on twenty-five acres, sporting activities such as pool tables, table tennis, tennis courts and a lake for fishing. We were quite relaxed about Bwembya going as he was on a plateau health-wise, and he was going with staff from school who knew him almost as well as we did.

The staff gave us a scrap book compiled for Bwembya to commemorate his time at camp. It has beautiful pictures of him having fun. There was a picture on the first page of the eight kids on the trip with the six staff who went with them standing by the bus. The rest of the pages have pictures and compics stuck around it to denote what was happening on each page. The kids used pictographs to tell their story and the staff stuck a few paragraphs of the activity and the day on the opposite page. There were pictures of Bwembya having his face painted, playing tennis, playing pool, sitting on a cooler box with a cushion on it under an umbrella on the beach, feeding a member of staff ice cream, playing in a covered playground, watching other kids swim, dancing on a stage with musical instruments that look like a live band was about to start playing, and a picture of him getting ready to come home on the bus.

When we moved to Baulkham Hills, we started attending the Anglican church at Crestwood. We took a little while to warm up to the church as we had loved our church in Bexley and had made many special friends there. Bwembya was the only one who seemed to have no reservations, he loved Crestwood Church. The minute we turned into the church driveway he would begin to clap his hands and sing. As soon as the car door opened, he was out like a shot, and ran into the church. In the church, he always sat next to me and often he would end up sitting on my lap so he could see the front better, as he was such a short little guy. He would hum out loud with the rest of us, usually following in tune and clapping as appropriate. His favourite song was, 'Shine, Jesus, Shine'. He loved Sunday school, especially observing other people doing things and he sat like a king in a chair often in front facing the others and smiling his little smile.

In 1996, when he was ten, Bwembya changed a lot. He was quieter and spent a lot of time sitting quietly and observing. He lost a lot of his energy and got tired more easily and there were many bleeding noses and chest infections. The downturn in his health had started. During this time, I guess people did not fully know the extent of what was happening because every time people called to ask how I was, I did not want to consistently narrate my late-night vigils, I just said Bwembya had been in hospital and was now out and that was that. It was the same with Mwango, when he called, I did not elaborate what was going on, how tired I was, how long I had stayed at the hospital, sometimes with the girls sleeping on the lounge in the emergency room. I just sorted it all out and got on with it.

As Bwembya was changing, I was changing. I was becoming more courageous in many ways. With Mwango travelling so much I learnt to step out of my comfort zone more. I had to make decisions for both of us and not wait for consultation from him about things: like if the electricity fuse blew. I learnt when I could fix it or when I had to call an electrician. If the fridge broke down, I had to decide if I should have it fixed or buy a new one. When our house on the street was the only house that had a garden that looked like an abandoned paddock on a farm, I had to go to Bunnings and buy a whipper snipper and cut the grass. We had a mower, but I did not know how to use it, but at least I could keep the lawn at a reasonable length. I bought a blower /vacuum that I used to collect all the leaves and twigs from the gum trees around the house. I kept the house looking lived in.

I also learned to find my voice, to speak a little louder. On one of our visits to a specialist, I was in a room and Bwembya was having an ultrasound when the technician looked at the screen and said she had to call the doctor. The doctor walked into the room, took the probe from the technician, and started pressing it on my son. I looked at Bwembya and I could see he was uncomfortable. His eyes were wide open, and I knew he was not happy. The doctor poked and prodded, printed out some images and left the room. I sat there feeling annoyed. When we went back to the desk, I told the staff there that I wanted to make a complaint. I felt that when a doctor walked in the room, he needed to acknowledge the parent and the child. Even with a nod of the head or a smile. My son was already scared, and it would have been nice if the doctor had greeted my son and made him feel welcome and safe. We were in a situation where we needed assurance and acknowledgement. My complaint must have been addressed because the next time we saw that doctor he made it a point to stop and say hello to Bwembya, smiling as he did so. Any time we had to see him he was very present and welcoming.

Things in our life quietened down. We did not go out as much, all our party time and friends seemed to have been left in Bexley. I was watching and waiting for the next stage in our life, and I finally started to understand the whole MPS thing. Having been on the MPS committee for a while I could see deterioration in the other MPS kids. The people on the committee started to lose their kids. The first funeral I attended I bawled my eyes out at the church because it was so beautiful. The next funeral I attended I felt like my heart broke because that little boy had MPS II and was almost the same age as Bwembya. I looked at his mother and I saw myself standing there as if it was my son who had died. Our lives were so parallel, that I realised it could have been me, and I wondered how I would cope. I knew when she looked at me, she knew how I felt, just like I knew when her husband, looked at Mwango, he knew how he felt. They had probably been in our shoes at other funerals. They were comforting me, and I found it difficult to stop the tears. We were walking the same path; they were leading the way.

Chapter 11

In February 1997, after four years of enduring living in limbo and not knowing if we would have to pick up our lives and leave the country, we finally got our permanent residency. For most people getting your residency is a good thing, a great thing. For me, it was bittersweet. Dealing with immigration had not been a pleasant experience for me. It was demoralising and frustrating. It felt like every time I stepped up to the desk at immigration the person at the desk started shaking their head before I had even finished what I was saying. It was as if I couldn't possibly have anything valid to say. I came to dread walking through their door and the day we got notification I did not feel any jubilation. The process was so tedious it did not feel like a win. The sticking point with our application was that we had a child with an illness who would grow up to be a burden on taxpayers. We had been living our lives in hope that a cure would be found, or that a miracle would happen, and our son would live a long life. We tried not to imagine a future where we had lost our son. But to show that Bwembya would not be a burden on taxpayers we had to prove that he did not have a future, that he was not going to live long enough to become a burden. In the end, we got our residency because our son would die, so it was bittersweet.

I immediately decided I was going to Zambia with the kids. Mwango had just taken leave at Christmas and wanted to wait for September when he had some leave due, but I decided I was going in March. I felt strongly that I had to go on this trip as soon as possible. Mwango knew me well enough to let me follow my instincts. Since Bwembya was virtually nonverbal I had to develop uncanny sensitivity to him. Most people with chronically sick kids are in tune with their kids and their needs. Starting about 1995, I started to pay attention to my gut instincts. Even when Bwembya looked fine I would sometimes say, 'I am taking him to the doctor, he is not well.' Mwango would look at me like I was crazy. There was always something wrong with him. He would have a chest infection, sore throat, or earache, and by night-time would have a high temperature. This happened a few times before Mwango stopped second-guessing me.

The first time I was alerted to something serious was one evening when we were all at home. Bwembya had started showing reluctance to go to the hospital and usually had to be made to go. One evening, I was changing him into his pyjamas and noticed his breathing was slightly off, like he had been running. I got that feeling in the bottom of my stomach and told Mwango I was taking him to the hospital because something was wrong. Mwango listened to his breathing and said he sounded alright, and that we should take him in the morning as emergency was always so full, we would be standing around forever. I decided I would take a drive and see if the emergency department at the hospital was busy. I called Natasha and she hopped in the car with me, and we drove to the hospital. I double parked near the entrance, and she went inside the hospital and had a quick peep. Emergency was relatively busy.

We were driving home, and a voice whispered in my ear, 'Just take him, just take him' repeatedly until I got home. I did not try to explain the voice because I couldn't. I got inside the house and told Mwango the hospital was busy, but I was taking him, anyway. Mwango had already put Bwembya to bed, but I switched on the light and said, 'B, let's go to the hospital'. Without hesitation, he got out of bed put on his slippers and gown and walked out to the car. I opened the door and he got into the backseat. No bribe or explanation was required, which I found strange. This would usually have caused a few unhappy whinges. It was totally out of character. He strapped his seatbelt on and sat waiting for me to get in the car and off we went.

We were a few blocks from the hospital when Bwembya suddenly took off his seatbelt and slumped in the middle between the two front seats gasping for breath. I wanted to stop the car to help him, to call to someone, but I knew I had no time. I don't know how I knew but I did. I stepped on the accelerator and prayed to God all the while talking to Bwembya. 'We are almost there, B. We are almost there.' It was the longest couple of kilometres I have ever driven. I could hear every breath and willed him to breathe like I had so many times before. I made it to the short-term parking outside the hospital.

I got out of my seat, opened the back door, and tried to lift him out and we both fell onto the driveway. I started shouting. A lady passing by from the car park rushed in and called the nurses at the triage desk who hurried over with a wheelchair and oxygen. Bwembya was taken straight into the emergency ward and a team of doctors, nurses, etc., appeared as they got him on the bed. The oxygen in his blood had fallen to a dangerous level and he was not getting enough oxygen in his lungs. I had apparently just made it in time. He had pneumonia.

We started to make plans for my trip to Zambia with the kids. I knelt and prayed to God. Please make our trip safe. I asked that there be no sickness and no deaths while we were there, only a great holiday for the kids and me. I bought tickets for myself, and three kids aged 11, 10 and 7. We were all excited and as usual we made it an adventure. Since they were little, we had been taking the kids away at least once a year to the coast, so they were used to travelling on long trips in the car. They had not been in a plane for a long time and certainly not for thirteen hours. We got our travel inoculations after a little drama.

Bupe had a big fear of injections. We were at the Vaccination Centre in Parramatta getting our injections. The doctor had the injections ready for us in the room. I went in first, followed by Natasha as we were both having more injections. When it was Bupe's turn she had one injection and ran into the bathroom and locked herself in, crying. The doctor tried to tell her she would be gentle, that it would not hurt that much when a little voice shouted, 'It's alright for you to say, you're grown up and I am only 7.' The doctor had to concede defeat and use other tactics like bribing her with jellybeans and a numbing patch. Bwembya had his injection and had a minor tantrum all the way to the car. Before we left for Zambia, I made sure I was well stocked with every foreseeable medication I might need from our family doctor to cover diarrhoea, vomiting, antibiotics, plus other things like bandages, Panadol, etc. However, we did not end up using any of the medication or first aid kit.

Our flight was on a Monday morning and Mwango was leaving for Brisbane that same morning too. It would have been too much drama to wake the kids up at all hours of the morning on a day we were flying so far, so we decided to book into a hotel near the airport. At four in the afternoon on the Sunday we got a minicab to the hotel. Kenny came over to the hotel when we got there. We bathed and fed the kids early. Mwango and I left the kids with Kenny, took his car and we went out for dinner at Bondi Beach, which gave us time to catch up before I left. We were going to be away for four weeks.

The flight was pleasant enough as flights go. We sat in a row of four, with Natasha in the aisle next to Bwembya, then me and Bupe in the aisle on my other side. Bwembya had a sedative prescribed for him and he slept most the way to South Africa. Natasha and Bupe also had travel sickness medication which made Bupe sleepy most of the way to South Africa, too. Natasha mostly watched movies with me throughout the flight. Sitting between two kids who are leaning on you either side is difficult especially if they sleep for hours. In Perth, we had to get off the plane for two hours, and I had to carry two sleepy kids into the terminal. They slept on the chairs in the lounge area, and I had to carry them back onto the plane again.

I was exhausted when we got to South Africa. Fortunately, they had a wheelchair waiting to put Bwembya on and wheel him to the international transit lounge. A couple of hours later we re-joined the Qantas flight to Zimbabwe and Bwembya slept all the way. We stayed in Zimbabwe overnight and left for Zambia the next morning. I had a cousin who was a nurse, married to a doctor in Zimbabwe. I was comfortable with a stopover in Harare as we were staying with people with a medical background. I felt safe being there with Bwembya. My cousin picked us up from the airport. They were able to have a wheelchair brought out to the plane for Bwembya, so he did not have to walk from the plane to the terminal. When we got to the house, the kids had a bath, dinner and we put them in bed. They woke up refreshed and back to their active selves.

The flight from Zimbabwe to Zambia caused a bit of anxiety. The plane was smaller and Bwembya did not like it at all. You had to walk from a bus to the plane and climb the steep stairs to the aircraft, which was not good for a kid with a heart problem. He was puffed by the time we got on the plane and sweated and whinged for the two hours we were in the air. I could not wait for the plane to land. Fortunately, on the plane was an old friend of ours who now lived in Zimbabwe. When the plane landed, he picked Bwembya up and carried him down the stairs for me. This flight was the only unpleasant part of the whole trip.

When we arrived in Zambia most people had not seen me for about seven years. I arrived there feeling happy with myself as I had lost some weight before we left. But every time anyone saw me, the first thing they would comment on is how fat I was. I had put on some weight in the seven years I had been away from Zambia, people would certainly have noticed the difference. I had worked so hard to lose weight. I had a babysitter come to the house three evenings a week while I went to the gym, did an aerobics class for an hour, then the treadmill for half an hour. I also swam a hundred laps in the pool (our pool wasn't very long) every other day and danced for an hour on days I didn't do either.

Bwembya enjoyed watching me exercise, he would come and dance with me and we would twirl round the room. He would put his bare feet on top of mine, and we would dance. When I got to the stage where I was doing sit-ups, he would sit on my knees and run off laughing when I failed to complete a sit-up because he was sitting on me. We had such fun dancing. He loved to turn while I held his hand up in the air like they do when dancing ballroom. The fun was when it was my turn to go under his arm as he was so short, but we managed.

We all had a ball in Zambia. We stayed with my brother Reggie who had three boys who were then eight, seven, and three. Natasha's brother, Big Kay (Kaoma), who was seven, came over for a long weekend in Zambia. He lived with his mother's sister in Swaziland at the time, following the death of my brother. My sister Bwalya came over every day with her son, little Kay (Kaoma) who was two years old. Both Kays were named after my brother Heckie, whose middle name was Kaoma. Bwembya and Bupe also met their half-brother (Mwango's son) for the first time. He was twelve at the time and he came over almost every day, too. The backyard was like a large playground with seven boys playing with swords and cars.

The house had a large garden with garden beds and lots of fruit trees. There was a security brick wall around the house. Two days after we arrived, it was Good Friday, and we had an Easter egg hunt on the Sunday. My sister and I bought lots of Easter eggs and hid them around the garden. The kids had a wonderful time looking for chocolate eggs. The first day we arrived, my brother's two oldest boys came and asked, 'Aunty Patricia, why doesn't B talk?' I told them as simply as I could that the nerves that help us send messages to our mouths to talk were blocked with something like glue so they didn't work, so when he thinks about it, he can't talk. If he does not think about it, he can talk. They got it straight away and that was that.

Taking a terminally ill child to a Third World country isn't exactly a decision most people would encourage but it was one of the best things I did to improve Bwembya's quality of life. He had a great time from the day we arrived till the day we left. Growing up among girls, he always played girly games, with dolls and make-believe. Seeing him in the middle of a sword fight, running around uninhibited with six other screaming boys warmed my heart. He fitted in so well. It made me wonder whether we had somehow been negligent in what his needs as a little boy were. Whether he would have developed his potential more if he had more male role models. For the first time in a long time, I was able to be completely relaxed about where he was and what he was doing. I could go out for the whole day with my sister and come home at night just in time to give him his evening medication and not be fretting about how he was.

My brother had three people working at his house. A maid, who took care of the kids, a housekeeper, and a gardener. There was always someone keeping an eye on the kids to make sure they were safe, fed, and clean. My clingy, holding-hands-with-Mum-all-the-time little boy had gone. In his place was a pirate, a ninja turtle, a cowboy, or a racing car driver. One night, an old friend of mine invited me and the kids over for dinner and Bwembya made it real clear he was not going if the other boys were not going. I put out the clothes the kids were going to wear on the beds for after they had a bath but a few minutes before we were about to leave Bwembya's clothes were missing. The car arrived to pick us up and he had no clothes to wear that were ironed. I got the message loud and clear when he looked at me with a twinkle in his eye when I asked where his clothes were, and he ran off with the boys to watch *Wild World of Wrestling* or something. He was watching rough boy programs on TV and loving it. There's would be no more *Sound of Music*, *Pollyanna*, or *Brady Bunch* for him.

We visited a few relatives in different towns and like at my brother's house Bwembya just did his own thing and usually hung out with the boys. I would only see him at mealtimes and at bedtime, and half the time did not know where he was. We went to visit my parents in the village. Chipili was a real village, not a quaint could-pass-for-a-village town, but a real village with no electricity at the time, except for solar panels at my parents' place. A village with people, washing dishes, washing clothes, and swimming in the river. Barefoot villagers walking with water containers to get water from the river. Ever since I could remember, my dad had planned to retire in Chipili, which was an old Anglican mission where he and my mum were born.

Chipili is in the Northern Province of Zambia about fifty kilometres from Mansa, the nearest place you could call a town. My dad's vision was always to return to his birthplace and improve the lives of people there, and he did. As with some African villages a river runs through a village. My mother's people were settled on one side of the river and my father's on the other side. We felt like we were related to half the village most of the time with all the extended family and family by marriage. It was where my parents came from, a village in the back of beyond, no electricity or running water at the time of our visit.

My brother Reggie drove Bwalya, her son Kay, my kids, and I to Chipili. All seven of us in a five-seater. I sat in the front passenger seat. Bwalya and the kids sat in the backseat with Kay on Bwalya's lap. It seemed like a long trip with frequent stops for toilet breaks. The landscape on the trip was no different to a drive to Dubbo from Sydney. Lots of open spaces. The only difference were the people we saw along the way. School kids in the middle of nowhere in little groups, carrying their books in bags or in plastic bags. Women walking alongside the road with goods on their heads. Men and women on bicycles. Some carrying big bags of charcoal, corn, or vegetables. There were areas with stalls where vendors were selling tomatoes, pumpkins, onion, sweet potato, Irish potatoes, groundnuts, beans, and other vegetables. We stopped at a few police roadblocks along the way where they checked driver's licences and where people were going.

We stopped off in Mansa, the last town before Chipili. The kids used the toilet, we filled up petrol in the car and bought some groceries. The road to Mansa was tarred but had sections of the road that had potholes. The road to Chipili was not tarred and had a lot of potholes. It took us almost an hour to drive about fifty kilometres. There were more people walking or riding bicycles along the road. Driving down this road was a little more difficult, as well as potholes we had to avoid, people, and bicycles. Sometimes the potholes were so large we had to leave the road and drive off road for a few metres.

As we got closer to Chipili there were more people walking along the road and the number of houses started to increase. We arrived in Chipili around four in the afternoon. A lot of people were waving at the car and shouting greetings. Reggie and Bwalya called out to a few people as we slowed down and drove forward carefully. I was surprised to see a satellite dish next to a mud hut with a thatched roof. I asked my sister how that was possible to watch TV with no electricity. She said you just used a big car battery. It warmed my heart to see progress in a village so far from major cities. We turned off the main road that passed through the village and went up the road that led to my parents' house. We could see the house through the hedge as we drove up.

The white rendered brick house with a large front yard with barely tamed ankle-length grass stood in the middle of the fenced-off property. There were Mango trees and other fruit trees along the side of the house. The windows at the front of the house were open and curtains flapped in the gentle breeze. There were many different coloured flowers along the driveway and big pots of green plants on the veranda at the front of the house. My brother told us to stay in the car and pressed the horn.

Mum did not know we were coming. Dad had kept the secret closely guarded. He had told her that my brother Reggie was coming over with some friends of Bwalya's from Australia to make sure the beds were made, and food was prepared for visitors, so she was not caught off guard. Mum came out of the house expecting to greet visitors from Australia and we all stepped out of the car. You should have heard her screaming. People came running from their houses to see what had happened, was it bad news? Why was Martha screaming so loudly? Had somebody died? There we were, my kids and I, my sister and her son and my brother. Mum did not know where to look or who to hug first. It was fun seeing her surprised; she was simply thrilled, although I did think for a moment that she was going to have a heart attack.

The kids enjoyed every minute of the stay in Chipili. Bwembya and Bupe celebrated their eleventh and eighth birthdays, respectively, in Chipili, and Mum made a beautiful cake, and we had a small afternoon tea for them. The kids were pampered and spoiled and over fed. I had not seen so much Zambian food in a long time. Every relative, friend and acquaintance brought some item of food for us, cooked or uncooked. Fortunately, the kids ate everything. They love Zambian food and were not fussy at all. Bwembya, who was eating dried fish, fresh fish, chicken, meat, caterpillars (Yes! Caterpillars are a delicacy, I ate them, too) and he ate lots of cooked pumpkin leaves despite normally never eating vegetables. Each meal was like a feast with food of different colours and delicious smells. In Zambia, we eat pumpkin leaves, they are my favourite vegetable. You lightly blanch them, drain the water, then add onion, tomato, salt, a little oil, and let it cook for a few minutes.

My dad's sisters and my mother's sister came to visit us. I liked that my aunties came with food in enamel dishes wrapped in a square cloth with the edges tied in a knot at the top of the dish. In the dishes, there was food like cassava leaves in peanut sauce, cooked dried fish, stewed chicken, a whole roasted chicken, groundnuts, sweet potatoes in peanut sauce and my kids' favourite, homemade peanut butter that was dark brown and very crunchy. Dad and I were happy when people brought *tute* (cassava) as that was our favourite foods. It went well with the homemade peanut butter. Other people came with other gifts. The kids were given a live chicken each. They were shocked one day to find out that we had eaten one of the chickens for dinner. They should not have named the chickens.

I felt quite guilty looking at some of the people who were giving us food. Some people had no shoes, no money, and no food themselves, but they'd brought us the last crop of corn from their field; it was humbling. We had chickens that people could not afford to give away, but that was the tradition. To welcome visitors, you give them anything you can. I was so touched. I, in turn, gave everyone a little something. Some money, some bread rolls as Mum made and sold them, and some drinks for people to take home. It was sort of like a barter system. I had also brought lots of head scarfs and clothes that I gave away to the women.

We had good times sitting at the back of the house where there was an outdoor kitchen to complement the kitchen in the house. There was not enough power from the solar panels to use for most of the cooking. Outside, there was a kitchen with a clay oven, which made the kitchen very hot, so we sat outside between the kitchens. Food was cooked on braziers with charcoal as the fuel. First thing in the morning, two middle-sized braziers were lit and a kettle was put on one of them to boil water to drink. At least one of the fires was kept alight all day and used to cook different foods across the day. The clay oven in the outside kitchen was used for baking. The smell coming out of the kitchen was mouth-watering because Mum baked bread rolls and scones in the oven. I did not know how the baked goods didn't come out of the clay oven smelling of smoke. It was clear you did not need electricity to bake and cook great food.

My girls taught my mother's three sisters how to dance. We had a demonstration from the girls, then the aunties got up and started dancing. They did not do too badly for women in their sixties. The girls where shouting 'go auntie, go auntie' as the aunties shuffled their feet and circled their arms towards them and then out in front of them. A bit of hip hop. Mum sat on the sidelines laughing as she shelled some groundnuts in a shallow basket. The aunties also gave me cooking lessons, each teaching me her specialty. I did well while they watched and instructed me. When I later tried to cook the chikanda, which is made of a small round bulb found in the ground, cleaned, cut, and dried then pound into a powder, I failed miserably. I failed to replicate the vegetables in peanut sauce, too.

While we were sitting outside the kitchen, my aunties' daughters also dropped by to hang out and join in the fun, but they were not brave enough to join the girls dancing with their mothers. We started talking about the kids, what they were doing and life in general. They wanted to hear all about our life in Australia. What food we ate, where we lived, if I had a colour scheme? What?

'Bana Bwembya, what is your colour scheme?' asked one of the cousins.

I was shocked. 'What colour scheme?' I asked.

'For your kitchen. Mine is yellow.'

'Where did you hear about colour schemes?' I asked.

'On Oprah,' she replied.

Of course, on Oprah!

Bwembya had no problem communicating with people in Chipili. He was talking more than I had ever heard him talk. In Australia, he would say a word occasionally, but it was usually 'mum', 'home', 'yes', but mostly 'no'.

One day we were standing at the door greeting the local priest. The priest greeted me and then turned to Bwembya and said, 'Mulishani (how are you), young man?' Bwembya answered in Bemba, 'Ndifye bwino (I am fine).' I was stunned. The boy who hardly spoke was speaking Bemba. Where did he learn it? How did he learn it? Mwango and I spoke Bemba around the house but not to the kids. Due to Bwembya's problem with speech we had been advised to stick to one language with the kids. We liked that we could talk about them and make decisions without the kids understanding what we said. But there was Bwembya having a conversation with the priest while I stood there with my mouth wide open. They had a proper conversation that lasted a couple of minutes. Wait till I tell Mwango when I got back to Sydney, I thought.

On the first day, I had talked to Mum about who would look after the kids while I was there so I could have a break from constantly being on the lookout. She identified a couple of people and I paid them a daily rate to have eyes on the kids all the time. Chipili was a big village and I needed to know my kids were in safe hands. Bwembya would go down to the river with some older cousin or uncle to fish, watch people swim and wash clothes in the river. My parents' house is right next to the river. You can see the river from the front and side of the house. Very occasionally the river flooded, and water came close to the house. Bwembya spent some days at my parents' shop/restaurant with Dad, sitting in the little rotunda outside, sipping lemonade. He was also taken bike riding (as a passenger) around the village by one of the older cousins and visited relatives in their homes.

The girls followed the women to the river where they washed clothes and collected water in large containers. They especially loved filling a big drum with water and rolling it up to the house. This was the water used for cleaning and bathing. They got water for drinking from the well with a smaller container. There was also a rain tank next to the outdoor kitchen that stored water and when the pump was working water was pumped up from the river a few times a week.

The kids helped to open the chicken coups and let the chickens and ducks out in the morning. They also got to go into the hen house and collect eggs. There was a lot of screaming and shouting involved, and the chickens would not be too happy with their eggs being taken. Some chickens and ducks would chase the kids. At the end of the day, they got to round up the chickens and ducks and make sure they were all in the coop before it was closed for the night.

We went to church on Sunday. The church, which was an Anglican cathedral on a hill opposite my parents' house, was built in 1928 by an Englishman. The service was the longest service I had been to in a long time. We could not stay the full four to five hours. The kids got fidgety and hungry, so we left after three hours and went home but Mum did not come home till mid-afternoon. You could hear the singing from the church well into the evening.

The people in Chipili were fascinated With Bwembya's LA Gear Light-up sneakers, which had little red lights going on and off in the heel when he walked. Everyone in Zambia was fascinated by them and I was impressed he had them at all as they were very expensive shoes. There is a story to these shoes. Before we went to Zambia, we went to a shoe shop we knew was having a sale to get designer sneakers for the girls. After buying tickets and presents, etc., I was on a tight budget, so we headed off to the sale. We were fitting the girls with sneakers, and they were all excited. We were not in the market to get Bwembya sneakers as he had not outgrown his shoes. The owner of the shop came with a box to where Bwembya was sitting and started to take off his sandals and put the sneakers on. Horrified, I dashed over and said we were not buying him sneakers. They looked as expensive as they were. The quiet Lebanese man packed Bwembya's sandals in the box the sneakers came in and said he did not want any money for them, they were his sneakers. Mwango opened his wallet and tried to pay for the sneakers, but he would not take the money. We almost fell over backwards trying to say thank you. That's how the sneakers came into our lives. Bwembya loved his shoes and walked with a spring in his step, like he was walking on air. The sneakers had an added benefit, they were very good for the tendons in his ankles. They were high top and prevented him from walking on tip toe.

We stayed in Chipili for eight days. While there, we took a day trip to a town called Kawambwa, where my mother-in-law's family came from. Dad drove us up for the day and we got to meet Mwango's grandfather, his aunt, and some cousins. His grandmother had gone to a funeral in another village, so we did not get to see her. Halfway to Kawambwa Bwembya indicated that he wanted to use the toilet. Great, I thought, in the middle of nowhere, how was this going to work? Bwembya always peed sitting on the toilet. Anyway, we stopped and walked into the bush, surrounded by grass almost taller than I was. Thankfully, it was daylight. I was busy squashing down grass to make a place for Bwembya to squat in and when I turned around, he was standing there peeing into the grass. I was so amused. He had probably seen the other boys pee like that at Reggie's place. Mission accomplished, one more skill learnt. I could not wait to go home and tell Mwango about it.

The Chipili experience was worth the trip. We were in a real village with none of the city trimmings, but I could walk into my parents' house and there was electricity from their solar power. I remember after visiting Australia on holiday, that I'd carried one of those solar panels back to Zambia. I was glad to be able to go into my parents' pink bathroom to have a nice hot bath or use the guest shower and not have to go down to the river for my daily bath. I could also watch TV or videos on the VCR and listen to tapes in the house. Entering my parents' house was like entering a different world from the one outside where people lived such different lives.

In Lusaka, we went to visit Uncle Linus and Aunty Janet. Aunty Janet had expensive furniture, including a lovely, imported glass coffeetable which was her pride and joy. Bwembya would slowly approach the table, stand in front of her and slowly start to lower himself onto the table, all the while looking directly at Aunty Janet and smiling his silly little grin. Aunty Janet would get up and lead him away from the table, flustered. He would wait a while and do it all over again just to watch the expression on her face. He was a little devil sometimes. I had a glass coffeetable in Sydney, and he tried that when we got back and I just told him a couple of times, 'Don't even think about it,' with a straight face and the novelty wore off.

I took a risk taking Bwembya to Zambia but oh what a wonderful time we all had, and best of all, Bwembya was not sick a day in those four weeks, he didn't even have any of the frequent bleeding noses he normally had. He also smiled, laughed, and had a lot of fun being a little boy. He was also surrounded by people who loved him, some who saw him for the first time and most who saw him for the last time. I remember that I wanted people to know him, to see him, to know he was a person, not just a sick child who they heard was often sick or in hospital.

Chapter 12

When we came home, it was amazing how quickly things changed. After about a month, Bwembya started to deteriorate quite rapidly. I used to dread the phone calls from his school. It got so bad that if there was a call from school about anything else but Bwembya being unwell, the first thing the caller would say is, 'It's not about B, I am just calling.' There were frequent bleeding noses that would be so bad he would end up in hospital. I remember getting one call and driving from work quickly not realising how bad the bleeding was until I got to school. Bwembya had a big wad of cottonwool on his nose. I did not think too much about it. I put him in the car and put his seatbelt on, but the teacher handed me a large roll of cotton wool as I got in the car. I was thinking surely, I didn't need that much cotton wool. We were almost at the end of the street when Bwembya put the wad of cotton wool he had on his nose onto the tray between the two front seats. I looked at it and it was completely soaked in blood. I quickly unrolled a big wad of cotton wool and handed it to him as blood ran down his nose. I realised it was very serious and drove as fast as I could to the hospital which was about a ten-minute drive (if you drove fast). On the way, I had to hand him wads of cotton wool about six times, at every stop sign or traffic light.

When we got to the hospital, there was no parking anywhere nearby, so I parked two streets away. By the time I parked the car, Bwembya was looking worn out and tired and I was anxious and starting to panic. I half-carried him to the emergency room and people looked at me as if I had beaten my child or something. No-one offered to help. I struggled to half-drag and half-carry Bwembya with both of us soaked in blood. The last wad of cotton wool had fallen somewhere on the road. I felt really annoyed with all the people walking by and not doing anything to help. We finally got into the emergency department and the triage nurses saw us. Bwembya was in my arms, eyes closed and not moving. They dropped everything, took him from my arms and ran with him into the emergency ward.

There was a flurry of activity as the doctor took the scissors and cut off his navy school track suit top, blue pullover, and white vest. I stood aside as they worked on him, answering questions about his condition. What medication did he take? How long he had been bleeding for? I could hear the doctor telling the team to 'hurry, we are going to lose him!' His body temperature must have been very low as one of the nurses rushed to get a heated blanket and another one of those silver blankets. They put him on a drip, and I remember being asked if he had ever been intubated before. I answered that he had not but that he would be hard to intubate as his airways were restricted. There was a lot of drama involving a lot of people but finally things settled after about an hour.

Bwembya woke up and looked really frightened and shaken. He wanted to get off the bed. The doctors were not having that, but I said I would sit in one of the large leather chairs and he could sit with me. I sat down and with tubes and wires everywhere, they sat Bwembya in my lap. It was against their better judgment I am sure, but anything to keep Bwembya calm as he had been getting really distressed. He had five litres of fluid pumped into him as he had lost a lot of blood and looked very pale. I could feel myself breathing again. The calm after a storm.

We sat there for a couple of hours and Bwembya dozed off. I was very uncomfortable, but not complaining; he was going to be okay. When his breathing settled and he was looking more like himself, I eased myself out of the chair and left him with a nurse. I went to call Mwango who was working in Sydney that week. I told him an edited version of what had happened and asked if he could pick up the girls from after-school care. By the time he left work, picked up the girls and arrived at the hospital, Bwembya and I had both calmed down and had had some catnaps.

Following this incident, Bwembya had an operation to have his nose cauterised to reduce the severity of the nose bleeds. Having an operation was considered quite risky due to his precarious health. I never told Mwango all the gruesome details because I did not want to worry him too much and I did not want to force him to give up the job that he loved which kept him away from home so much. If he changed jobs, it would be because he wanted to, not because he was made to. There was a lot he did not know about how things were for me during those difficult years. I just did what needed to be done.

The next couple of months were very difficult ones with Bwembya being so unwell with respiratory infections. The clingy little boy who had disappeared in Zambia appeared again and he became my shadow. One night after I had put him to bed, and I was watching TV in our bedroom, he came into the room with his chest sounding very congested. He got into bed with me and held my hand. He lay there looking at me breathing heavily with a sort of rattling noise coming from his chest. We had been to the doctor in the afternoon, and he had prescribed some antibiotics. Bwembya slept and I tried to go to sleep, but his breathing was so laboured and loud I was afraid he was going to stop breathing. I was terrified and felt powerless. I wanted to pick up the phone and tell Mwango to come home because I needed him home, because I was scared. But I didn't. I said a little prayer and then slowly, Bwembya's breathing quietened down and I was able to relax and go to sleep in the early hours of the morning.

After a night like that, Bwembya would sleep in in the morning and I did not have the heart to wake him up. I would get the girls ready, get myself ready, pack his breakfast in his bag, then wake him up at the last minute, get him dressed and we would leave. He would have his breakfast at before-school care, or at school. I would write a note in his communication book that he had not had breakfast. Bwembya was getting tired and lethargic, and things were becoming more difficult for me. Trips to some medical appointments became harder as Bwembya did not like to go in lifts, so we had to use the stairs in some areas of the hospital. Previously, he had been active and going up three flights of stairs without any problems. I had to carry him up three flights of stairs to get to the dental clinic for his check-ups at Westmead Dental Hospital or to other appointments such as the hearing centre. Fortunately, most of his appointments were at the children's hospital and it had ramps.

I was slowly getting chronically tired and in June 1997 Mwango went to Asia for five weeks, so I did not get to relax even at the weekend. There were a lot of trips to appointments and to the emergency room. Fortunately, the girls were wonderful and did what they were asked ninety-nine per cent of the time without prompting. They had started taking part in Saturday activities. Natasha had started tennis lessons again and Bupe had started ballet lessons. I was very lucky I had someone who babysat for me often. Lilly was doing her teacher's placement at the Hills School and that is how we met her. Her wonderful mother was a teacher at the school. For a few years Lilly helped me by babysitting the kids. If I was with Bwembya at the hospital I could phone Lilly to pick the girls up from after-school care, take them home, feed them and put them to bed. If for some reason we ended up spending the night at the hospital, Lilly would spend the night at our house and drop the girls off at before-school care in the morning.

In August 1997, I left my job in Burwood after about six years with the organisation. I needed a change and the travel to Burwood in peak-hour traffic was stressing me out. I joined a Christian not-for-profit organisation as a deputy regional manager in Rooty Hill. Rooty Hill was easier to get to, as I was travelling against traffic and had a good run. Because of the change in direction, driving to Rooty Hill instead of Burwood, Baulkham Heights before- and after-school care was no longer on my way to work so Bwembya started utilising the school bus. He was picked up about fifteen past seven in the morning, so I had to get him ready early. On days when he was having a sleep in, I would drop him off at school before I went to work, or drop him off with one of the teachers who lived nearby and had offered to take him in to school if he was tired and needed to sleep in. I would drop the girls off at school on my way to work.

But I was becoming really run-down and I was beginning to feel it. Working full time in a busy job where you are managing disability services and helping to run a busy centre is hard work. Having a sick child who was continuously sick made things twice as hard. I was being professional and did not let my personal life get in the way of my work. Much of the time the staff at work did not know I had been at the hospital half the night and only had two to three hours' sleep. Or I was up half the night with Bwembya who had a raging temperature at home and was restless. I just continued to do what I was doing.

As a result of all this, I started to fall apart, and it took me a while to realise it. I thought I was just being overly tired. One day driving from work, I experienced a panic attack. I could not breathe properly or feel my hands on the steering wheel or my feet on the pedals. I parked the car on the side of the road and stayed there till the feeling passed. When I started to drive again, I turned the air conditioner in the car on full, drove carefully, afraid the feeling would come back, and I would not be able to get to after-school care in time to pick up the kids by six in the afternoon. I experienced these panic attacks a few times, and I was also starting to feel depressed. One evening, I put the kids to bed and felt so overwhelmed I could not think straight. I went to the kitchen to make a cup of tea and dropped the cup. I wanted to scream and shout but the kids were sleeping. I had to get it together. I was the adult in the house. I asked myself what advice I would give someone in my shoes. The answer: talk to someone, get help. I looked in the phone book and got the number for Lifeline. I picked up the phone and called the number.

I knew what other people should do in these circumstances and who I would refer them to, I just never saw myself as someone needing professional help. The lady at Lifeline talked to me and referred me to several services, the first being to a family centre for counselling. Apparently, I needed grief counselling. Silly me, I had done counselling courses and knew about grief counselling. The counsellor was wonderful and after a couple of months attending weekly sessions, I was well on the way to getting my act together. Lifeline made referrals to a homecare service, and I started getting help four days a week for Bwembya. A homecare lady came an hour a day on Monday to Thursday to give Bwembya a shower and get him ready for bed. We had some lovely ladies come into our lives who came to love Bwembya and the girls.

The call to Lifeline also resulted in a referral to a respite care service. Before this, I would never have dreamed of letting Bwembya go away alone for respite. The anxiety attacks and depression made me realise I had to take care of myself first before I could take care of Bwembya. This was the same rhetoric I was dishing out to our clients at work and ignoring in my own life. I needed someone on the outside to point the obvious to me. Bwembya started going for respite in Northmead and he loved it.

The kids Bwembya were grouped with for respite were kids from his school. When we went to drop him off, he would be waiting impatiently for me to go. He would keep shaking my hand and trying to lead me out while I was still talking to the staff and sorting out medication sheets and payment. But I could go home knowing he was in good hands and happy to be there. At work, only the regional manager knew what was going on in my life. I had to leave early on a Tuesday to attend the late afternoon counselling session, otherwise it was business as usual.

At the beginning of 1998, we went on our usual annual family holiday, this time to Forster on the central coast. I spent most of the time swimming with the girls in the pool at the hotel and reading books. We went to family fun parks and had a good time. We still had to take things easy with Bwembya as he still had occasional bleeding noses, but the adult-strength drixine nasal spray prescribed was working quite effectively most of the time. A few squirts before the bleeding became heavy and usually it would be alright. We also learnt how to manage his nose bleeds by keeping his fingernails short, keeping the nostrils lubricated with Vaseline and giving him plenty of cold water and ice blocks in the summer.

When we came back from holiday on a Friday, I took the kids out for a movie. Bwembya had developed a very strong opinion on what he wanted and when he wanted it. The movie was called *Spice World*, starring the Spice Girls. We walked into the movie theatre and the girls sat down. I stood behind Bwembya waiting for him to sit down, too. He stood in the aisle with his hands on his hips waiting. The movie started. A look of utter disgust spread over his face, he turned, looked at me and simply walked out as if to say I am not staying to watch that. My normally placid child who would watch anything the girls were watching, had drawn a line at having to watch *Spice World*. I told the girls to watch the movie, followed him out and surprisingly I got a refund for the two tickets. Bwembya and I then went for a walk around the shopping centre until the movie finished and the girls came out.

The most unpleasant thing in his life was swimming lessons. Since the incident at the pool in Bexley, he was still wary of water, but we all thought he should be water safe, so the lessons continued at school but under moderate protest. He would hide his swimmers and towels where no one could find them when it was swimming time. It took the teachers and I a little while to catch on, but we did, and he knew it when we saw the mischievous grin on his face.

✦

Chapter 13

Bwembya's life improved when his heart medication was increased. The breathing problems and the respiratory infections stopped. He was now twelve years old and for almost two years he had no serious illness, just your usual cold and flu. I had one unsettling day when he was at respite for the weekend. I got a call to let me know that he had been given a double dose of medication. One of the staff had not documented his morning medication, so when the next staff member came on duty, he was given the medication again. They had called the hospital and were told it should be fine but to keep an eye on him. They apologised profusely. I told them it was ok and to let me know if anything happened. There was no point being upset. I had managed a residential group home and was aware of how easily this could happen. It was why there must be policies and procedures to avoid incidences such as this. I provided some advice on how this could be done. The service subsequently changed its policy and procedures for medication to require two people to sign off and check the medication when it was given.

Bwembya had a full life going to a school that he loved, and to after-school with his sisters and kids who obviously loved having him around. On Saturdays, on a fortnightly basis, he attended the Junior Activity Group (JAG). He was going to his beloved church at Crestwood on Sundays and at the end of the service he could go up to the kitchen and get a nice piece of cake with a variety of other sweet items. The ladies in the kitchen spoilt him.

On Sunday evenings on a fortnightly basis, he went to teen club at a church in Baulkham Hills where some kids from his school, including kids from his class, got together with church members and had all sorts of activities. They had dinner and then a church service, although he usually did not stay for the church service as he was exhausted by then and needed to go to bed to be ready for school on Monday. In addition to teen club, he had respite care on a regular basis, usually for one weekend a term and a few days in the holidays, and he also attended vacation care with the girls at Baulkham Heights and for one week during the holidays with the Children's Services Program at Rooty Hill. He was a busy, happy little chap.

These were the good years and Mwango and I were cheerfully devoted to our role as chauffeurs. Bwembya had more birthday parties than most kids. He had a party at school, a celebration at Saturday club, at teen club, at JAG and at home as well. He was also active, running around the garden playing basketball, hitting his cricket bat and playing T-ball at school.

In September 1997, there was a big production of *CATS* at school. Performing arts at The Hills was taken very seriously. The teachers spent a whole term making costumes for the performance. The make-up was superb. Bwembya's costume included black tracksuit pants and a black skivvy with a brown fluffy fur like material covering his stomach and chest. He had a hat made of the same fluffy material in a leopard skin pattern with two little black ears on either side of the hat. His nose was painted black as were the whiskers on the sides of his mouth. There were little bits of hair painted on his chin. But when it was time to go on stage and all the kids were ready behind the curtain Bwembya was nowhere to be seen. Finally, one of the teachers found him at the back of the hall and the students walked slowly onto the stage. We could see that Bwembya's makeup and costume looked different from everyone else. He had transformed himself. The makeup was a little smudged and pieces of the costume were missing, but he stood on the stage with a cheeky smile, looking very smug.

He was maturing and changing. He was also becoming more independent and doing things for himself such as clearing his place at the table after he finished eating, using a napkin to wipe his hands and mouth after eating instead of his shirt. Most importantly, he was closing the door to the toilet when he was in there. One winter evening, my daughters had their friends sleeping over and usually in winter after a shower Bwembya would dress in the living room in front of the heater. This night he refused to go to the living room and headed for his room and did not come out until he had his undies and PJ bottoms on – such modesty.

Bwembya was maturing so quickly, I was amused by some things and alarmed at others. One afternoon I had taken him to a specialist appointment at some private rooms in Westmead next to the Children's Hospital. We were siting in the waiting room waiting to see the doctor when he indicated he wanted to go to the toilet. I stood up and led him down the corridor to where the toilets were. He took off in front of me and quickly went into the men's toilet. I was shocked. I had always taken him into the women's toilets as he was just a little guy. I stood there wondering if I should just barge in. But it was a men's toilet. I decided to just stand close to the door and listen for any unusual noise and I would rush in. My heart was racing thinking of all the things that could go wrong. These were private rooms, right, he should be ok. The door opened and there he was wiping his hands on his navy-blue jumper. 'Oh B', I said and followed him back to the waiting room.

Mwango and I decided to spend some quality time together while things were going so well. I was tired and had been having problems with my blood pressure. Our GP put me on medication to control the blood pressure. In early March 1998, Mwango was working in New Zealand for three weeks, so I decided to go over to Auckland for a long weekend. I had my hair done and bought some new clothes. On the Thursday I flew to New Zealand after organising with Lilly and my brothers to look after the kids. I managed to upgrade my economy seat to business class, so it was my first-time flying business class. I was impressed. After a quick check-in where there was no queue, I was able to go to the business class lounge and have some breakfast from the buffet. Champagne was served as soon as we took off. I had orange juice. The lunch was delicious and well presented. So, this is how my husband travelled! But it seemed that as soon as we took off, we were landing. The flight was too quick, I was just starting to enjoy myself. Damn!

When we arrived in Auckland, I was singled out and led to a quiet spot where I was asked a lot of questions. Where was I coming from, where was I going, how long was I there for, how much money did I have on me, where was I staying and who was picking me up? 'Did I look like someone who was trying to sneak into the country? For goodness' sake, I just came business class, don't spoil my experience,' I thought. 'It must be my Zambian passport.' The customs officer was polite and inquisitive, but she listened carefully, checked my ticket, my passport, and the Australian visa in the passport. I was legitimate. I could go.

Mwango was waiting for me at arrivals. His face lit up when he saw me. Seeing him wiped out the unpleasant last half hour. I walked into his arms and returned his embrace. I loved the way he missed me. Like I had been on another planet and not just a few hours' away. He took the luggage from me, and we went out to the rental car. We drove back to the office and Mwango went back to work until it was time for him to call it a day. I sat in the lounge area having a cup of tea and reading a book.

While I was in New Zealand, we relaxed and did some touristy stuff, savouring the time together. On Saturday, we caught a ferry from Auckland and spent the day at Waiheke Island. We caught the first ferry to the island with a small group of people. There was a hop-on, hop-off bus, but we decided to walk around the island to enjoy the scenery. The island was very green, and we saw birds everywhere. The sound of birds followed us on our walk. There were lovely beaches and a few vineyards on the island. We stopped at one of the restaurants for a leisurely lunch and visited three boutique wineries. Mwango got to do some wine tasting and bought a few bottles of wine. We got time to unwind and de-stress. I flew back to Sydney the next day, business class, and arrived home refreshed and relaxed.

When Mwango came back to Australia, we had a little dinner party at the end of March for his fortieth birthday. We had a few close friends at our house because that was all I was able to handle. I was learning to take care of myself and to not over-tax myself. I was busy with work, travelling up and down to Canberra, Melbourne, and Forbes for conferences and forums. I enjoyed going on trips to different places. Lilly continued to look after the kids for us as Mwango was usually somewhere across the country, too. In the April school holidays, Mwango was in Port Macquarie for a couple of weeks, so we decided the kids and I would join him there for a few days before heading off to the MPS conference in Ballarat Victoria.

We spent a few days in Port Macquarie, then the kids and I drove from Port Macquarie to Ballarat with a night in Albury. There was hardly any complaining or whinging on long trips. The girls liked to read books. I would buy them sets of books when we were going on holiday. Bwembya sat in the middle of the back seat, quite content to sit and watch the road and listen to me singing my way along the freeway. He would hum along or play with a ball or car all the way. We arrived in Ballarat mid-morning, had lunch, and went for a swim in the pool at the hotel. Bwembya of course just watched on the sidelines. He enjoyed watching us in the pool. The pool was an indoor heated pool with a spa at one end of it. The pool and spa were most welcome after the long drive. Our suite had a big spa in the bathroom. The girls and I made good use of it. We sat in the spa reading our books. Bwembya just sat on the edge and watched, occasionally splashing us with little bits of bubble bath. He only got into the spa when we stopped running the jets and everyone got out. He stood in the spa to have a quick shower and out he came.

The formal part of the conference started on Friday. The kids went off prospecting for gold or something on the organised trips that were on offer for the children. I was one of the speakers for one of the sessions that morning, talking about community services. In the afternoon, I drove to Melbourne to pick Mwango up from the airport. We both felt it was important for us to attend these conferences. We learnt a lot from other families and professionals. It was at an MPS conference that I learnt why Bwembya could sometimes talk. No one had been able to explain that to me before. We were in a breakout session, and I was in a room with a doctor from Scandinavia. I asked him why my son spoke sometimes and not all the time. He explained how the nerves that carry the message from the brain to the mouth were blocked with glycosaminoglycans. He had what they called spontaneous speech. If he did not think about it, he could talk. As he was not relying on the thought being transmitted to the mouth.

I picked up Mwango from the airport and we drove straight back to Ballarat. When we got back to the hotel, I went straight into the spa in our room before we went for dinner. The kids had spent a fun-filled day and were exhausted by the end of the day. It was nice not to have to worry about where they were or who was with them as care was all pre-arranged.

Mwango continued travelling and I continued doing the things I did. James and Shaunagh had another little girl at the end of May called Gabrielle. We were happy to have another little angel join our troops. In September, Mwango and I decided we had to have some time away by ourselves, a sort of second honeymoon that we had promised ourselves long ago and never got to do. Bwembya's health was stable, and we seized the moment. We left for a holiday resort (suite complete with spa) on the Gold Coast on a Thursday morning after organising a tight schedule for who would look after the kids. The schedule went like this:

- Left kids at our neighbour Gina's in the morning, she put B on the bus and dropped Bupe off at school.
- Tasha to catch the school bus as normal.
- Lilly picked the kids up from after-school and stayed with them till Saturday when Kenny came over.
- Clementine a family friend came Sunday to Wednesday.
- Lilly took over from Clementine Wednesday to Friday.
- Friday, James picked up the kids to stay at their place till Saturday.
- Saturday evening, we picked up the kids when we came back.

I can't draw or paint, but I can organise my life and anyone's life if they let me. On the Gold Coast, Mwango and I hired a car and did all the usual sightseeing, ate out and generally lounged by the pool or read in the spa. We came back rejuvenated.

Our family had lots of happy times. The kids and I did some fun things such as attending parties at different places. We went to the end-of-year Christmas party at Baulkham Heights. The girls danced in the concert and Bwembya had fun running around and disrupting the dancing. From there, we proceeded to attend a twenty-first birthday party for one of the girls I worked with. It was the first time I had been to a party with a real live stripper who was dressed as a policeman. I had not laughed so much in years. I was screeching like a teenager and loving every moment of it – as were all the other women! The kids were safely in another room watching a movie with one of the older teenagers and were in bed by the time the stripper arrived. Bwembya was good. Normally there was no way he would sleep in a strange bed at a party with fun going on. But I guess it had been a long day with all the fun earlier at the Christmas party. A little fellow can only take so much excitement in one day. Mwango missed all the fun and games as he was at the usual round of cocktail parties and dinners bankers attend at the end of the year. But maybe it was just as well, I would not have been able to scream so loud and be so uninhibited if he was around.

In the second half of 1998, Mwango changed jobs and was no longer travelling back and forth out of Sydney. The first week he was home on a Friday evening, he was eager to help with the cooking and bathing of the kids. He walked into the house, put his briefcase away, changed into casual clothes and came into the kitchen where I was clearing up afternoon tea dishes. 'Bath time, guys, where are you?' he called out. Bupe walked into the kitchen and said, 'We don't have a bath on Friday's.'

Mwango said, 'What?'

'We don't bathe on Fridays. On Fridays, we go and get videos from the video club and have whatever food we want. Mum, can we have hamburgers tonight?' she said.

Mwango looked at me like his jaw was going to fall off. 'Honey, the kids do not bathe on Friday. What does that mean? They are dirty after a long day at school. Come on!'

I turned around and faced him. 'Honey, we have a routine around here. We rush around all week, so Friday is our chill-out evening. We get home, have afternoon tea, go to the video club, get videos, and then go and get some food like hamburgers from the deli or chicken and chips at Crestwood shops. The kids have activities on Saturday, that is why they have a bath in the morning. On Friday, they just have a sponge-type bath before they change into pyjamas. In summer, they have a swim and then they would take a bath.' He did not look convinced but went with the flow.

✦

Chapter 14

On 31 December 1998, we moved to Wandella Avenue in Northmead. It was nice to see the New Year in a new house. The landlord in the house where we were living had put the house up for sale and I was getting tired of having to leave the house tidy everyday just in case people came to look at the house. With three kids to get ready in the morning the last thing I needed was to spend more time getting the house looking shipshape for people I did not know. One day, I woke up and decided enough was enough; we were moving. I called the real estate agent we rented from and told her we wished to move. She had a house to show us the following day in Northmead in a similar price range and size.

The house at Wandella Avenue was supposed to be our interim house for a short stay. We did some minor renovations. We removed the wallpaper and the carpets which were all different colours in different rooms. Bwembya enjoyed helping pull the wallpaper from the wall after Mwango had softened the glue with a steaming machine and when Bwembya went to respite one weekend, we bought two single beds and changed his room around so he would get a surprise when he came in. Well, we thought he would be happy, but he just glanced over the room and walked out, so much for that. I did miss the double bed as I was the one who would always bounce on it while Bwembya looked at me with amusement.

At Wandella Avenue, we had some of the best times in our lives and the saddest times in our lives. When we moved to Northmead, Bwembya was in relatively good health. I would have a few breathless mornings walking him to the school bus on the street when he would take off in a sprint with his bag on his back while I was opening the door to the bus. He would run down the street on people's lawns, and I would have to race after him to catch him. He thought it was all hilarious and would have a big grin on his face. He really pushed the limits with this running down the street.

I was having issues with my health again. For so many years I had put my health at the bottom of the to-do list. I kept going even if I was sick and saved my sick days at work for when Bwembya was sick. I had glandular fever and problems with controlling the thyroid levels with medication and I was so sick I quit my job in Rooty Hill in April 2000 and stayed at home recuperating for a few months, unable to move or do much. I decided to get a less demanding job to enable me to get my health back to a stable place.

Mwango was busy with work during the week. He left home early and arrived home usually after the kids had bathed and had dinner, but he did spend a lot more time with the kids at the weekends. Because I was unwell and I also had to spend time with Bwembya at the hospital, Mwango started to take an interest in cooking. This was probably because he had to if he wanted to eat a proper meal and not have things cooked by the girls. Once he started, he loved to cook. Tash was studying hospitality at school, so the two of them started experimenting with food and watching cooking shows religiously. They would cook meals for the family and took over cooking the Christmas lunch. Christmas lunch was always a three- to four-course meal.

Mwango loved to play golf with a group of guys from work on a regular basis. Golf was his time to focus on something he loved and get some stress relief after long days at work. We still had a group of great friends. Old friends from our Bexley days and new friends made in the area. Friends like Callum and Yasmin, who we met through the after-school care at Baulkham Heights. Their two girls, Ruby and Kirby, went to after-school with our kids. This worked very well for both families as we could pick up each other's kids if we had to. If Yasmin was running late at work or they had a night out, I would pick up all the kids and take them to our house. If I was running late or had something planned, she would pick up all the kids and take them to her house. We spent a lot of time together.

Our friends were all unique and important in different ways. They came from all walks of life, and we met them in different ways. They were not just friends to eat and drink with, but also with whom we could have stimulating conversations. They were an educated group of people who made any picnic, barbeque, dinner, or party worth attending. A few of these friends have fallen away due to moving to other parts of Australia or overseas, but most of them are still sitting beside us eating, drinking, and having stimulating conversation.

The year passed quickly and before we knew it, we were at the annual bush dance at the Hills School where we could let our hair down, dance uncoordinated without fear of being ridiculed, and have a ball through it all. As usual, Bwembya and I did our little ballroom dances with its twists and twirls. The year ended quietly. I took the kids to the children's service on Christmas eve at church like we did every year. On Christmas day after church, we had lunch followed by a quiet relaxed day with friends.

On the second day of February 2000, I took Bwembya to the cardiologist and he said everything was fine and that they would see him again in twelve months. That was good news because it meant less trips to the hospital. That Saturday, two ladies from Make a Wish Foundation came to interview Bwembya, Mwango and I to meet us and see how they could help to get Bwembya his wish. For months, Bwembya had been walking past an old mini-stereo system and switched it on and off, trying to get it to play. The girls had cassette players in their rooms and CD Walkmans. We finally let him take the old mini system to his room, but it was really on its last leg.

Bwembya was disadvantaged when he wanted to watch TV, despite our having three TVs in the house. Since our trip to Zambia, he was no longer happy to watch whatever the girls were watching. There was a TV in the living room, a TV in the family room, and a little TV in our bedroom. There was only one video recorder in the family room. Weekends were a big problem as the girls loved to watch their girly programs in the family room, where Bwembya loved to watch his videos. There were always unhappy faces when I told the girls to put on Bwembya's video. I acted as referee and tried to keep the peace. My husband watched anything sports related in the living room on weekends.

Make a Wish Foundation got Bwembya a corner cabinet with a TV, a DVD player, a mini-stereo system, and some DVDs. His life improved tremendously but the girls' life did not. He would watch DVDs for hours and then decide he wanted to watch a video and go and stand in the family room with the video until the girls put his video on. But he would still have the DVD playing in the sunroom where his system was set up and would be hopping between the two rooms, much to the girls' frustration until I stepped in to put a stop to it. He just needed someone to watch the DVD with, so I ended up sitting with him. His favourite video was *Grease*, and the favourite DVDs were *Jack* and *Billy Madison*.

Mwango and I were able to go out without worrying too much about Bwembya as his health was stable. Lilly, our babysitter had gone overseas, but we had two young ladies whom we met through programs at the school. They helped us with the kids when we wanted to go out. For the first nine months of the year, we were able to do just that. Dinner, jazz clubs, parties, and have fun in a relaxed atmosphere. I also liked to curl up with a good book and a glass of my favourite sparkling wine. Occasionally, I could get drunk on one glass of wine as I could go as long as six months without a sip. I was particular about my drink. I drank moscato, preferably Brown Brothers or sweet champagne.

My New Year resolution in 2000 was to start drinking; it was a family joke at the time. What was funnier was that when I first came to Australia my dad served me wine and I told him I did not drink. He was amazed I didn't drink. He could not have been wrong. 'No, no, no, no. Patricia, you drink, it's Bwalya who does not drink.' My gorgeous sister had been living under my parents' roof, drank a little, well, drank like a diplomat's daughter, and my dad had no idea? My siblings thought this was the funniest joke of the year. But I did not blame Dad, as people had always assumed I drank, because I used to hang around people who drank and loved going to nightclubs and parties. I had a long conversation with one of my friends from school after she offered me a drink and I declined. She was obviously not a close friend of mine. She was like, 'Girlfriend, stop being coy. You drink.'

'No, I don't really drink.'

'Girlfriend, you drink, why are you denying it.'

I asked her, 'Have you actually seen me take a drink?'

'No. But you drink.' I turned around to the other people in the room who had known me for a long time and been with me in the clubs and parties.

'Has anyone actually seen me take a drink?'

'No. But you do drink, don't you?' they said. I rest my case.

I started drinking so my lovely husband would not drink alone. I thought it would mean we could be merry together. One evening, Mwango and I went out for dinner for our anniversary, and he convinced me to have a glass of red wine, but after half a glass I could not get up to leave, and Mwango had to half-carry me to the car. When we got home, he went inside and called the girls to help him carry me inside. I had laughed all the way home in the car and all the way into the house where I kept telling the girls how much I loved them. The girls had to change me into my pyjamas and put me to bed – and they have never let me forget it. That was my first and last glass of red wine. From then on, if Mwango wanted me to join him in a drink he would have moscato with me. I would have one glass and he would have the rest.

In June, I started a job as community aid coordinator in Chatswood. As with my other jobs, I loved my work because it gave me so much satisfaction helping people get services that improved their life. But I had to make a few changes to the family routine. I had to teach Bupe to catch the bus to and from school. She also learnt to catch a bus to her ballet class on Tuesday afternoons. On Tuesdays, I would leave work, pick up Bwembya at after-school, then pick up Bupe from ballet. I was lucky to have flexible working hours.

Chapter 15

I turned forty in August 2000. I had been planning to have a big bash, but it didn't happen because I was still not well, and my blood pressure was playing up a lot. The weekend of my birthday Bwembya went on a weekend away to Terrigal With peer support group. Bupe and Tasha had gone to their friend's house for the weekend as pre-arranged. I had spent months talking about what I was going to get up to, and my workmates had also been giving me ideas about what I should do, but I was too tired to do anything but lie on the couch and watch TV. Mwango and I spent a quiet evening at home. He cooked me a lovely dinner and we watched some movies.

The girls auditioned to be in the Sydney Olympics and they both got selected to be in the opening ceremony. Bwembya and I once again spent a lot of time together in the car, taking the girls to different locations where they were picked up and bused to the secret places where the rehearsals took place. We could be driving to Quakers Hill one day and to Silverwater the next day. They danced in the opening ceremony around the float representing Africa. Each participant was given two tickets for the dress rehearsal. Since we had two kids in the ceremony, we got four tickets. We were proud of our girls, and they had a lot of fun, making new friends and meeting famous athletes.

Mwango, Bwembya, my brother James and I attended the Olympic Ceremony dress rehearsal in September. We were also fortunate enough to see the gymnastics, baseball, basketball, and track events. Even though Bwembya was healthy at this time, he still got tired easily, so while we were at Homebush, we would get a golf buggy to drive us from where the bus stopped to the building where the events were taking place. Sometimes, we would use one of the wheelchairs they had on offer if we were moving around a little. By the time we got home after ten at night, Bwembya would be exhausted. Mwango would have to carry him piggyback from the bus stop on Windsor Road to our house.

We enjoyed spending this time together, shouting in the stadium. We shouted with the rest of Australia, Ozzie, Ozzie, Ozzie and proudly sang our national anthem. We had never thought about it before, but we realised we were now Australians and proud of it. We wanted whichever Australian was competing to win. Lady-like manners all but disappeared as I shouted till my voice was almost gone. Sitting beside me, Bwembya held my hand and made almost as much noise as I did. We all loved it and went home almost as tired as the athletes who had put in the work. All the excitement made us decide we should go ahead and get our citizenship, so as soon as the Olympics were over, we began the application process.

At the time, Bwembya was continuing with his many programs and having his own fun. When he was away at respite, we made sure we spent quality time with the girls, such as taking them out to dinner or to shows, and I would do a girly thing with them like go to the Majestic Hotel in the Blue Mountains for lunch, while Bwembya was at vacation care for the day. On the last day of the Olympics, James and Shaunagh welcomed another baby girl. They named her Zahra. We were all delighted to have another girl to join the family. Our Australian family was growing.

The major incident that year was in October when Bwembya had to go to theatre to have eight teeth removed under general anaesthetic. Most of his baby teeth had not fallen out and were hindering the teeth that were ready to come out under them. I was at the hospital with him for the duration of his stay. For the girls it was school and business as usual. After having eight teeth out, Bwembya was a very sick little boy.

Somewhere in the middle of the night, as the anaesthetic wore off, Bwembya felt some thread irritating him in his mouth, so he pulled the threads right out, but they were the stitches holding his gum together. I woke up to him whimpering and trying to get onto the little fold-up cot that I was lying on next to his bed. There was blood on his bed and when I got up to clean the spots of blood on the floor, I realised they were pieces of flesh with thread through them. I called the nurse, she had a look and put some wads of cottonwool or something in his mouth and I let him climb into my little bed, curl up next to me and fall asleep. He slept comfortably, I did not. It was a fold-up cot. Two weeks after this operation, he got pneumonia and for about five months we were in and out of hospital. He was admitted into hospital three times in the first two weeks. He was lethargic all the time and always had some chest or respiratory infection.

Because he was so unwell, we decided not to go away for a holiday at the end of 2000 and to stay at home for Christmas. We had Christmas lunch at home with the family. After Christmas, the girls flew to Queensland for ten days to see their Aunty Mary, who was my sister-in-law Mwenya's cousin. We needed our family to keep functioning as well as it could and the girls needed a holiday. Mwango and I took the opportunity to spend some quality time with Bwembya. We took him shopping and to the beach and had lunch at Doyle's at Watson's Bay.

At the end of January 2001, we become Australian citizens. We all proudly showed up at the Hills Centre for our citizenship ceremony. All four of us walked up onto the stage as a family to receive our certificates and a plant each. We were excited. After dinner, some friends came over and we opened a bottle of champagne to celebrate. Four years later, in May 2005, at my graduation for my master's degree, I found myself sitting in the Hills Centre again. Mwango and Kenny came to see me graduate and were seated up in the wings with the usual digital camera and video cameras. As I was led to my seat, memories from the day of our citizenship ceremony flooded back. I was seated in the same row in almost the same seat I had been seated in then. It disturbed me for a little bit but then I got on with the program.

When the guest speaker was giving her speech, she started talking about how many of us had made sacrifices to get to where we were today, and what a struggle it had been for so many of us. Her speech took me back to the days I had to leave Bwembya in the hospital and go to university and then back to the hospital late in the evening after class. It made me recall the day the school bus arrived home and no one was there to meet it. The carer who met the bus on the day I had classes, thought she started work the following week, so there was no one home. I had to anxiously call Shaunagh to leave work, get to the house and connect Bwembya to the oxygen condenser machine. As I was in Milperra, which is over an hour in peak traffic from home,

I had to give her instructions over the phone. I also remembered the citizenship ceremony and Bwembya walking up those stairs to receive his little plant. How he had been so full of mischief and so full of life. Yes, getting to where I was that day had been a struggle.

I sat there weeping silently, tears flowing continuously for the rest of the speech. People must have thought I was crying with joy. I was crying for me, for this woman sitting there who had struggled so hard to get the degree, who had sat in the hospital with books around her writing papers while her son was asleep leaning against her in a hospital chair. I cried for the woman who stood behind her son while he got an x-ray as he wanted her to hold his hand while it was done and who once stood next to an MRI scanner so she could keep him calm while he had a scan. He was claustrophobic and did not want to stay in the machine. I cried for the irony of sitting in the same row I had sat in with my son a few short years ago, when we drank champagne and celebrated our citizenship. I cried because I was proud to get my degree despite how hard it had been. Graduating was bittersweet because God closed one door and opened a window. I had lost so much and gained this degree.

It took a major effort to get myself together and try to appear excited to Mwango and Kenny and to enjoy the lunch Mwango took us to. It was one of the hardest days I had to live through because of the raw emotion that came to the surface at a time that should have brought me my greatest joy. It felt as if I was on the edge of sanity. Thankfully, times like those were few and far between and didn't last more than a few minutes most of the time. I don't know whether the boys saw my tears or knew why I was crying. All they could see was my smile through the tears.

The year 2001 started off with Bwembya not well. I hated to see him feeling so unwell. I kept telling the doctors there was something wrong with him, but I got the feeling they thought I was neurotic and imagining things. Deep down in my gut I knew something was wrong and I kept taking him into the hospital if I was unhappy, and he always seems to be diagnosed with respiratory infections or pneumonia. He was sick from mid-February for a week. A month later, Mum arrived from Zambia to visit us for a few months. Bwembya loved his grandma, and it made him smile as if all his birthdays had come at once. He was quite sick again in the first two weeks in April.

On the day before Anzac Day, Bwembya was unwell and became worse on Anzac Day itself. I took him to the children's hospital at Westmead as he had a temperature and was vomiting. One of the junior doctors in emergency examined him and told me to bring him back the next day as the hospital was very busy on a public holiday. I took him home with apprehension and kept an eye on him. The next morning, Mum went to Dubbo with my brother James and his family for a long weekend. As mothers do, she wanted to stay behind when she saw Bwembya was unwell. I reassured her he would be okay, and that we had an appointment at one in the afternoon in emergency to see the doctor we had seen the day before.

In the morning I got a phone call from his paediatrician who was overseas at the time. We had met her on one of our trips to the emergency department when the staff had trouble assigning Bwembya to a speciality to put him under for that visit as it was not clear what was wrong with him. She was in the room and had a talk with the staff looking after us. That was the day she offered to have Bwembya under her team if he came in with nonspecific symptoms. On the phone that morning, she told me she had been in touch with the hospital and her department had been alerted that Bwembya had gone to emergency. She had called to see how he was. When I answered all her questions, she advised me to take Bwembya to the hospital right away and she would alert the hospital that we were on our way. I set off to the hospital with Bwembya earlier than the appointed time, he was becoming sicker and sicker by the minute. The hospital emergency room was full, but fortunately the doctor we had seen the previous day was waiting for us and took us into one of the treatment rooms almost as soon as we arrived. She ordered x-rays and other tests. While we were sitting waiting for the x-ray to come back just inside emergency, a nurse who was passing by took one look at Bwembya and asked me to bring him over to a bed that was in the corridor and lay him on it. She went and called a doctor, and he was finally admitted.

We went up to the ward much quicker than usual. There was often a long wait in emergency before a bed was found. We were put into the cardiac ward in a multi-shared room at the end of the ward. We were not up there very long when I realised that Bwembya was extremely ill. He would not respond to my voice or my touch, so I quickly called the nurse and things fell apart. I had had a few close calls with Bwembya, but this was the first time I consciously thought we could lose him. He was barely conscious, not responding to voices or touch, and his eyes were rolling. The knot in the pit of my stomach felt heavy and hard, but I could not afford to crumble. The next day he got progressivity worse. He became incontinent and had to be put into nappies. It was touch and go with his life for a few days. He had an infection in his heart and had to go into theatre to have a central line inserted into his chest to get the antibiotics directly to his heart.

It was a few weeks later that I learnt by accident that Bwembya had had a stoke caused by an aneurysm. One of the signs was that he had developed night blindness a few weeks before. I had seen him walk into the screen door at home. During assessments while he was in hospital it was discovered that he had lost his peripheral vision, so an appointment was made for him to see the eye specialist. When I arrived, there was another person in the room and the specialist asked me if the student doctor could stay for Bwembya's appointment. I said it was fine. She started giving a history of Bwembya's current admission and his background. She then said, 'Bwembya had a stroke caused by an aneurysm.'

I said, 'What did you say? Bwembya had a stroke?'

She looked at me and realised I did not know. 'What were you told?' she asked.

'That he had an infection in his heart,' I answered.

'He has, but it also looks like he had a stroke sometime in the last few weeks.' That explained why he had become clumsy and was bumping into things.

Bwembya stayed in hospital for six weeks until the beginning of June. I spent all but two nights at the hospital. Mwango stayed there for two nights and complained about how uncomfortable the fold-out cot was, but I was fine staying overnight as I was used to the whole thing. As he got better, Bwembya started attending the hospital school a few hours at a time until he could stay for most of the morning. He even got to have his whole class visit him with homemade get-well cards.

Despite all this, the lives of our girls still had to go on. I would leave Mum or Mwango and slip off to take Bupe who was in year six, to her year seven interviews. I also dropped the girls off at the Macquarie Ice Rink where they met with the youth group. Life was still going on around us. My nieces were still having birthday parties and christenings that I attended totally exhausted and worried out of my head, because I didn't want to be away from the hospital for a minute longer than necessary. It felt like I was on high alert all the time. My heart would miss a few beats each time the phone rang.

Mwango and I did all we could to keep the family going, with the help of family and friends. I tried to keep our family life as normal as possible because I never wanted the girls to look back and only remember how their brother's illness defined their lives. I made sure we did all the things we could do, when we could, for as long as we could. Hearing them talk about something that happened on one of our trips warms my heart. A few months ago, I heard them comment about what a lovely childhood they had and all the fun they had on holidays, and it reaffirmed that I had done what I had hoped to do.

In the first week of June, the antibiotic course Bwembya was being given through the central line finally finished. The next day he had to have the line taken out. The doctor and the nurses took him to the suture room on the ward and I went along with him as I usually did to hold his hand. The doctor was not the person who put the line in. The central line had been put into his chest in the theatre. He was busy tugging at the canula and Bwembya started bleeding.

I watched closely against my better judgement, holding Bwembya's hand and calming him down as he was whinging a little. The nurses asked me if I wanted to go out, but I refused. I was not going anywhere, although I felt like I was going to pass out at the sight of the blood and the skin pulling away from the stitches. But nothing would drag me away from my son. Bwembya was so brave to lie there and take all that pain. There was no anaesthetic. We all found it difficult to look at what was happening. I held Bwembya's hand and talked to him. With the other hand I patted his head and wiped his tears. I focused on him, willing him my strength, willing the procedure to finish quickly. When it was all done, he got up off the bed, stood there with tears on his face and he smiled. He turned around and walked slowly out of the room. He could have been carried or put on a wheelchair, but he walked!

Mum had been waiting in his room while this was going on in the treatment room. We got our bags and walked out of the hospital. My son and I hit the road running. He was in his wheelchair and very eager to get out of there after six gruelling weeks. It was a traumatic experience for all of us. A little red book got me through those difficult weeks. I have a little red Gideon's International Bible that my brother Heckie gave me when I was going to college in America. I think he was given it when he was getting confirmed; it was dated 11th July 1975. He would have been sixteen going on seventeen then. I carried this little Bible everywhere with me in my handbag. It was worn-out and fragile. I had stuck the cover on with a bit of cello tape to hold it together. In the Bible, I had a Psalm that I had marked with a blue pen around the edges. It is Psalm 46; it calms me and gives me peace.

Bwembya stayed at home for a few days with Mum. When Mum went to stay with James, I had a carer provided by Carer

Respite to help look after him. During that week, Bwembya was petrified at night and came and slept in our bed. He would sleep on my side of the bed with me in the middle. Some part of his body had to have contact with me all the time. Normally his foot would touch my leg, or his hand would touch my arm very lightly. If the contact was broken, he would immediately move to restore it without waking up.

On Monday during the second week of June, Bwembya went to school for half the day. I worked for half the day, so I was able to pick him up. Mum left for Zambia in the third week of June. Her departure nearly destroyed what strength I had left. I wanted to beg her not to go as I did not feel Bwembya was well enough. I felt like he was on the brink, still vulnerable, but I could not ask her. I am not good at asking for help. Instead, I dug deep within me, and talked to God. He always comes through for me, maybe not immediately but he does. Caring for a sick child was not easy and having Mum there seemed to alleviate some of my anxiety, like someone was helping lighten my load. With her there, I was able to let go of the caring role when I was at work for half the day as I knew B was in as safe hands as he could be. Even the nurses were no match for Mum when she refused to let them wake him up for therapy after he had a bad night; she simply told them to come back later. Granny power.

I had to make decisions about my job. I loved it but I was realistic enough to know that we were getting to a stage in Bwembya's life where my caring role was going to increase. I decided to look for a part-time job and went for an interview as a volunteer coordinator at a hospital in Dundas for twenty hours a week at the end of May. I got the position and started work the day after Bwembya left hospital. I was able to pick him up at lunch time every day from school and we would go home and have a rest until the girls came home. Eventually, Bwembya was able to go back to school full time, although he was fragile for a while and never fully recovered his strength.

For about five months after the stroke, the twinkle in his eyes was gone. There was no spark; then suddenly one day it was back, the mischief, the daring, the half-smile, and we all breathed a sigh of relief and said, 'He is back.'

Once he was out of hospital, Bwembya refused to wear pyjamas. He slept in t-shirts and soft sports shorts, or long-sleeved t-shirts and track pants and he completely changed the way he ate and what he ate. Things he had previously refused to eat were now being eaten without us resorting to ingenious ways of making him eat. No one told him what he needed to do to get healthy – he just changed his eating habits.

To begin with, he had a strange fetish. He wanted chicken for dinner every night and for it to be cooked differently. There were to be no leftovers, he had to see the food being cooked. He would go to the freezer, get the chicken, bring out the pan or the pot or the baking dish depending on the flavour of the day. If he did not want to wait for the chicken to defrost, he would get the car keys and my handbag and lead me to the car and point what direction he wanted to go. We would end up at Woollies and he would pick out the chicken in the fresh chicken section and carry it to the counter.

We were amazed when he started eating vegetables, drinking milk (lactose reduced), and eating fruit. For the past couple of years, he would not eat a variety of foods, only specific things. We had assumed he was allergic or had problems with some foods like most MPS kids do, so we never fussed. But it was like the penny suddenly dropped and he decided he was going to eat properly. From then on, he took whatever medicine was put in front of him and drank it without a second look, and he would also get into a lift and keep as far away from the stairs as possible.

By mid-August, he was back at his Saturday peer support group. The girls were back at their activities, which I had suspended for a month, and we all went back to some sort of normality. In the October school holidays on a Thursday, the kids and I went to Kilcare to spend a few days at a holiday house. We had been going to Kilcare for several years, usually in the Easter holidays. Mwango came up by train on the Friday after work and we had a nice weekend before going home on Sunday. Kilcare is a lovely area, with the house being a short walk to the water. There we relaxed, ate a lot of take-away food, and spent the day by the water. Bwembya and I usually sat under an umbrella. I would read while Bwembya watched Mwango and the girls playing in the water. I took the opportunity to recharge my batteries while Mwango took over the cooking and care of Bwembya. The house had a big deep bath, and I had a bubble bath or used bath oils to help me unwind.

At the end of October, I started writing a book. I found it hard to put on paper how I felt about my son, how he touched my life. How could I put into words how I felt? Especially about the little things, like when we eskimo kissed and he would laugh his little laugh, a laugh that brought a twinkle to his eyes and a smile to my soul. Or how he would stand there watching with a silly little grin as I put my face powder on. I would lean over and put some powder on his nose, and he would squeal and run off very amused. Or how he would go through silly phases like sleeping with his school cap on his head. It was ridiculous, but he insisted on sleeping with a school cap for a little while, and we let him. Or I could write about how he would give me little light butterfly kisses on the cheek, kisses so light they were barely there, and how he would help me brush my teeth because I brushed his teeth or would share the last chip from his little bag of chips, the chip he had already half eaten. Or I could write about the boy who would offer to share his drink when only the ice was left at the bottom or stand on guard when I was cooking like he was making sure I was doing the right thing and not burning the food.

There were so many stories, but I never did get the book quite off the ground as it proved too hard to start writing things down when I was not sure where we were heading. We were still leading busy lives as people with children do. I was still active in all the committees, MPS, Hills School Council, OOSH – and I was getting involved in community disability forums and trying to get safe playgrounds and parks in Baulkham Hills where kids with disabilities could play safely.

The rest of 2001 passed without any major drama. Mwango and I were a little more relaxed and were able to go out with friends and leave Bwembya with babysitters or carers. Christmas day was spent at a friend's townhouse in Clemton Park. There were bush fires that year. I remember seeing ash and smoke everywhere. It felt like the fire was only a stone's throw away. It was unsettling.

The townhouse was in a complex and the communal pool was covered in ash as was the grass and the driveway. On New

Year's Eve, we went to Yasmin and Callum's place for a party that lasted until the sun came up. We all had our kids, spouses and partners with us and had a lot of fun. I despair to think what the neighbours thought we were up to, but I dare say they were used to it.

Chapter 16

At the end of 2001, Bwembya's health seemed to have stabilised although he still looked fragile. The year 2002 was filled with many changes and lots of activities. We had decided to keep acting on our conviction to have the best possible time we could while we could. We would go on holiday with the kids as we normally did. The place that had so far been ideal for Bwembya was Merimbula. It had lovely shallow water beaches That he could wade in and feel comfortable and the girls could go out to the deeper water to swim.

We set off to Merimbula on Sunday early in January 2002 and stayed at a lodge. The lodge had a lovely pool with a little kid's pool beside it. We were able to see the kids from the window in the unit. Bwembya was quite happy wading in the little pool while the girls swam in the big pool and there were barbeque facilities near the pool, and it was family friendly.

Bwembya spent a lot of time sleeping under the beach umbrella with his head in my lap or sitting on the edge of the little wall by the beach watching his sisters swimming. The school had lent us a little wheelchair that came in very handy as Bwembya was too tired to walk more than a few hundred metres.

The holiday went alright except for the first night when Bwembya had difficulty breathing. When we put him to bed, he became short of breath and started making a sort of wheezing noise. The holiday unit had two bedrooms, with a double bed in one room, and two single beds in the other room. The fourth bed was an unstable fold-up bed. Because Bwembya was so unwell at night, I felt it would be safer for him to sleep in the double bed with one of us. Mwango slept on a mattress on the floor the first night, but he complained of a sore back the whole of the next day, so by default I ended up sleeping on a very uncomfortable, compact two-seat sofa in the living room. It did not faze me. I had been sleeping in uncomfortable positions for a long time, so one week of discomfort was like business as usual. Tasha offered to sleep on the little fold-away bed, but I did not want her spending her life taking on things that were uncomfortable, that was my job, I was the mother. She used to offer to sleep at the hospital with Bwembya instead of me when he was sick. But I did not want her to become the carer for her brother, no matter how tired or stressed out I was.

I guess I had reached a stage where I was very aware that we were in the last chapter of Bwembya's life, and that every minute counted. I was going to be there at his side as much as I could be, to give him strength and to be the constant thing in his life. I was also very aware that he could die in his sleep. I don't know why I thought that, but I did. Even when we were in Zambia in 1997, I made sure Bwembya slept in the room with me, when he could have slept with the boys or with the girls in their room. I thought it would be too traumatic if he died where they were, so I decided to keep him where I was or where I was handy. Apart from the little drama on the first night, which we reported to his doctors, the holiday in Merimbula went well.

Back in Sydney, Bupe was starting year seven at the high school, where Tasha also went, so there was all the excitement of buying uniforms and books ready for the school year. She auditioned for the Rock Eisteddfod at school and got in. I decided to study for a master's degree and enrolled in February. My husband rolled his eyes when I made the announcement I was going back to school, but he knew better than to try to talk me out of it. I think even he was amazed that I finished the degree and achieved good grades. Studying for a master's degree made sense to me. I was in a job that was not challenging me, and I was so used to working under pressure at different organisations, that I felt like I needed something to take my mind off my life, off the inevitable that was surely and slowly rolling towards me, so school it was.

In February, the downturn with Bwembya's health started and my unease and tension increased. The school term started with Bwembya having fluid in his lungs and having problems breathing so he was put on antibiotics and his medication was increased. He now had to have medication given to him while he was at school. For years, we had been able to have the medication in the mornings and evenings only, but the goal posts had shifted. Two weeks later, Bwembya was crying all day as if he was in pain, so he was admitted to hospital where he stayed for four days.

In March on the day of the school swimming carnival, a note came home with Bwembya. It seemed he was having little turns at school and that we should keep an eye on him. A few days later, he was up all night unsettled, walking around the house. The next day I took him to our GP, and by the evening he ended up in emergency at the children's Hospital. He had the same symptoms as the last admission and was discharged the next day. During this time Bwembya was not getting a lot of sleep and was eventually prescribed sleeping tablets to help him sleep, but it meant I was up half the night making sure he was alright. He was sick a lot with never-ending coughs and chest infections that seemed to go on and on. The notes from school suggested that he was distressed once or twice a week. This was a very worrying time for me. Every time the phone rang, my heart missed a few beats.

On one of the visits to emergency, Bwembya picked up one of the teddy bears in the toy box and held on to it throughout his hospital stay. It seemed to give him comfort and he held it tight as he slept. On his birthday a few weeks later, I got him a light brown teddy bear, JT (Jack Teddy) and this bear went everywhere with him when he went to hospital or respite, but when he was well, he did not seem to even pay attention to it. It just stayed on his bed.

I was getting busy with school assignments as the weeks rolled by. I worked for five hours over four days, so I had a lot of time to work on them. One of our MPS kids, a son to one of the ladies on the MPS committee, died. That stopped me in my tracks. I felt like I was standing in front of a big boulder that was slowly but surely rolling towards me. It seemed inevitable that I was going to be squashed, but I was determined to meet it head on. I was at Yasmin's house after picking up Bwembya from peer support one Saturday when she told me the news. She knew the family. It was there that I decided I would have a party for Bwembya the next Saturday, even though his actual birthday was the following day. He was turning sixteen and that was a milestone for him.

I spent Sunday ringing friends to invite them to Bwembya's birthday party. We were going to celebrate and celebrate big. The party would start at two in the afternoon and continue until the last person left. People could come and go when they wanted. There would be a birthday party followed by a barbeque. However, through all of the mad planning and preparation, I forgot that Bupe's birthday was three days after Bwembya's. I was just focused on Bwembya, but Bupe was not one to let things pass her by. While we were in Castle Towers on the Thursday night getting supplies and ordering the cake, someone rang me on my mobile to talk about the party. When I finished talking to them, Bupe turned around and said, 'Mum, it's my birthday too.' The penny dropped, and I had to refocus. I let her choose the cakes and she chose two matching cakes that looked like wrapped up birthday presents, one pink and one blue. The cakes were beautiful.

Saturday was a lovely day. It felt like I had ordered the weather together with everything else. We had people coming in and out of our house all day and you could see how Bwembya was revelling in all the attention and enjoying all the presents. I had to keep repeating that it was Bupe's birthday, too, and a few people got an envelope and put money in it and gave it to her as she only had presents from close family and friends. Normally, I would never forget birthdays – except for the one time I forgot Mwango's birthday when we were in Scotland. His birthday is ten days before Bwembya's birthday and the year Bwembya turned one, I was so focused on B's birthday that I completely forgot Mwango's birthday until the day.

The birthday party was a success and both Bwembya and Bupe had a great time. The grin on Bwembya's face was worth all the rushing around I had to do in a week. Bupe happily stashed the envelopes full of money in her room. There was more money than she had ever had at any one time. On the Tuesday after the party, I had a day off and took Bwembya to the genetic clinic. While we were there Bwembya had trouble breathing. The doctor watched him for a while until it settled. We thought it was just the excitement of the day.

I was driving to Castle Towers with Bwembya sitting in his usual spot at the back in the middle of the seat in the Magna. He took off his seatbelt and leant against the back of the two front seats. He was breathing heavily and gasping for air. I told myself not to panic and looked for the ambulance station that was supposed to be a few hundred metres down the road next to the Shell station, but the station had moved. There was a medical centre on the ground floor of the shopping centre, so I headed for that, parked outside it and rushed in to get a doctor. There was no doctor there. I asked the receptionist to call an ambulance 'NOW!' and quickly went back to the car where I started talking to Bwembya calmly, telling him to breath and that everything was going to be alright.

The paramedics arrived a short time later after coming to the wrong side of the shopping centre. They looked him over and gave him some oxygen and we went in the ambulance for the first of numerous ambulance rides. I had been heading to the shopping centre to pick up the girls who had gone to watch a movie, so I called them on the mobile phone, and they came to the car. I had the car and the girls at the shopping centre, but I had to go with Bwembya. An off-duty paramedic who happened to be in the car park and knew the paramedics who came in the ambulance, offered to drive my car. He said he would drop the girls off at home as it was on the way and bring the car up to the hospital – and that is what he did. He brought the keys for the car to me in the emergency room at the children's hospital. We stayed in hospital for two days while the doctors tried to determine what had happened. Medical staff could not work out exactly what was happening, and I sometimes felt like some staff thought I was exaggerating, even when it was so clear something was happening. Bwembya's paediatrician believed me and instructed her staff to pay attention to what I told them as I knew my child best.

Following this incident, I went to the Baulkham Heights equipment pool and hired a shower chair. Working in disability services made me aware of equipment requirements and where to access equipment. This chair made things easier on Bwembya as he was getting breathless every time we had to give him a shower.

He began to have one chest infection after another and was in and out of hospital. I started calling different respite services trying to get in-home respite because I knew that the time for the different activities Bwembya was involved in was coming to an end.

Bwembya started having shorter school hours as he was so unwell. I was now working five days, from nine in the morning to one in the afternoon, so he would be the last child the bus picked up before it went to school, and I could pick him up from school after one. Mwango and my social life had become almost non-existent. When we did go out it was very reluctantly. In early June, the South African musical *Umoja* came to the Sydney Casino and Mwango booked tickets for the two of us as we needed to get out of the house and one of the teachers from

Bwembya's school kindly offered to look after the kids while we took the night off. We went and had a wonderful time knowing Bwembya was in safe hands.

For Bupe's thirteenth birthday that year, I bought two tickets to *Swan Lake* by the Royal Ballet at the Capitol Theatre in Sydney. I had always wanted to see *Swan Lake* and paid premium price to get good seats. On a Saturday in June, Bupe and I got all dressed up and went to the ballet determined to enjoy the afternoon, but true to form, I was asleep before the opening curtains had stopped swinging. In those years from 1996 to 2003, I fell asleep watching movies, DVDs, and videos. It was probably because at home and at the hospital I was a very light sleeper. I would wake up if there was a sound from Bwembya or the wind shook a branch outside.

At the end of June, Community Options accepted Bwembya onto their program and initially provided a carer for him on Saturdays. It was usually a young male who would take him out to the movies in his wheelchair. Mwango would drop them off and pick them up, but unfortunately this only happened a couple of times because Bwembya's health deteriorated quickly. After that, they stayed home and watched videos, until even that did not work for very long.

Mwango and I plodded along trying to keep our life as normal as possible. While our life was slowly changing, our friends were falling in love and getting married. I attended a hen's night for Addie, a good friend of ours at the end of July and had a lot of laughs. Mwango was with Bwembya, and I was able to relax and let my hair down without worrying about him. The next day, Mwango and I attended Addie and Brice's wedding with Mwango officiating as the master of ceremonies. We had a carer (registered nurse) with Bwembya, so we were able to relax and enjoy ourselves. Mwango looked dashing in his suit, and I felt like a million dollars. It was amazing what a new dress and hairdo can do. We ate, danced, and socialised with our close friends, and managed to snatch a little happiness along the way.

The highlight of the year was my sister Bwalya's visit with her son Kay. It was a very different visit, just moments snatched away from my caring role for brief shopping sprees. Surprisingly, Bwembya became vibrant and chatty – even noisy. He started talking a lot more. It was not my imagination as the teachers at school also heard him. Especially the word mum. He slept in the same room as Kay, who said that Bwembya would call out his name and talk to him all night long, but he ignored him because he wanted to sleep. I thought Kay would be terrified of the CPAP machine as it was an awful sight, but he was okay with it when we explained what it did. Bwembya seemed very happy to have another boy in the house.

While Bwalya was here, Bwembya was admitted to hospital and spent five days there with breathing problems. It was during this admission that I was asked what the resuscitation orders for Bwembya should be. I checked with Mwango, and he said he wanted everything done to resuscitate Bwembya. That week was Bwalya's birthday and my birthday. We decided to have a picnic in the hospital gardens for lunch as we could not celebrate it properly, then Kenny took Bwalya and Kay to the Blue Mountains for the rest of the day.

On the Thursday of the following week, I had an interview with a health service for a project officer position. It was time to move jobs again. Being a volunteer coordinator was difficult when you are not there to coordinate the service because of a sick child. I therefore felt I needed a job that would not require me to go into work at specific times. I thought project work would give me the flexibility to plan my own hours and work. In the interview, I explained that I may need to drop everything I was doing if I was needed for my son. The panel understood. The project was a palliative care project for people from culturally and linguistically diverse (CALD) communities. I got the job and started working in September. The evening of the interview, an ambulance rushed Bwembya and I to hospital as he was having problems breathing.

We spent another few days in hospital, came out for one day and were back in the next day. Bwalya and Kay left for Zambia while Bwembya was still in hospital. At this stage, there was no consensus as to what was causing the breathing problems. Neither the respiratory nor the cardiac team could find the cause. One evening, while he was having one of the breathing attacks, his cardiologist walked into the ward to see one of his other patients in the room. He noticed the nurses fussing around Bwembya and came over. He examined Bwembya and was able to make a recommendation to the respiratory team regarding what he thought was happening. Finally, someone believed me after months of my saying Bwembya was having these incidents where he could not breath properly, and it seemed like he was running fast. He was diagnosed with pulmonary hypertension.

We had a case conference with all the parties involved in Bwembya's care, including Community Options and staff from the school. Bwembya's cardiomyopathy had reached a stage where there was no more that could be done to stop the deterioration. The specialist made sure I understood that and asked me to tell them what I had heard them say. I left the meeting facing up to the fact that Bwembya was now under another new team, the palliative care team. I worked in a health facility; I knew exactly what a palliative care team did. I had turned the corner and found myself in a place very different from where I had been before this hospital admission.

Bwembya also seemed to understand exactly what was happening. We left the meeting and back in his room one of the doctors and I were discussing it. He was checking to see if I understood where we were and what was going to happen. Bwembya was lying in bed watching TV.

'We have reached the limit to the amount of medication we can give Bwembya. We cannot increase his medication anymore due to his weight.' Bwembya had lost a lot of weight and was quite thin. 'There is not much that we can do for him on top of what we are doing. The palliative care team will manage some of his symptoms as they arise.' We heard a little sob. Bwembya looked at us and tears started falling down his face. He started sobbing and got out of bed. He had understood everything we had said. He walked to the small, enclosed balcony at the back of the room and stood there sobbing. I went over and pulled him into my arms and we both cried.

It was ironic that the day I got the call that I had the palliative care project officer's position, was the day Bwembya was discharged from hospital under the palliative care team. I was told that my son was being discharged but that he would need oxygen every day for a few hours in the morning and after school. The hospital was going to set us up with a home ventilation system. I worked in a hospital, and I had managed a service where we had purchased oxygen for our clients. I knew exactly what they were talking about. Things had changed, there was no going back. I was shattered. Even though I knew what was happening, it was still so unreal. I could not begin to explain how I felt, and I did not even try to tell anyone how I felt at hearing the news.

I dug deep within myself to find the courage to know what I needed to do. And to focus on what was ahead. It was not the time to peel back the layers of my life or to feel sorry for myself. It was not the time to think about what my child's life should or could have been. Not the time. It was time to just be Bwembya's mum. I looked at him with tears in my eyes. He looked up at me, got up and flicked the oxygen cord to untangle it and went to get himself a drink. It was business as usual for him, what is the problem? I burst out laughing and shook my head. Nothing seemed to faze him, he was here, he was alive and that was that.

So, we went home. The oxygen cylinders, an oxygen concentrator, and all the required attachments were delivered to the house. Some small oxygen cylinders were to take to school. In the last week of August, Bwembya was back at school for half the day. Staff from the children's hospital came to the school and held a case conference with the staff involved in Bwembya's care at school. They showed them how to change the oxygen bottles and monitor the oxygen levels. A procedure was developed in case of an emergency. In the morning, when he woke up and the home care lady bathed him, Bwembya was put onto oxygen until the bus came to pick him up. He was able to go to school on the bus as he was the last child picked up and the school was a couple of streets away. Someone would be waiting for the bus at school with a wheelchair and then eventually as he got sicker with the oxygen. He would also come home on the bus. He was the first drop off and was put straight onto oxygen when he got into the house.

We had a few minor incidents with the concentrator. One night about two in the morning, a loud noise woke us up and we jumped out of bed. The alarm on the concentrator had gone off. I panicked and stood in the doorway as Mwango rushed headlong into Bwembya's room, but he was sleeping peacefully. He shouted, 'He's fine!' We headed towards the sunroom where the concentrator was situated. The tube had twisted and had caused the alarm to go off. We looked at each other with relief and went back to bed without a word. Another incident was not so minor when the electricity went out in the neighbourhood because it meant there was no concentrator, and therefore no oxygen. We had one small cylinder which was three-quarters full but as Bwembya had woken up afraid in the dark, he needed higher levels of oxygen than normal. We had no plan. The cylinder was the backup plan. We tried to settle him down so that he was using less oxygen and hoped it would last until morning, or the electricity would come back on. Bwembya didn't like the dark, but we could not use candles in the house where there was oxygen. Fortunately, we had a big flashlight and left that on in his room. I lay on the twin bed next to him to give him reassurance and he went to sleep eventually. The electricity came back on after a couple of hours and we were able to hook him back onto the concentrator. We did learn a lesson from this incident. We made sure we always had two full bottles of oxygen as a back-up, and we bought little portable oyster lights that work on batteries that could be stuck on the wall next to Bwembya's bed.

By October 2002, Bwembya's breathing problems had become worse. He had to be on oxygen almost twenty-four hours a day, except when he was having a shower (by December, he was on oxygen all the time). With Bwembya constantly sick, we finally agreed to go to Bear Cottage, which is a hospice for children with life-threatening illnesses. The nurse in charge of the cardiology ward had been trying to get us to have a break there since the Cottage had opened a year or so before. We gave in and decided we really did need a rest. In mid-October after much drama, we went to Bear Cottage. Even as we were setting off to go a new problem arose. Bwembya started having problems with breathing in the car.

Those few months were very difficult for me. Seeing my son deteriorate at so rapid a pace and not being able to do anything about it was terrible. Watching him struggle for breath and coughing during the struggle was difficult to handle. I held his hand and felt like I was trying to breathe for him. I breathed deep breaths myself, probably to keep myself calm more than anything else. We connected on a level where he understood what I was feeling and that I was urging him on without words or sometimes, if I was driving him to the hospital, with glances.

The day we went to Bear Cottage, we were in and out of the car about five times before we set off because Bwembya couldn't decide which car he wanted to go in. We decided to take two cars to give him the space to breathe. The first time I only got to the edge of our driveway before the breathlessness started. We stopped and tried again. He then decided he was going in his dad's car, got in, saw I was in the other car and came back. Eventually we left with Bwembya and Tasha in my car. There were a few minutes of hair-raising gasps, but I put on his favourite music by Brandy and talked to him quietly. By the time we got to Bear Cottage, things had calmed down a bit and he was humming to Brandy. I had discovered by chance that Brandy's music calmed him down. When we bought him a cassette player and put it in his room, he would get the Brandy tape for me to put on and hum himself to sleep.

Bear Cottage was a wonderful place. It was in Manly at the top of the hill overlooking the sea. It was purpose-built and was opened in March 2001. It looks nothing like a hospice for sick kids. The staff wore everyday clothes, and the atmosphere was like a holiday resort. There were rooms and suites that families could stay in. We met a lot of different families from different parts of the state. There were activities for the sick kids and their siblings. Bwembya felt completely at home from the first day because he already knew most of the staff at the cottage as they had worked at the children's hospital and attended to him there. The palliative care doctor who visited Bear Cottage had also worked at the Children's Hospital. If he did not know the staff, he soon had them wrapped around his little finger.

When he started going to the cardiology ward, he met a formidable member of the nursing staff. A no-nonsense, do-this type of nurse. Without a word, Bwembya showed her, her place. Using a few looks and gestures he asserted what he wanted and made clear what he was not going to do. Mwango and I walked out of the room laughing. We heard her laugh out loud and from that day he was her pet patient. Every shift when she walked onto the ward, she would make a bee line for his room and say a cheerful hi to him. She always called him Ben, though, for some reason, despite our numerous efforts to get her to say Bwembya or B. Maybe she was having the last laugh.

I spent the first day at Bear Cottage up in a glass atrium overlooking the sea and trees, where Bwembya could see me from the balcony below. I would wave down to him. I was in my second semester at university and exam time was drawing near so I had assignments to complete. Mwango had taken the girls down to the beach. Later in the evening when we got back to the living areas, I heard one of the nurses telling another nurse that it was their turn to push Bwembya around.

I asked why they were pushing him around and discovered that they thought Bwembya could not walk because he had kept signing that they should keep wheeling him around. My husband and I had a good laugh because Bwembya could still walk. At school and at home he would use the wheelchair to wheel his oxygen bottle around the room, and the cottage was sizable enough for him to wheel his bottle around unless he was going out. He looked at the staff and had a big grin on his face. He got up, held the handle of the wheelchair, and took off to the lounge area where all the other kids were. Mwango and I took the opportunity to spend a little time on our own. We took a drive down to the shops at Manly, had dinner at an Indian restaurant recommended by the staff, and had a quiet evening.

The following weekend was Tasha's seventeenth birthday. She had a few friends come for a sleep over. The girls watched movies and had pizza and the usual party food. The house was abuzz with screeching girls and Bwembya watched the comings and goings with amusement. When it was time to cut the cake, Tasha decided she would let him blow out the candles for her. He was happy to oblige, and I took off his oxygen leads and switched off the oxygen for a little while. He tried hard but could not even get one candle to waver. He made the right face, the right sound but not a breath of air came out. We still laugh about it, and every time we have a cake in the family with candles to blow out, we remember that day and do a lot of huffing and puffing and smiling. Laughing was often how we coped.

Bwembya's determination to keep living, to keep doing what he could because he could, continuously amazed me. One day, I walked into the kitchen, and he was standing on one of the dining room chairs, complete with oxygen tubes, looking in the cupboard for something specific he wanted to eat. A few days later I heard the back door open and went to have a look and there was Bwembya going down six stairs to the backyard, tugging his oxygen cord as he went. I stood by the window and watched him slowly walk and tug until he got to the back of the garage and got himself a bottle of lemonade from the fridge. His sisters wanted to rush out and help him, but I stopped them. I understood that he needed to have some control over the things that he could still have control over.

I started trying to prepare the girls for Bwembya's decline. I would talk to them about how he was and what was happening to him, to gently introduce the idea that things were moving forward, that there are life cycles and sometimes things end. I talked about God and how he loved us and how we belonged to him, about how sometimes things do not always work out the way we would like them to. About grief and loss and new beginnings in a place where there was no pain. I did not know how much this helped or didn't help but I tried, anyway. I also talked to Mwango about how Bwembya was deteriorating, and about what we needed to do. For years we had been driving past Castlebrook Memorial Park and commented how peaceful it was. We decided we would bury Bwembya there when he did eventually leave us. We discussed whether we wanted to bury him or cremate him and decided on cremation although it was not something Zambians did. This was our son, and we would choose how we laid him to rest. These discussions were brief and to the point, to ensure that we agreed. We also had a brief discussion with my brother James, so that he knew what we would like in case we were too distraught to think straight.

✦

Chapter 17

At the beginning of November Bwembya was in hospital for five days with breathing problems. November was the month my brother James, his wife Shaunagh, and their three girls, Malaika seven years old, Gabrielle four years old and Zahra two years old, moved in with us while their house was being built. Bwembya was happy to have the girls live with us. It was like a reality show to him. He loved to watch them play and fight. He especially loved it when they got into trouble and were sent to the bedroom. He would stand at the doorway with a grin on his face and a twinkle in his eye. We had a full house, but we hardly noticed it. Everyone blended in well. We all woke up at different times, went to work or school at different times, and slept at different times.

The house may not have been huge, but it was roomy enough to cater for all of us. Whoever got home cooked, which was usually me as I was at home after one in the afternoon with Bwembya. But on the days, I was at appointments or in hospital with him, Shaunagh would cook. We were lucky that our family members got along so well. Shaunagh and I would sit in the sunroom on the couch watching TV in the evening. We loved watching *Desperate Housewives* and *ER*. Kids in bed, cup of tea, and a biscuit in hand and we sank into the sofa and watched TV.

The last day of school in 2002 was a Friday, a week before Christmas. When Bwembya came home I looked in his school bag as I did every day. I read the communication diary. I was overcome with emotion at the love and compassion of those wonderful people at the Hills School. The things my son had done at school that year were in the annual report folder, complete with pictures and commentary. There were pictures of Bwembya at ten-pin bowling, in the swimming pool, at the beach, at the Easter hat parade peddling a tray of goodies, at the ice-skating rink on a plastic chair being pushed by a staff, gardening in his class greenhouse, playing the guitar at music therapy, painting with the art teacher, riding a three wheeler bicycle, shopping at Woollies, paying at the checkout counter and playing with a kangaroo at Featherdale Wildlife Park.

There were pictures of Bwembya in the Hills School soccer team, playing T ball, cooking sausages, playing games on the computer, using the microwave to heat up his lunch, shredding paper in a shredder, taking shredded paper to the pet shop, playing with a rabbit, and tickling its nose. There were pictures at a Variety Club Christmas party, playing a drum and asleep on the classroom floor after a long day. There were pictures of him packing his bag at the end of the day and one of him patting a horse when he went to watch his classmates horse riding. There were pictures of him all dressed up for the performing arts night, jumping on a trampoline at the Castle Hill Show, patting little baby chicks and puppies. There were pictures of Bwembya at a school sleep-over, in the 'Cats' performing arts night, at a Wiggles concert at school, and at the Hills School Olympics dressed in an African print outfit looking very dignified and attending the Paralympics.

The last report for the end of 2002 was the most significant of all. Bwembya handed it to me. He wanted me to look through it. I got a pleasant surprise to find that in the report was his School Certificate and that he 'has met the requirements for the award of a School Certificate'. Record of achievement in the eight key areas were satisfactory for all of them. He had such a big grin on his face, it was wonderful. We celebrated and made a big fuss over him. I told everyone about it. I was chuffed my baby had passed his school certificate.

Christmas 2002 was spent at home with all the family. My brother James and his family were house sitting in the northern beaches. The girls and I went to church in the morning and Mwango stayed with Bwembya. James and his family, and Kenny all came over on Christmas day for lunch. It was a hilarious day with the kids putting on dances and singing; even Bwembya joined in with a little jig or skip now and then. We captured it all on tape, but I don't think anyone has been able to sit down and watch it yet. Bwembya had lots of fun opening presents. He helped me open all my presents. Mwango and Natasha cooked lunch. Tasha was studying hospitality management in North Sydney. They had been experimenting and had planned the whole meal to perfection. All three courses.

Boxing Day in the afternoon Bwembya had breathing problems. By late afternoon, I was in an ambulance with Bwembya on the way to hospital where we stayed for four days. On New Year's Eve, I decided the girls needed to get out of the house and I accepted the invitation to Yasmin and Callum's for a New Year's Eve party, like the one they had the year before but a little tamer as we were getting older. Mwango stayed home with Bwembya, and we made sure we were at home by midnight to cheer in the year with him, but when we arrived, we found Mwango fast asleep in an armchair.

The following day since Mwango had missed out on the fun, Callum came to pick him and Bupe up to spend some quality time with him and have a drink. About ten in the evening, Mwango called asking if they could be collected because Callum had been drinking and could not drive them home. Bwembya was watching TV with Tasha so I thought I would duck out for a few minutes and pick Mwango and Bupe up. I had driven three quarters of the way when Tasha called on the mobile to say that Bwembya was breathing funny. I told her to turn up the oxygen, walking her through it and did a u-turn and headed home. I tried to keep to the speed limit with difficulty, talking to Tasha all the time to keep her calm. I got home, rushed in, picked up the phone and called an ambulance.

We spent two days in hospital but this time instead of going home, we were taken by hospital transport to Bear Cottage as I seriously needed a break, and we had missed our last booking in December as Bwembya had been in hospital. The trip was harrowing as even in an ambulance Bwembya had problems breathing, but the medical team in the vehicle had all the protocols and medication ready to be administered. I held Bwembya's hand all the way to Manly and was relieved we got there in one piece as I was not sure who would have heart failure, him, or me. I was exhausted. When we got to Bear Cottage, I was able to get a massage and then get into the spa. I felt calm and in control once again. Mwango and the girls came to Bear Cottage later that day.

During this visit I woke up on the Wednesday knowing there was something wrong. I went into Bwembya's room and waited for him to wake up so I could give him a bath. I looked at him and felt deep within me that something was very wrong. All the time I was giving him a quick shower my heart was breaking although I could not show it. I was blinking my tears away as I bent over to pat him dry with a towel. I got him ready and took him in to breakfast. My whole day was ruined. Sometime during the day, I ended up in the staff office crying, telling the staff something had changed in Bwembya and I was afraid of whatever it was.

One of the senior staff who had known Bwembya and helped nurse him back to health after his long stay in hospital in 2001 took me to the door, where we looked at Bwembya who was happily pushing the wheelchair that held his oxygen bottle down the corridor. She said she had never seen Bwembya looking so well since his stroke, and what was I worried about, he looked fine. I was not convinced. There was something in my gut telling me something was not right.

We took the time to relax and Mwango and I went out for dinner to a seafood restaurant while the girls watched movies with the other kids there. On the Friday, since it was so difficult for Bwembya to travel in our car due to breathing problems, we had to look for an alternative way to get him home. Bear Cottage staff had arranged a trip to the beach that day and had taken the kids out for the afternoon. I drove home on my own and the bus took my girls and Bwembya back home for me. It saved me another hair-raising trip home with a child who was gasping for air. He seemed to do better in a small bus with windows open than in a car.

I went back to work on the Monday and Bwembya had a carer (a nurse) looking after him for the few hours I was at work. The following Monday I was at home sick and ended up home the whole week with very high blood pressure that made me dizzy. I realised I was exhausted again and needed a break, so I reluctantly agreed to have Bwembya go to Bear Cottage on his own for the long weekend. A minivan taxi took us to Manly on the Thursday. It was another horrendous trip for me, and that did not help my blood pressure. Bwembya gasped for breath halfway there then settled. I did not have the Brandy tape on me, and it was a cab that did not have a tape player, but we got there in one piece. I was shaking when I got out of the cab, but more importantly I was glad to see the look on Bwembya's face. He had been looking like a deer caught in the lights of a car in the dark. His eyes had been wide open. But he was now back to normal.

I spent the night at Bear Cottage in a room down the other end of the building from Bwembya, as the cottage was full. He came to my room and saw where I was. I explained what was happening and he seemed fine with it, but I hardly got a wink of sleep, I was so on edge due to being so far from his room. I had spent a lot of time on the last visit teaching him how to press the panic button if he needed someone. He was fine in the morning and ate a little breakfast. Mwango picked me up in the evening after work and we went home. We took the girls to the movies to watch *Lord of the Rings*.

There were no words that can describe how I felt leaving Bwembya on his own, although I knew he would be fine. I was so uneasy, but I knew it was something I had to do because I needed to get some strength to see me through what was coming, whatever it was. I didn't think the whole experience was a great benefit for me as I spent the entire weekend worrying and not sleeping, waiting for the phone to ring. I felt fragmented and like I was being pulled in two, trying to relax but feeling agitated with worry.

Mwango and I drove to Manly and picked Bwembya up. I sat in the back with him. He had problems breathing despite us turning the oxygen up, playing Brandy and having all the windows open. Finally, half-way through the drive he settled. Manly is a long way from Northmead and I felt like each time I did the trip I was leaving little pieces of me along the way. But thankfully we made it home and I was glad to have Bwembya sleeping in his own room with my door open so I could hear his CPAP machine going, and knowing he was there.

On Tuesday, it was back to work and business as usual. It was still school holidays, so we had a carer with Bwembya while I was at work. After work, I walked into the house with my usual chirpy, 'Hello, darling' to him. The nurse who had been looking after him said he had been fine all day. I took one look at him, and my heart skipped a beat. The unease I had been feeling was stronger than ever. I called Yasmin and asked her to drive us to the GP. The doctor asked me what was wrong. I told him I did not know but I thought Bwembya was coming down with something. He listened to his chest and said he seemed fine, only slightly noisy in the chest and that he would give him some antibiotics just in case to ward off any infection.

The school holidays were over and Bwembya went to school on Thursday. All seemed well but I was very anxious. The whole week I kept waking up at night to check on him almost every hour, or I would lie in bed listening for any noise in his room. Strange things happened on the Thursday night. I went to bed early as soon as I had put Bwembya to bed. I climbed into bed and switched off the light in the bedroom. The door of the bedroom was half open and the light from the hallway filtered in. I was lying in bed when I saw a dark shadow, like a black tumble weed, at a fast speed racing in and out of the bedroom. It sent a shiver down my spine. I felt knots in the pit of my stomach. It scared the life out of me. I got on my knees and said a prayer. I knew Bwembya was very sick, and we were getting near the end of his life. I asked for three things if the inevitable was going to happen. I wanted his death to be painless, I did not want him to die at home as it would traumatize the girls, and I wanted to be there when he died. I was there when he was born, and I needed to be there when he left the world. Saying the prayer helped. The fear and the unease left me. A sense of peace and calm came over me. The dark shadow left, and it was just a normal night. I fell into a deep sleep and did not stir till morning.

The next day we got on with our usual morning routine of getting ready for work and school. Mwango left for work at about half past six in the morning. The girls left to catch the bus for school after seven. As I was getting ready to go to work, Bwembya was standing by the kitchen counter. He looked fine and I went to give him a kiss and for some reason I felt like I wanted time to stop. It was as if I saw his tired soul, from all the effort to live. I wanted to tell the homecare lady who came to give him a shower to leave him alone, not to give him a shower, so he could save his energy, but I kept my mouth shut and just kissed him goodbye. I left home feeling very uneasy, not wanting to go, because something was not right.

I was about two kilometres from home when I heard and saw an ambulance go past me driving very fast. My heart missed a beat. The ambulance was going down Windsor Road towards home. I panicked, was it going to our house? I was looking for a way to turn around and go home when I remembered I had a mobile phone. The homecare lady would have called me it there was a problem with Bwembya. During the past few weeks any sign of an ambulance when Bwembya was not with me caused me slight anxiety. I turned up the music in the car and started to sing to calm myself down.

It was a very rough day for me. I was trying to prepare a six-month report for my project at work because I had to present the report at a meeting the next Thursday at ten in the morning. That afternoon, I was in the director's office packing my things away when I had a strange thought: 'I would not be at that meeting on Thursday, because I would be at the funeral. What were the girls and I going to wear at the funeral? We would definitely not wear black.' I was not thinking whose funeral, just the funeral. I did not know where the thought came from as I was busy on the report and focused on getting it right. I got in the car and drove home in a flood of tears, really sobbing, although I didn't understand why. I managed to compose myself before I got home by telling myself it was ridiculous because Bwembya was ok.

I met the bus at three in the afternoon outside the house and took Bwembya in as usual. He had not had much breakfast and did not want anything but the lollies I had been buying for him every day that week on my way home. His favourite snakes and jellybeans. I was sitting on the couch, and I asked him for a lolly. He had half a snake that he was chewing on and had a whole one in the bag. He took the whole one out of the bag and gave it to me. I was amazed and laughed as he always gave me the one he had chewed on and kept the others. As per our usual afternoon ritual over the last couple of months, he came and lay on the couch, leaned on me, and fell asleep. I studied this child who had his head on my lap, stroked his hair, ran my finger along his hairline and studied the little moles on his neck. I watched him sleep and thought how much I loved this child of mine.

He woke up when the girls walked in from school and started making a racket around the house. The homecare lady came and gave him his shower and dressed him in his pyjamas, or what passed as pyjamas, a t-shirt, and shorts. We had dinner although he hardly touched anything on his plate. The rest of the evening I was on the computer checking my emails while he sat squeezed beside Mwango on one of the armchairs leaning his head onto his chest. I had never seen him do that before this week.

About ten to nine he got up and indicated to Mwango that he wanted to go to bed, I could hear Mwango asking him, 'Are you sure you want to go to bed now?' as it was a little early for him after all the late nights we had been having on holiday. On Fridays, we usually went to bed a little later. I got off the computer and followed them to the bedroom and unwound the tubing from the oxygen concentrator. Bwembya sat down on the bed breathing heavily. We watched him for a few minutes and decided to hook him straight on to the large oxygen tank we had for emergencies, but despite the Oxygen level being increased the breathing did not settle. He paced up and down the bedroom, then went to the dining room and back with Mwango following him around with the large tank.

Bwembya moved to the dining room again, pacing between the chair where I was sitting and the chair he normally sat on at the breakfast bar. He leaned on me and looked at me. This was unusual because he normally did not like contact when he could not breathe properly. He normally just stood leaning over his chair like he was catching his breath, until the breathing settled, or we called an ambulance. I asked Mwango if we should call an ambulance, but he thought we should try to manage it ourselves because that was why we had been given the oxygen in the large tanks to manage incidents like this. We swapped the nasal cannula for the oxygen for a mask, but there was no change. I was overly concerned with his breathing as I could see his chest moving in and out in the front and at the back. He was so thin I could see his ribs through his t-shirt as he struggled to breathe. I also saw a look in his eyes I did not like. He looked scared and I felt a chill go through me. I figured this was different, something was not right, so I called an ambulance.

The ambulance arrived within five minutes and the two ambulance officers, started the usual procedure. They thought he might be having an asthma attack and gave him some Ventolin. This did not help, nor did the oxygen they supplied. They decided to take him to the hospital right away. I quickly packed a light bag with just JT the bear, a couple of changes of clothes for him and the CPAP machine, as he had to take his own when he went into hospital. My usual routine was forgotten, no toiletries, no pyjamas, no book, just my handbag and a sweater.

Bwembya's breathing was so bad that in the ambulance he could not even sit down. He leaned over the table breathing with difficulty. I was strapped into the side chair and Bwembya refused to sit on my lap like he usually did if he did not want to lay down. I felt helpless watching him struggle to breathe. I could not even reach out to hold his hand as I was seated too far to touch him. The driver started to tell the paramedic in the back that he needed to strap Bwembya in. He answered that we needed to go right now, and the flashing lights and siren were turned on. We drove as quickly as we could. I heard the driver talking to someone urgently, but I was not paying attention to what he said because I kept talking to Bwembya all the way.

At the hospital a few things happened that were unusual. When the ambulance stopped and the doors were opened, the paramedic in the back picked Bwembya up and carried him into the hospital. Bwembya was seen by a doctor in emergency as soon as we arrived, as if the doctor had been waiting for us. The cannula for an IV was put in his arm as the doctor finished examining him. A portable X-ray machine was in place and the X-ray taken almost before the nurse had finished putting the medicine into the canula.

Several doctors came to see Bwembya, and I could hear his name being mentioned over the phone and someone talking to his paediatrician as I heard her name and Bwembya's name mentioned in the same sentence. I did not pay too much attention to everything going on around me as I was focused on Bwembya. An hour later, things seemed to settle down, his breathing eased, and he relaxed a little. He asked to go to the toilet. I pulled the curtains around his bed, got him a bed pan and he did a big wee. I was relieved as after the X-ray I had asked the doctor what was on the X-ray, and she had said he had a lot of fluid in his chest.

For the next hour I sat and stared at him, and he stared at me. After years of hospitals and emergency rooms, I would have packed the usual bag with the usual things in it. Normally I would have had a book to read in my overnight bag. I thought 'no book, I might as well look at Bwembya and talk to him', so

I did. We stared deeply into each other's eyes, leaning across the little hospital table. He sat in a big comfy chair with two pillows behind him, leaning onto the table with a pillow on it to rest his arms. All the time we had been going to emergency, no one had ever brought that big chair for him. He was normally forced to sit on my lap or get onto the bed which he hated. I sat in a hard normal chair and leaned across the table looking at him and talking to him. He looked at me in that thoughtful pensive way of his. During the last year with all the visits to emergency, Mwango usually rushed to the hospital in the car after us. Today, he thought we should have stayed home and tried to manage the incident ourselves. He stayed at home because he thought it would be the same as always. The breathing would be managed with oxygen and medication and the crisis would be over.

At about midnight, Bwembya indicated that he wanted to go to bed. He stood beside the bed, very calm and peaceful and looked up at me. I said, 'You want to go to bed?' He started to raise his leg to get up onto the bed. I picked him up and put him onto the bed. I walked up to the desk and asked the nurse if it was okay for me to get him a blanket. She waved me on, and I got him a blanket from the linen cupboard. I covered him with the blanket. He looked into my eyes; he was very tired. I kissed him and he turned over and went to sleep.

This was unusual as usually the last thing he wanted to do is get into bed in emergency. He would usually sit up in bed or in a chair until he was practically falling over, or sleep in my arms until I put him into bed. Within ten minutes the porter came to take us to the ward. We were accompanied to the ward by a couple of nurses. Bwembya opened his eyes on the way up to the ward. I touched his forehead and said, 'I am here, B, go to sleep' as I walked beside him. We got to the ward and were warmly welcomed. We knew almost all the staff, including the porter who took us there.

Bwembya was taken to a single room near to the nurse's station. This was only the second time he had had a room that close to the nurse's station; the first being after he had the infection in the heart. Bwembya hardly woke up, he just looked around, curled up and slept. I kissed him, put the teddy into bed with him and made my bed. The nurses were eager to help me make my bed, and I kept saying I would do it as I knew exactly how I liked my bed made. After years of experience, I used a towel and a pillow stuffed at an exact spot where a metal pole or wooden bracket was on the fold-out bed. After making the bed, I realised I had to sleep in my clothes. This was about half past midnight and the ward was quiet. I must have slept the minute my head hit the pillow as I don't remember anything after that.

✦

Chapter 18

I was woken up by someone shaking me roughly. I lay there feeling like I had to catch my breath as the room came into focus and I remembered where I was. I shivered as I pulled the thin white cotton hospital blanket up to my neck. The room felt cool, as if there was cold air coming in from somewhere. I sat up clumsily on the flimsy little fold-up bed, holding on to the edge so I did not fall off. I was groggy and drowsy. I blinked a few times to get the room into focus. The room was dark with a little light filtering in through the half-open door; there was just enough light to see the outline of everything in the room. There were little green, orange, and red lights on various machines in the room. I had been shaken out of my sleep but there was no one there. The room was very, very quiet, which was disconcerting. I was in a hospital room and usually there was always something beeping somewhere, but it felt like you could hear a pin drop. I wondered what had woken me up in the empty quiet room.

I looked over to the bed next to where I was sitting, to where Bwembya was sleeping and quickly stood up. I tip-toed round to the other side of his bed and stood close to where his head was and looked down at him. He was lying on his side facing the door. His face was half covered with a face mask connected to

220

the CPAP machine that was helping him breathe while he slept. As I was looking down at him, I saw him take one breath and then nothing. I picked up the cord with the red duress button and pressed it quickly. It was a reflex action. I did not stop to think about what I was doing. I just knew I had to press that button. I felt a strange calm, like I had been here before and knew exactly what I was supposed to do.

As I stood there quietly, I heard voices. Although I could not hear what was being said, there was an urgency to them. A nurse ran into the room, switched on the lights by the doorway as she came in, and stood over where my son lay. I heard her say, 'He is not breathing.' She pulled the pillow from behind Bwembya's head and threw it to the side, then removed the mask from his face as another nurse ran in. They turned Bwembya over onto his back and started trying to resuscitate him. I stood on one side of the bed feeling like time had stopped. Like everything had stopped. Another nurse rushed in wheeling a trolley with all sorts of equipment on it. One of the nurses checked for his pulse. She said, 'No pulse.' She grabbed a resuscitation bag and placed a mask on his face as the other nurse positioned the ECG machine. I moved round to the other side of the bed, trying to keep out of the way but still close enough to see everything that was happening. Two of the nurses kept talking to him, 'Come on, B, wake up, B, work with us, B', as they performed CPR. A few minutes into this a group of people rushed into the room and took over the CPR.

Within five minutes, there were about eight people in the room around the bed working on Bwembya or just watching what was happening. I kept talking to him as I stroked his head or any part of his body that I could reach. I stayed close to him, keeping my hand on his body without obstructing what was happening. I only stood back when they used the electric charges on his chest. At 1:37am, as I glanced at my watch, I heard one of the doctors say Bwembya had no pulse rate, no respiration rate, the oxygen saturation rate was not obtainable and there was no output even with the cardiac compressions. I watched as one of the doctors picked up what seemed like a big syringe and injected him in the chest with it. This was repeated after a short period. There was an urgency and a tense hopefulness in the room. I felt like I was holding my breath, hardly daring to breathe. CPR continued. About ten minutes into this, I said to no one in particular, 'I had better call my husband'. They kept working on Bwembya and I calmly walked to the desk in the ward and asked to use a phone. A nurse led me to a phone in one of the side offices.

As I was dialling our home number, I remembered asking my husband a few weeks earlier what he would want to be told if anything happened to Bwembya. I had asked him if Bwembya died when he was not there, should I tell him our son had died or something else. He had said to tell him the truth. When he answered the phone after a couple of rings, I calmly told him Bwembya had stopped breathing and the doctors were trying to resuscitate him. There was silence on the line for a few seconds, then he said he would be right over and hung up. I then called my brothers James and Kenny and told them the same thing I had told my husband. We talked for a little while as I explained what had happened and what they were doing to Bwembya. James who was spending the night at Kenny's place wanted to rush over but I asked him if he could go to our house to be with the girls.

I thanked the nurse who had let me use the phone and walked back towards the room. Outside the room there were a few people watching what was happening. I heard one of them say in a shocked voice, 'Is that Bwembya?' I looked at the person. It was the orderly who had brought my son to the ward from emergency earlier. I also recognise the cleaner, who usually chatted to Bwembya while she cleaned his room. They all looked shell-shocked. The whole night I had been calm and barely breathing, trying to take in what was happening around me. Watching this group of people desperately willing my son to live nearly broke me. There was so much tension in the air it almost overwhelmed me. Someone gave me a big hug and barely holding myself together, I walked back into the room.

Attempts to resuscitate Bwembya continued with me watching every move, holding or stroking any part of his body I could. A little while later I was called to the phone at the nurse's station by one of the nurses to speak to Bwembya's paediatrician. She told me the doctors had done all they could, and Bwembya was not responding. They needed to stop resuscitation attempts if that was alright with me. I agreed to that, and she talked to me for a few minutes. I did not take in much of what she said but she was calm, caring and obviously upset by what was happening. I assured her I was fine and agreed to call her if I needed anything. I handed the phone back to the nurse who was waiting beside the desk and slowly walked back to the room. Soon after I entered the room, they stopped all resuscitation attempts, unplugged the equipment, and wheeled the trolley away. Everybody quietly left the room. The last person to leave switched off the main lights in the room so that the only light left on was an effervescent light on the board above the bed.

The room was cool and quiet as I pulled up a chair and sat next to the bed where my son's body lay. A nurse walked into the room with a basin of water, some soap, and a soft white cloth. I helped her remove Bwembya's clothes and she gently wiped him down and cleaned him up. I took out a clean set of clothes from the little weekend bag that was on the floor next to the chair and helped her put the clothes on him. I put the dirty clothes into a plastic bag and put the plastic bag into the bag beside the chair. The nurse took Bwembya's arms and placed his hands gently one on top of the other. She put a hand lightly on my shoulder and looked into my eyes but did not say a word. There were no words to be said. She picked up the basin of water, the soap, the soft white cloth, and left the room.

I sat down in the chair and looked around the quiet peaceful room. I felt strange. There was no sadness, no grief, no shock. The thing I had dreaded for so long had finally come and gone. My son had died and all I felt was a strange feeling of peace. I felt like I understood things I could not explain. I felt humbled, insignificant, but still like I was part of something so much bigger than I could even begin to understand. Something timeless and infinite. There was nothing in this room but there was everything in this room.

I sat there quietly like I was keeping watch while Bwembya slept. How did we end up here? We had come full circle. I remembered the day you were born when you came in as quietly as you had gone out. You did not come in screaming and yelling, you came in quietly. I did not talk, scream, or shout during labour. I felt like I had to concentrate on bringing you into the world. Pay attention to what was happening and listen to the midwives who were with me for many hours. I was not one of those women I had heard about who made a scene. The ones who scream, swear, rant and rave. That was not who I was.

Seventeen years later, I have changed so much I can hardly recognise the quiet introverted girl who gave birth to you so many years ago. The girl who used to cry because a movie was sad, because someone said something that hurt her feelings, because her new husband in jest said she could not cook. I used to think when you died, I would be inconsolable and lose control. I thought I would have to be dragged screaming and crying from your body. But there I was sitting quietly in a dimly lit room in silence, as calm as I was the day you were born.

The chair I sat in was cold and hard. I adjusted my posture and continued to look at your body lying there. The room was still cool and quiet. But there were other sounds around me, the beeping of machines and muted voices in the distance. Life was still going on outside the room. I continued to watch your little body lying on the bed beside where I sat. I had spent a lot of time beside you, while you laughed, cried, played, ate, slept, and just lived. Even though you were a teenager you were still Mummy's baby. You loved to hold my hand and sit right next to me with your head on my shoulder. Your little body seemed to be smaller than it normally was. You were sixteen years old; you would have been seventeen in a couple of months. Your body was like that of a ten-year-old, all bony, thin little limbs with elbows and knees poking through the plain white sheet wrapped around your body. I noted your ash-grey face and the blue tinge of your lips. How could change occur so quickly from a living breathing person with pale brown skin to an ash grey colour?

I leaned back in the chair but stayed close enough to keep touching Bwembya's head and looking at his hair, his lips, his ears, at all of him. I looked at his long lashes and wondered how my son got the long lashes, big eyes and the silky black hair that curled into tight curls as it grew longer. He had his dad's hair. My daughter Bupe often complained that it was not fair that he got the long lashes and the good quality hair, and she did not.

My eyes travelled down the length of Bwembya's body to his feet. His small child-like feet. I always marvelled at his still baby-soft feet, while his sisters had normal kids' feet, rough around the edges feet. Like me, Bwembya did not like to walk barefooted, he always had flip-flops, slippers, gumboots, or shoes on his feet. When he wore sandals, he had a funny habit of wearing socks with them. He wore his flip-flops on the beach. I smiled when I thought of how he hated getting sand on his feet at the beach. He would rush into the water to get the sand off his feet. He would be clearly unimpressed when more sand got on his feet when he had to walk back up the beach. Like his mum, he loved the beach but not the sand. He was so like me in some things. I smiled to myself when I thought about how I too wore flip-flops to walk on the beach and how I hated sand on my feet and behaved exactly like he did. Loving the beach and hating the sand.

I looked around the room and at all the things I had brought with me. The teddy bear that was like your security blanket whenever you were in hospital, but not at home as it was not cool. Your CPAP machine next to the bed, switched off. You had reached a stage in your illness where you could not breathe well for long without oxygen. You will never need help to breathe again. You have died. I have known for years that you were not here to stay, that you were passing through, but I had not let myself dwell on your leaving, just on your being here while you were here. There were a few times over the years when I had thought we were going to lose you, or had lost you, times when I held my breath and waited for the unimaginable to happen and somehow it did not.

I looked at you lying there. You have finally gone. If I had the power to let you stay I would. I know you wanted so much to live. I know that if I had the power to or if I was God, I would wish you back, but I am only a mum who had to let you go. I thought about Jesus dying on the cross and what a big sacrifice that was. If I had the power God had, and I had the choice I would bring you back without a second thought. I am in awe of the God who let his son, who was a good man, die for other people's sins when there was so much else he could have done. That was the choice he made.

A child crying somewhere in the ward brought me back to the present. To the cool quiet room once again. I tried to imagine where you were, what had happened to you. I knew you were taken away gently but by whom and to where? You were ok wherever you were because I felt you were. I tried to reach into that dark space in front of me to feel you, feel your essence, but there was nothing, just a quiet peaceful feeling.

This was not how I had imagined things would happen when you died. I used to imagine the machines you were hooked up to going haywire and the machine that shows the heart rate flatlining as I watched it stretch from a zigzag to a straight long line. All the things I thought would happen were not what happened. I used to think I would lose all control and self-respect. I thought I would be wailing, the cry of a woman in mourning, the way

I had seen women cry in anguish and grief at the loss of loved ones. I thought I would be inconsolable, and that I would curl up in a corner and never get up. I thought I would have to be dragged screaming and crying from your body when you died. My eyes so swollen that I could not see out of them.

I have changed a lot over the years, in appearance and in character.

I have become this calm, tough-on-the-outside woman with an opinion and not afraid to say so if it concerned my children. I fought so hard to make sure you had the right to do what you wanted when you wanted. Some battles which I would normally have been too afraid to even contemplate, I took on without even thinking because it was for you. I took on education departments, after-school services, vacation care services, and medical services. I made sure you got to fully live your life the best way you could, so that there were no regrets.

I looked at your ash-grey face and thought of how much I would miss you. I could still see you smile even though when I looked at you, you were not smiling. You have barely been gone a few minutes and I am missing you already. Something is already missing in my life, even though I have not yet processed what has happened and had time to think about it. My life has changed, and I have not even left the room where your body lies. For so many years, I was Bwembya's mother. How would I know how to be someone else?

You taught me so much in your short life. I was supposed to help you grow and teach you about life, but it was you who was doing the teaching. You taught me to be brave, to be resilient, to meet my problems head on. I watched your battle from the sidelines. I watched you struggle and fall as you got weaker.

I watched you get up and continue to keep fighting. I picked you up and carried you when you could not get up on your own. Because of your courage and your acceptance of every twist and turn in your short life, I sat there and did not fall apart. I sat there and believed that we would somehow put one foot in front of the other and keep going, because that was what you would have done.

As I sat there quietly, I knew things were going to change dramatically in the next few hours. Life was never going to be the same again. I did not let myself think about my husband or the girls. How this will affect them, how we will handle your leaving our world, because that would have broken me. Instead, I focused on you and how you lived and showed us how to be strong and keep living through whatever life threw at us. I know I will have to face the rest of the world and deal with what has happened tonight but for the moment it is enough to sit in this quiet peaceful room to be near you, even though I know you are no longer there.

✦

Chapter 19

The room was still cool and quiet as I continued to sit on that cold hard chair. The light above the bed gave a radiant glow to Bwembya's grey-tinged skin, as if he had a bit of ash on it, with a little light blue lipstick rubbed into his lips. I heard a loud anxious voice with a mention of my son's name. It was my husband Mwango's voice, his anxious panicky voice. Then there was a sound of footsteps hurrying down the corridor.

I sat up when my husband came through the door. I looked up at him as he hurried over to the bed and stood beside it looking down at Bwembya. He looked like I always thought I would look, distressed and inconsolable, as if his world had come crashing down around him. He sat down next to me with tears running down his face. He kept saying that this was not how he wanted Bwembya to go, not like this. He was distressed and hit the side of the bed with his fists. I put my arms around his shoulders. As I was comforting him, talking to him quietly, saying, 'It's alright, honey, he was tired, he needed to rest', there was a noise beside us. I heard what sounded like a gasp and we both looked down at Bwembya, he was breathing, loud strong breaths.

For the second time that night without stopping to think, I pushed the duress button. My heart was racing. What was happening? I looked at Mwango and calmly said, 'Honey, we need to lift the bed off the flat angle and get some pillows as Bwembya cannot breathe properly on a flat bed.' Mwango composed himself and raised the top end of the bed, then we put some pillows behind Bwembya's head. A nurse came running in, took one look at Bwembya, picked up the phone and called someone.

I was not paying attention to what she was saying, I was watching my son breathe. This child who had been pronounced dead and taken off his oxygen, was breathing again, with loud strong breaths. The doctor who had been looking after Bwembya came back into the room and I could see the shock on his face, his disbelief as he checked Bwembya's vital signs. I watched him check Bwembya's pulse on his wrist, his neck and near his groin. He left the room mumbling that he was going to call someone. I was too distracted to pay attention to the name. He came back after a few minutes still looking perplexed and told us that Bwembya's doctor had said to put him back on oxygen, give him some Valium, and make him comfortable.

The nurse took a tube attached to a clear canister on the wall and suctioned some white froth that looked like bubbles coming out of Bwembya's mouth and she wiped his face gently. He was given Valium through a needle and put back on oxygen. Mwango and I then sat on either side of him, each holding a hand. The ash-grey colour in Bwembya's face and the blue tinge on his lips was gone. He looked more like himself again. His eyes were open but fixed, I did not think he could see anything. I could feel his essence again, he was back with us. I didn't question what was happening, I was merely observing and being present, holding his hand, being his mum.

Sitting on either side of the bed holding Bwembya's hands, Mwango and I talked to him about how much we loved him. I felt my hand being squeezed. I looked at Mwango, he nodded, and I could see his hand being squeezed, too. Tears were gently running down Bwembya's face and I knew he could hear us. I could see him trying to concentrate. His eyebrow lifted and made lines across his forehead, and then relaxed. We told him we loved him very much. We also told him it was okay to go, okay to go to sleep and rest if he was tired. We gave him lots of hugs and kisses and kept telling him we loved him; that we would always love him. I turned to Mwango while Bwembya seemed to doze off, and said to him, 'He will not die until the sun is coming up'. Mwango looked at me but did not comment, he knew I sometimes got these premonitions.

I did not know why I said what I did with such conviction, but the thought just came to me, and I said it aloud as I thought it. Bwembya was born when the sun was rising, and he would leave when the sun was rising. There was no time for sorrow and tears. I wanted to be present for this important moment in my son's life and not miss what was going on around me. Bwembya needed to know his mum was there, that she loved him and there was no need to be scared.

During what seemed like a long night, there were a few people walking in and out of the room to check on Bwembya. Around half past two in the morning, my brother James walked in and gave me a big hug. I had not expected him to come but he decided to come and see what was going on after he had sent the girls to bed. His face showed how worried he was, but I could see the relief on his face when he looked down at Bwembya and saw that he was dozing peacefully. He told us he had talked to the girls about what had happened, calmed them down and sent them to bed, promising them he would wake them if anything happened. He talked to Bwembya quietly, kissed him and we sent him home, promising to call him if anything changed.

I started singing to Bwembya. I sang all the songs I used to sing to him whenever he was sick, or to put him to sleep. Songs like 'Please Don't say Good Night' by Five Star and I sang all his favourite Brandy songs till my voice was hoarse. I was fine doing this until I started singing the song titled 'Everything I do'. In the last part of the song my voice broke. As I was singing, I was thinking that I would really swap places and die for you if I could. I had always been the mother who is always singing, in the shower, in the kitchen, in the car, and to my girls' embarrassment in the supermarket. I sometimes spontaneously danced to the music without a care as to who was watching. I felt like I had music running through my veins. Bwembya never seemed to mind, he would look at me with a grin on his face. He found it all very amusing.

As the kids were growing up, I would stand outside their bedrooms or sit on the step leading from the bedrooms to the living area and sing to them. When I stopped singing, Bwembya would continue humming songs until he fell asleep. From the living room we could hear the girls going 'B, go to sleep, stop singing', but he would continue to sing until he fell asleep. The girls were now grown, so Bwembya was the only one I still sang songs to whenever he was sick, or to get him to sleep. He was the only one who listened to me sing out loud in the car and he would hum along with me. He danced around the house with me. When he was little, he used to love following me around the house as I sang along to whatever music I had on. Tonight, I felt like I had been singing for hours, my voice was getting hoarse and Bwembya had fallen asleep. I sang to him until I dozed off.

It was early in the morning when Mwango gently woke me up from my light sleep and said, 'Honey, he is gone'. Bwembya had died just as the sun was rising. He had gone peacefully while his dad watched him go. We both had the opportunity to be with him when he was leaving the world. Mwango stood up, went to the window, and opened the blind, the sun was just coming up faintly on the horizon. The orangey pink colours of a beautiful dawn. He looked at me and said nothing, but his face said everything he felt. We looked at our son lying there with the pupils of his eyes fixed and dilated. Mwango reached out tenderly and gently closed his eyelids. Something shifted in me as I watched him do that. This man was the father of our son, who knew how I loved Bwembya, and who loved him as much I did.

There stood the man to whom I had been married to for almost eighteen years. He had shared my journey as we single-mindedly strived to give Bwembya the best life we could. He had always been a hands-on dad to our son. There are many memories of Mwango as a hands-on dad, particularly one of him with two large safety pins in either side of his mouth, as he expertly folded the terry cloth nappy and changed Bwembya's nappy on a fast-moving train from London to Edinburgh while I sat back and read one of those Mills & Boon books my mum used to buy and pass on to me. There were a few older British women looking at my husband, nodding their heads in approval and they gave a little clap when he finished changing Bwembya and started to feed him with a bottle. As I looked at him standing beside the bed, with a face filled with sorrow, my heart broke a little knowing how great his sorrow was. He was a wonderful father and husband, who loved deeply and who had never been afraid to show it.

The nurse turned off the monitor and removed the oxygen mask. She went out of the room and returned with the doctor. He checked the vital signs again, the pulse on the wrist, the neck and groin. He wrote something in Bwembya's chart and left after expressing his condolences. A few minutes later, I was called to the phone by one of the nurses. Bwembya's paediatrician talked to me, and again passed on her condolences and said she was there any time we wanted to talk to her, that we just had to give her a call and she would be in touch. I then called James and told him Bwembya had died and asked him to call the priest at our church to inform him of Bwembya's passing.

One of the nurses came back in the room and cleaned Bwembya up with a soft wet white muslin cloth. We changed him into the second spare set of clothes I had brought with me from the little weekend bag that was on the floor next to the chair. It was always cool in the hospital, so I had bought some warm clothes. We dressed him in dark grey trackpants and an orange top with navy sleeves and a square navy patch on the chest with the number '02' in white. The nurse lowered the bed and removed the pillows. She placed his hands gently one on top of the other and folded the bedding back, tucking it neatly around him. She gathered up all the things she used to clean Bwembya and quietly left the room.

Mwango and I sat side by side in the quiet room. I thought to myself, 'What happens now?' I looked at Mwango and he seemed to be thinking the same thing. It was daunting looking at our dead child lying in front of us and having no idea what happened next. In Zambia, other people would handle all the arrangements. The older family members who knew what needed to be done would take over the reins, after consulting with us. Here we were, we had never been in the position of being older members of the family, the ones who were involved in such decisions. Sitting there without a plan was unsettling for me. I usually knew a little about something or knew someone who had been through an experience who I could ask. I always did my research. The aftermath of a death was one area I had not thought to investigate thoroughly, maybe because that was something I had not been ready to face.

The hospital chaplain walked into the room and introduced herself. She explained what usually happened when someone died, and what the choices were. As she was talking to us, one of the pastors from our church arrived. We were very happy to see him. They both prayed with us and helped us make initial decisions about what we do first. We were told we could stay with the body for as long as we wanted, then the body would be transported to the mortuary where a funeral director would organise to pick it up for preparation for the burial. Our pastor suggested a funeral director who a lot of people at our church had used and we were happy with that. We agreed to meet with him and the funeral director the next day at our house, and then they left. Mwango and I sat back feeling grateful that things had been organised and we had a good idea about what was going to happen.

The news had already spread. For the rest of the morning, we had people coming into the room. Staff coming on duty came into the room to pay their condolences. This included doctors, porters, nurses, physios, and cleaners. People were standing in the corridor crying. I was the one comforting people. I was still very calm and had not yet shed a tear since Bwembya died. I was living in the now, not daring to go to that place that would leave me vulnerable to a tidal wave of grief that threatened to overwhelm me, to a place I was not sure I could crawl back from. I did not feel brave or strong or courageous, I felt like I had to be present to take in what was happening and to know what I needed to do to get us all through this enormous loss.

Later in the morning, Kenny and James came to the hospital with Natasha and Bupe. As they walked in, James who had the girls on either side of him, quietly told us that he had told them what had happened. I thought it would have been hard for me to do, but I would have done it. I was grateful to James for being there to do such a huge job. He could have waited for us to tell them when they came to the hospital, but he didn't. Both James and Kenny's eyes were bloodshot, and they were both sad. I looked at the girls who seemed hesitant to come further into the room. James had his arms around each of them, and gently urged them to come in.

They both turned and looked at the bed where Bwembya lay, then they looked to where Mwango and I were standing. I looked into their eyes, and I was filled with sorrow. Their red tear-filled eyes told me everything. I hurried towards them and hugged them. With a head on each of my shoulders, and arms hanging onto me so tightly, I felt like we had merged into one. Their tears slowly soaked through my clothes as I let them cry. I felt them trembling as they cried with heartbreaking grief-stricken sobs. My chest tightened and my heart broke as I took on their pain and my tears mingled with theirs. Tears for them, for their sorrow, their loss and for their future without their cheeky beloved brother.

After a few minutes I talked to the girls quietly and calmed them down. 'Bwembya has been sick for a long time,' I said. 'He was tired, and he needed to rest. His little body could not keep going. It would not have been fair to keep him here when he was struggling so much to even breathe. He needed to go and rest.' The sobbing stopped but the girls clung onto me. After hugs and cuddles all round, we stood around Bwembya's body and tried to come to grips with what had happened. We all took turns holding Bwembya's hands, kissing him and talking to him, telling him how much we loved him. Kenny took some pictures of Bwembya, and we sat around the bed and talked about Bwembya and his quirky traits, laughing through our tears.

We told stories about the things Bwembya had done. About what a naughty or cheeky boy he could be. 'Remember the time he put a whole big jar of Vaseline in his hair and on his eyes so that he looked like he had conjunctivitis. It took so long for grandma to get the Vaseline out of his hair,' said Tasha.

'Or the day we looked out the window and he was jumping on the trampoline with his legs in plaster,' remembered Bupe.

'What about when we were waiting to see the doctor at the medical centre and he went up to everyone who was in the waiting room and retied their shoelaces,' Mwango added, rolling his eyes.

'Some people were not too happy about that' Tasha agreed.

'Remember when he set fire to the Persian rug in the living room by poking a stick at the bars of the heater and touching the fringes of the rug? Or when his dressing gown caught fire because he was leaning back close to the gas fire?' Bupe said.

'He loved wearing gumboots even in summer,' Uncle Kenny said.

'Mum, you hid his gumboots one summer, but he went and found Natasha's old pair,' added Bupe.

'That is right,' I said. 'In winter I hid his sandals so he would wear shoes and then forgot where I hid the sandals when summer came. I eventually found the gum boots and sandals when I was tiding up the top of the linen cupboard, but by then they were too small to fit him.'

About an hour later we went down to the coffee shop on the lower level of the hospital. At the coffee shop Mwango and I went to the side to a little alcove where the public phones were and started phoning friends and relatives in Australia. Mwango used a mobile phone, and I used the pay phone. James had already called his wife in Dubbo, and the family in Zambia before he came to the hospital. I never imagined I'd have the strength to call people to inform them my son had died, but I did.

I kept it simple and just informed whoever I phoned that Bwembya had passed away this morning, and that we were all at the hospital and would let them know what was going to happen when we got home. When we finished calling everyone, we went back to Bwembya's room. We stood around his bed talking for a little while. We were all calm and composed from the feeling of love and peace that was around us. We were ready to go home and leave the room. Kenny, James, and the girls said their goodbyes to Bwembya, and left.

Mwango and I stayed in Bwembya's room until early afternoon when the nursing unit manager came and talked to us. She gave us her condolences and explained what was going to happen. A nurse and a porter came into the room and prepared Bwembya for the trip to the mortuary. They took his arms and put them under the bedding down the side of his body. They pulled the covers up to his chest. He looked like he was sleeping despite the colour of his skin and lips. Mwango and I carried Bwembya's belongings.

We followed the group as it proceeded through the hospital to the mortuary entrance. We walked through the hospital with the porter pushing the bed leading the way and the rest of us followed behind. As we walked through the corridor, I wondered if the people who were walking past could tell if Bwembya was dead. I recalled walking along this corridor and seeing a young boy on a bed who I had thought must be dead. His colour had been a greyish paste and he looked like he was sleeping. I thought at the time he must be extremely sick to look like that but realised now that he was probably dead, and that they were taking him where we were taking Bwembya.

When we got to the big doors in the section of the hospital where the mortuary was, we were told to say goodbye as we could not proceed past the doors. Everyone stood quietly around us. They stepped a few feet from the bed and turned away to give us a little bit of privacy to say goodbye. We kissed Bwembya and told him how much we loved him and would always love him and stood back. The group then proceeded to go through the doors and Bwembya was wheeled away. The doors to the mortuary area closed and Mwango and I stood there looking at the doors for a short while before we made our way through the hospital to the entrance.

As I walked out of the hospital through the big glass doors, my heart felt like it was going to burst open. Up until then I had not really cried about the death of my son. I had cried when the girls had arrived, but it was more for their loss and their pain. I thought I was doing okay until the doors to the mortuary area closed, and we started to walk out the hospital. My heart broke. I was carrying Bwembya's teddy bear, but I was leaving him behind. I did not want to leave him behind, but I didn't have a choice. That was when reality hit me. I hugged Bwembya's teddy bear and thought this was it; it was all over. I shall never walk out of this hospital with my son again. I thought of all the years we had walked out of those doors together, always happy to be going home. I was walking out of the hospital with the things that Bwembya had left behind, but not with him. Overwhelmed, silent tears rolled down my face and Mwango reached out and held my hand as we walked to the car.

I looked back at the hospital, to a place that used to be a haven, a place of healing but now all I felt was that it was a place of loss. I wondered if I would ever be able to walk through those glass doors again. I thought about how I had sat at intake desks at different times of my life in three different countries because of my son's ill health. A lot had changed over the years. There were no long benches, sparsely furnished rooms with red polished floors and pale green washed-out cotton curtains, but they were places where I found my voice and my courage. The environment may have changed but the feeling of my heart had stopped, like I was hardly daring to breathe had been the same wherever I was. I had learnt to face things head-on and sit on the fear until I was ready to let myself feel. I wondered when the dust would settle from this final stampede. I looked back at the hospital one more time and tried to see the building through my tears. If there had not been people with kids walking past us, I think I would have been sobbing and wailing because the thought of leaving Bwembya behind was almost more than I could bear. But even in my sorrow I was conscious of where

I was. I could not let how I felt alarm the sick children that I walked past.

The car was parked on a side street one block away from the hospital. When we reached it, I composed myself, dried my tears and got ready to face what lay ahead. I knew it was going to be a long afternoon. On the drive home, we were both quiet. Every now and then Mwango reached out and squeezed my hand and I squeezed his hand back. We would get through this. It was comforting and kept me in the present.

✦

Chapter 20

It was early afternoon when we pulled into our driveway. Mwango parked the car in front of a tall gate that led to the double garage at the back of the house. Everything looked the same as it did every day when we drove up the driveway. The tall Christmas trees on the left-hand side of the driveway grew tightly together, you could not see the house next door. The lawn on the right-hand side of the car in the front of the house was green and thick. I looked at the lawn and remembered how in the last two years every time I was outside in the evening, I would stand on the lawn and look for a star. The first bright star I saw was what I would focus on. I would make a wish that Bwembya would be well, healthy, and happy.

I looked at the house as if it was for the first time. It was a single-level four-bedroom double-brick house set on a seven hundred square meter block backing onto a nature reserve. The bricks were maple coloured and the roof had red terracotta tiles. The window frames were the same colour as the roof and had yellow awnings with a few horizontal stripes the same colour as the window frames. Our house looked solid. It was still standing; it had not gone up in flames or crumbled to honour our enormous loss.

We sat in the car quietly for a few minutes, lost in our own thoughts. I thought about how our world had changed and how life was going to be so different. There was life before Bwembya died, and there was life after he died. I did not realise that his death was going to have such a major impact on our life. That events would be marked according to whether they happened before Bwembya died or after he had died. We were at the beginning of a new journey; it was uncharted territory. We could grieve for him forever and remember him with sorrow, or we could grieve for him and remember him the way he was, the way he had lived his life, full of laughter and smiles. I had to set the standard of how we wanted Bwembya to be remembered – with a smile. Even if we would be smiling though our tears.

We got out of the car, took things off the back seat, and closed the doors. As I walked towards the house, I felt calm and in control once again. Mwango opened the front door and let me walk into the house before he followed me in. The house was exactly as I had left it. I was expecting something to have changed as I looked around, but everything was just where it was supposed to be. It was still home. The house was quiet which was unusual for a Saturday afternoon. The TV was usually going or there would be music coming from somewhere in the house. As we walked into the living room, Kenny, James and the girls came in and we all sat down and started to talk. James put on the kettle and made us all a cup of tea. Mwango and I explained what was going to happen for the rest of the day.

We told everyone to expect a lot of people in and out of the house in the next few days, as was our Zambian custom. Mwango and I explained what normally happened when a person died in our tribe. There are seventy-three tribes in Zambia. The Bemba people occupy the north-eastern part of the country. They are a matrilineal group for whom succession is passed on through the mother's line, unlike most tribes in Zambia where succession is patrilineal. Only sons of the King's sisters are eligible to succeed the Bemba throne as the Bemba chief called Chitimukulu. There are forty clans in the Bemba tribe.

When a person dies, people gather at the home of the deceased. Women sit in a separate area to the men. Men usually sit outside at the front of the house. They build a log fire that is kept alight until the funeral is officially declared over. Women usually gather inside the house and at the back of the house where the cooking takes place. Some people come for a few hours, some for the whole day and some sleep over during the night, while others, especially family members, stay over for the duration of the funeral.

People who sleep over, sleep in the area allocated, with women separated from the men. Some people sleep on mattresses on the floor in the funeral house. These are usually members of the family and close friends. Other people sleep in chairs, on the floor, in tents and even on the grass outside. Women wear casual modest clothing with the local chitenge fabric around the lower half of the body like a wrap to protect their clothing, and as a sign of respect. They sometimes also wear a head scarf. Men wear casual clothing so they can sit on the ground if they have to, on logs or wherever they can find to sit.

Zambian funerals begin as soon as a person dies and last until the person is buried. They usually last 3-7 days, depending on when the people who are required to attend the funeral arrive. Upon entering the property or the house, people start wailing or crying. Food and refreshments are provided. Donations are made by people attending, and sometimes by people who are not attending the funeral. Following the burial at the cemetery, people go back to the funeral house, have a meal and except for close family and friends, everybody offers their condolences, gathers their belongings and leaves.

I wrote a shopping list for James as we would need to have refreshments to give people when they arrived. I just had enough time to take a quick shower before the first visitors arrived. Many of our friends started arriving a couple of hours after we got home. Family friends, friends from church, from the MPS society, home care ladies, teachers from B's school, the girls' friends, and acquaintances. We did not light a fire to formally start the mourning period, but the funeral had commenced.

The phone started ringing continuously, and we got a lot of calls from all over the world as the news spread. People we had not heard from for years called to pass on their condolences. We spent the day telling people what had happened, how Bwembya had died because that was the first question people asked. My older brother Reggie kept calling to see how we were. I did not talk to my mum as there were no phones in Chipili. Dad, who lived in Lusaka, was out of the country but would be returning the next day. He was a member of parliament for the Chipili area and was the deputy speaker of the house (parliament), so he spent most of his time in Lusaka. There was hardly time for us to sit and reflect as we had people in the house around the clock.

The rest of that day was one big haze. I was very tired but too hyped up to sleep. My sister-in-law Shaunagh and her three girls arrived to find a busy, full house late in the afternoon. I had not had time to think about the impact Bwembya's death would have on my three little nieces. It was about eleven in the evening before all our visitors left. We were all exhausted. I brushed my teeth and kissed the girls good night. I had extra-long hugs from the girls and had to peel myself out of Bupe's arms and tuck her into her bed. I walked past Bwembya's room. The door was closed like it had been all day. I thought about going in and decided that that would not be such a good idea. I did not feel ready to face how I would feel if I opened the door. It might be the one thing that would break the wall that is keeping the dam of water at bay.

I walked through the house switching off all the lights except the light in the toilet. We normally left that light on because Bwembya had developed night blindness after his stroke eighteen months ago. With a little bit of light, he was able to find his way to the toilet. I went to my room and got into bed. I was just falling asleep when I sensed someone standing next to me. I looked up and there was Bupe standing there looking miserable. I lifted the bedding, moved to the middle of the bed and she climbed in. She pulled my arm around her, and we fell asleep.

✦

Chapter 21

The world did not stop like I always thought it would when Bwembya died. Dawn arrived on Sunday like it did every day. It was sunny and beautiful. I woke up squeezed between Mwango and Bupe. As I lay in bed, I could hear children's voices and little feet running around the house. The little girls were awake. I got up to face the day, a day without Bwembya. Friends came and took over the running of the house, which was fine with us as we did not feel like cooking or eating for that matter. The pastor from church and the funeral director came to help us plan for what was to happen.

The funeral was arranged for Wednesday at eleven in the morning. The service was to be at the church in Baulkham Hills. We picked the readings, Psalm 46 and Romans 8: 31-39. The hymns we picked were 'Shine, Jesus, Shine', 'Rejoice, Rejoice', and 'Father, I Thank You'. Bwembya loved church. He especially loved the singing. 'Shine, Jesus, Shine' was one of his favourite hymns. He would clap and hum along with the song. We picked a brown shiny casket with silver handles. I thought it might be difficult for me to pick a coffin, but it wasn't. I knew all about coffins from my job as pensions officer in Zambia. I knew what coffins were made of and what made some coffins better than others, so I knew what I was looking for. We chose an arrangement of flowers that had yellow roses in it. Yellow roses because my son had brought so much happiness into our lives. Yellow was the colour of sunshine. A happy colour. I used to sing 'you are my sunshine' to Bwembya. I called him sunshine as a term of endearment. The cremation was to be at Castlebrook Memorial Park. Mwango and I were happy with the arrangements. I thought about singing 'The Rose' by Bette Middler at the funeral but knew I would not have the courage to do that. I felt that song exemplified how I felt – that my Bwembya had been a rose, prickly and thorny, but beautiful for a while in bloom. It was all as if I was in a dream that I was afraid of waking up from because I was unable to handle the truth. In the dream world I had the strength to keep going on.

On Sunday evening, Penny, a friend of mine from Brisbane, flew down for one night. Penny had been a year behind me in high school in Zambia. She walked in distressed and crying. I hugged her and told her it was ok, Bwembya was fine where he was. She sat in the nearest armchair and continued to weep as if her heart was breaking. As I was comforting her, I sensed someone standing close to me, almost touching me. I looked to where they should be standing but no one was there. As I looked away the feeling came back. I knew almost immediately that it was Bwembya. I could feel him. It was hard to explain, but it was him standing beside me, only I could not see him. I could hear his thoughts and knew what he was doing. He was standing beside me watching Penny.

I tried to think about what was happening. How could he be here? I didn't cry. I couldn't cry. I heard him ask, 'Mum, why is Aunty Penny crying?' I felt him standing right there and I could not understand it. It was like how you feel when someone walks in the room. You do not always have to see them to know who is there. It was as if he was there, but just out of the line of my direct view. I comforted Penny and she stopped crying. Then as quickly as Bwembya had come, he was gone. The space was empty once more. The women were looking at me and probably wondering how I could be so strong. I should have been greeting people as they walked into the house crying and weeping with them. But I couldn't. I was not shocked or surprised this happened, although I had not been expecting it to. It was not the only time someone who died had been around me. The first time was the day my sister-in-law, Mwenya, died. I had been terrified because in the dim light of my bedroom no one was there, but the voice talking to me was unmistakeable. The second time was three years later when my brother Heckie died. Two days after he died, I was walking to the garage to get the car out. It was early evening at dusk, not yet dark but shadowy. I felt as if someone was walking behind me and assumed one of the kids had followed me out of the house. I looked back, ready to tell whoever it was to go back into the house, but there was no one there. I felt the hairs at the back of my neck stand up. There was a cold chill like I had walked into a cold room. I manually pulled up the garage door and as I walked in, I had that sensation of someone following me again. This time I felt the presence, I knew it was Heckie as clear as I knew who I was. I could not explain it, but I knew it was him without a doubt. Like he was right there behind me and that if I looked back, I would see him. I was not terrified. There were many times I wished I had not been frightened the night Mwenya died, how I should have listened to what she had to say. I was simply scared. I was not ready to deal with what was happening, not ready to see Heckie or experience something so unreal. I was still grieving.

There were six children in our family. We were all born within eight years, so we had always been a close-knit family. Heckie and I were very close, but everyone in the family would probably say they were also close to him. He was always my protector. Everyone at primary school knew I had a big brother who they would have to answer to if they messed with me. After a few incidents where he walked into class and confronted a bully, I never had any trouble from anyone. The year he left our primary school and went to high school, one of the boys tried to bully me and Heckie heard about it and came back to the school during his lunch break and made it clear that he was still watching.

Even after we had grown up and were in different high schools in different towns, he still looked out for me – except the time I discovered he had printed dozens of copies of a picture of mine taken in a photographer's studio, and was selling them for 1 Kwacha, which was a lot of money in those days. I only heard about it because one of the girls at my boarding school told me her brother, who did not even live in the same town we lived in and was not Heckie's friend, had a picture of me. I asked her where he got the picture from, and she told me he bought it from my brother. I did not know why people would buy my picture. It is not like I was drop-dead gorgeous or anything. I looked ok but was not anything to write home about. I was quite plump and, in the picture, wore an ordinary crimplene white dress.

He was my confidant and life coach. It was nice to have someone I could confide in, and who would not judge me.

Heckie would tease me but not judge me. Nothing shocked him and he would tell me exactly what he thought and not sugarcoat it. He would tell me if what I wore made me fat and advise me on what to wear that looked good. He would tell me if he thought the boy I was dating was a waste of space. He influenced my taste in music because I hung around him and his friends a lot. He influenced my taste in clothes because he had a good eye for fabric and fashion. When he died, I lost not only a brother but a great friend and confidant. His death was a great loss to all of us. He was the funny one, the musical one, the all-rounder. He could take any electrical or mechanical object, pull it apart and put it together, most of the time successfully. We cooked together, sewed together, permed hair, and listened to music together. He did different things with different members of the family. He was at home talking to the guy on the street who sold cigarettes individually out of a packet, or the conductor on a bus who spent his day packing people into buses. He was equally comfortable playing tennis with members of the diplomatic corps in Canberra and attending cocktail parties with important people in society. Out of all of us six children his personality was the one that was larger than life. That is why he was missed by lots of people for vastly different reasons.

Heckie's death was almost too difficult to bear, especially when I thought of how it would be affecting my mum. Heckie was very close to Mum; he could do no wrong. She gave him the world. She would have given us the world if we had needed it. She gave him the world because he needed it and she saw he needed it, so she gave it to him. Her time, her energy, her money, her car, whatever he needed. We were comforted by the thought that short as it was, he had had a charmed life.

When he tried to communicate with me, I was not open to what was happening, it was too much for me to cope with. I refused to listen or acknowledge what was happening. For a couple of weeks after he died, I would feel him following me around. Always outside the house and usually by the garage late in the day. I always wondered why it was in a specific place and never in the house or away from the house. Even when I was with other people, no one else seemed to notice or experience what I experienced. I never told anyone about that incident. I did not think anyone would believe me.

The third time I had something unusual happen to me was in 2001 when the son of one of the MPS families died. Vince was a remarkable young man who had MPS II like Bwembya did. He had a special relationship with Bwembya. He would send him postcards on his travels and would talk to me about what it was like living with MPS II. I was in the car on a Friday evening coming from youth group with Bupe and Natasha when I told them Vince had died. The girls burst out crying. I had to stop the car to comfort them. I let them cry until they quietened down and then we went home.

As I was driving home, I had a vision of Vince. It was like someone switched on a projector on the windscreen in front of me. There in front of me was his face. He smiled at me and said to tell the girls not to cry, that he was happy where he was. He was surrounded by yellow flowers. I had been sad when I had heard the news Vince had died, but having this vision made me shake off my grief. It made me think maybe it was ok up there.

We got to the house and as I helped the girls out of the car, I had the sensation of someone standing by the backstairs watching us. I looked up at the small veranda at the back of the house and there was no one there. As we walked towards the backstairs, I felt two people walking with us. I knew who it was right away. My brother Heckie and my sister-in-law Mwenya. So close, so comforting. I knew exactly where they were, on either side of Natasha as she walked into the house. I heard what they were saying to her, even if she did not. They comforted her, saying it was alright, Vince was fine.

The girls did not seem to notice anything. I followed Natasha into her room. We sat on the bed, I held her close and comforted her until the tears stopped. For the rest of the evening, I could sense Heckie and Mwenya following Natasha around the house wherever she was. In the morning they were gone, the space around us was back to normal. I thought for a few days that maybe it was all an illusion, until Mwango, Natasha, and I walked into the church for Vince's funeral, and I saw the flowers on his coffin. The same flowers I had seen around him in my vision. I did not tell anyone about that vision either.

Natasha insisted on going to Vince's funeral. It was her first funeral, so I was a little apprehensive about taking her after all the loss she had experienced of important people in her life. Mwango and I sat on both sides of her in the church, and she was fine holding my hand right through the service.

The Monday after Bwembya died, like the day before, was sunny and beautiful. I woke up early and let the girls sleep in. James, Shaunagh, and their girls had left early for school and work. I called the girls' school to let them know what had happened and that the girls would not be at school this week. I called my office and informed my director that my son had passed away and I would not be at work all week. I had called the principal at Bwembya's school on Saturday, and she came to the house on the Saturday itself, so she would let everyone at the school know.

The day was quiet with not many visitors. During the morning the funeral director rang to inform us that the only way they could fit everything in between the church service and the service at the crematorium was to have the church service at ten in the morning on Thursday. As soon as he said that I remembered my premonition that I would not be at the meeting at ten on Thursday because I would be at a funeral. When I hang up the phone I sat down and went through what had happened on Friday. I thought that my premonition was not a coincidence. Penny and I spent most of the day with the family unwinding, watching TV, cooking, and taking it easy before people started arriving in the late afternoon.

In the evening when everyone had gone to their rooms, I closed up and checked the doors. I went to the back of the house to the sunroom and checked the back door to make sure it was closed. I switched off the light and left the room but as I went out, I heard music playing. I switched on the light to see if something had been left on, but the computer and music systems were off. I unplugged them from the socket, switched off the light and again the music started. As I walked through the dining room, I felt as if a crowd of people was following me. I looked behind me but there was no one there so I continued to walk slowly through the house switching off the lights. From the dinning to the kitchen, to the living room, to our bedroom. Mwango was in bed fast asleep. I got into bed and felt the crowd standing at the foot of the bed. I was not afraid. I stared into the open space. I still could not see anything, but I could feel the crowd. There was a little light coming in through the half-open door from the light in the hallway. I felt one person from the crowd walk towards the bed. I knew who it was immediately. It was Bwembya. I felt him lean over and something touch my forehead very lightly. Like the touch of a kiss. I put my hand on my forehead but there was nothing there. I just felt a little pressure. He walked back to the crowd, and they all left the room, and it was still once again.

The next morning, I was up early and making breakfast in the kitchen when Mwango and Tasha walked in, and I started to tell them what had happened, and how strange it was. Mwango said it was probably all a dream but just then Bupe walked in and interrupted us. 'Mum something really strange happened to me last night. I had just got into bed, and I was trying to fall asleep when there were all these people in my room at the foot of my bed. I recognised some of them but not all of them. Bwembya was at the front. There was Uncle Heckie and Aunty Mwenya. They looked like the picture Tasha has in her room but a little older. B stood there with his hands on his hips as usual. They told me not to cry as B was going to be ok, he was with them.' Mwango, Tasha and I looked at Bupe with astonishment. I told her what had happened to me. This could not be a coincidence. Later in the morning I went and checked my email. I opened one of those musical cards from a friend in Zambia. The music was the same as I had heard the night before.

The day was another beautiful sunny day filled with visitors. Flowers continued to arrive in masses. There were flowers on every table around the house. Yasmin drove me to a gourmet deli nearby where we ordered food for the wake. We were in the car at the traffic lights when I saw a mother and her two boys walking along the road. I watched her play with them, and I could see the younger boy who was about six cuddling and curling into her as she tried to walk. I thought about how Bwembya used to do just that, cuddle so close in seemingly impossible situations like when I was walking down the road. There is something about boys that is so different when they are with their mothers. I had seen my brothers with my mother. I would miss having Bwembya around; having girls was different. Between a mother and a son there is a unique bond, like sons would always stay close but girls could always leave. Mothers with sons will know what I mean. I felt sad because I would never know how we would have been when he was older, when he was a man. Would he have been too shy to curl up into me without a care as to who was watching when he was all grown up?

Wednesday was a busy day. Mary, who was my sister-in-law Mwenya's cousin, came from Queensland in the afternoon. She helped me organise dinner and sewed a chitenge material wrapped around skirt for me to wear to the funeral. She also helped the girls choose clothes to wear the next day. My sister Bwalya arrived from Zambia in the evening. I was apprehensive about seeing her. I thought my strong resolve would crumble and I would be a mess. I was surrounded by our daily visitors when she came. I walked into her open arms, and she broke down sobbing. I comforted her; my eyes filled up but did not overflow. I had this unshakable strong belief that Bwembya was fine. Somehow, we kept it all together.

The evening went well and true to Zambian tradition, to my surprise, a few ladies slept over. To have women sleep over at my house when I'd lost my son was a privilege. I felt honoured to have ladies sleeping on my living room floor on the carpet the night before the funeral. They would not let me get mattresses for them, or use the bedrooms, they were fine on the floor. It may have been a sad time, but I had rarely laughed so much at a funeral. The ladies were hilarious. They had us in stitches, and we forgot where we were.

✦

Chapter 22

The day of the funeral was a lovely day. I felt fine and that everything was going to be okay. We woke up early and lined up for the bathroom and breakfast. We fussed with our clothes and our hair. The girls and I wore dark colours, but not black. Bwembya was a sunny character, and we did not want this day to be dark. I put his teddy bear along with a box of tissues in my big navy woven bag. The car from the funeral home came at half past nine in the morning to pick up Mwango, Bupe, Natasha, and me.

There were a few people at the church when we arrived, mostly part of the congregation. We walked in and there was the coffin in the front of the church. It looked so small, but beautiful. We had decided to leave the top part of the coffin open before the service began, to give people who wanted to the chance to say goodbye. I went straight to the front of the church and put the bear on the bottom half of the coffin beside the flowers. I touched Bwembya's forehead and then kissed it lightly. It was my baby's body, the body in which he had lived for so long. The skin felt cold. Frozen really. There were small beads of water running down his forehead as if he was sweating. I gently wiped the beads of water as they appeared.

I did not for one minute think the body in the coffin was Bwembya. I did not feel him. He was not there. There was just his body, the vessel that used to hold him. The emptiness had been evident from the first few seconds after his death. It was like a shell when the spirit had left – but a shell that was still beautiful and significant. From the moment Bwembya died I had not thought he was still in his body or expected him to suddenly appear. He had left and was somewhere else. I wondered if he could see what was happening, and if he would remember how I loved him. I stood there for as long as I could while people came to look at him and to pay homage. I stroked his forehead and talked to him in my mind. I was talking to my son out there, somewhere. I was a mother packing up the pieces of a life left behind and saying goodbye.

The service was beautiful. It really was a celebration of Bwembya's life. I had not thought much about funerals before. Maybe because I had been grieving for so long and had accepted what was to come after looking at that thin body and feeling the strain he was going through just to keep breathing. Sometimes it was kinder to let people we love go than keep them alive to keep us from the pain. Sometimes keeping people in pain is not loving them enough to release them.

I loved my son enough to let him go. I loved him enough to not let him keep struggling to breathe. The relentless days and nights I spent with him while he struggled to catch his breath were sometimes more than I could bear. If I could have breathed for him, I would have. If I could have died for him, I would have. But sometimes it was about making different kinds of decisions, like telling him with love and compassion it was okay to go. I missed him a lot, but I never asked why he died or why it happened to us. All I know is that I felt privileged to have known him and have loved him, to have been his mum.

The service started off with 'Shine, Jesus, Shine.' We knew it was one of his favourite songs because he always caused a lot of commotion in church when we sang the song. He clapped at the wrong time or after everyone had finished and just by the look of joy on his face, you could tell he loved it. The pastor started off by telling us that this was a time to remember Bwembya and look back on his life. The eulogy was given by my brothers Kenny and James, followed by Jean the principal at Bwembya's school. Bupe read a poem she had written, then we sang a song called 'Rejoice, Rejoice'. The Bible readings Psalm 46 and Romans 8: 31–39 were read by our friends Tess and Thorton. The pastor gave the message and the prayers, and we finished off with the song, 'Father, I Thank You'.

Kenny who was Bwembya's godfather talked about Bwembya's life.

'How would I describe Bwembya? Everybody who has been touched by his life will have different descriptions. There was the cheeky B, the joyful B, the playful B and the loving B. Bwembya gave me the first experience at changing nappies. I had no problems changing a wet nappy, but a soiled nappy was a bit of a challenge.'

'One evening a couple of my friends came over. They got a bit of a shock to find me in the bathroom with rubber gloves and a face mask, such a pitiful sight. I was dressed up ready to go out. I had a date; I did not want to get myself dirty. I was on the floor with Bwembya on a towel, changing his nappy. I was shouting to them that I would be there in a minute. They saw me on the floor and had a big laugh as I looked so pathetic.'

'There were interesting times when we tried to put Bwembya to bed. He would pull me to the car, and we would take a drive round Woden Valley, or around Red Hill until he fell asleep. I would think, this is great! I would drive slowly back, hoping that I could lift him out of the car and put him into bed. We got home; he was wide awake.'

'How will I remember Bwembya? To me he was a fighter. He was my godson. A godson that I dearly loved and will miss. I know he is up there in a better place and probably looking down on us with his cheeky little smile. That is how I remember Bwembya.'

James talked about his experience with Bwembya. 'As Kenny has mentioned, we have all had our unique experiences with Bwembya. Firstly, I would like to congratulate Patricia and Mwango for allowing Bwembya to have such a wonderful life. It would have been tempting to wrap him in cotton wool, but they let him live a full life, one full of love and joy. He enjoyed his life like any boy did. Playing cricket, T-ball, basketball, having tantrums, doing whatever he wanted to do that he was allowed to do.'

'Bwembya had some amusing habits. When it was time for dinner time, we would call him to the table. He would stand there looking at everyone eat, smile, and not touch his dinner. When it was time for bed around 9.30, Mwango would be pulling his oxygen tube, saying, "Ok B, ready for bed". Bwembya would come out to the kitchen, get his dinner plate, and start eating. He would eat slowly and an hour later he would still be eating.

He would end up having an extra two hours before he had to go to bed.'

'Last Christmas was a really good Christmas with Bwembya. We had a great time and I remember sitting down an hour after lunch and listening to music. The girls had a concert, and we all decided to have a bit of a dance. Bwembya got up and did a few dances and we captured it on video. We were very pleased we had managed to do that as we could see him enjoying himself and having a laugh.'

'On behalf of the family, the Kasengeles, we would like to thank the church, MPS society, the Hills School staff and the principal. He loved school so much that even in the school holidays he would get up, get his backpack, put on his school uniform, and get ready to go to school. Everyone would say Bwembya it's not school today, it's school holidays. But he would want to go to school, that's how much he loved school. I would like to thank Westmead Children's Hospital, the respite carers who have been with us and were always there. Friends and family, of course, for all the help and support. Let us celebrate his life and cherish his memory, thank you very much.'

Jean, the principal at Bwembya's school, talked about Bwembya's life at school. 'So much of what we saw at school, you obviously saw at home. It is my privilege to share a message from the Hills School on behalf of the students, the parents, and the staff. I would like to thank Mwango and Patricia for that privilege.'

'I guess in sharing our thoughts with you today, we share some images of a journey. A most amazing journey of the human spirit. Bwembya's journey with us was a short journey by normal standards, but significant in its impact. And I guess if I were to comment on that which speaks strongly of Bwembya, it would be his prevailing spirit. A spirit that was amazingly strong, free, pensive, patient and persevering. And despite the trials of his deteriorating health and the discomfort that he experienced, his tenacious spirit made him keep bouncing back, and I guess that is what we remember of Bwembya.'

'But there were many faces of Bwembya as we have heard this morning, and I thought that I might just share with you some of them from his school. I guess the first face of Bwembya that we remember was B the ace. His first teacher and her first experience was when Bwembya came running out of the classroom bouncing a tennis ball. He did that most of the day and he almost bowled her over. He also became a bit of a frontrunner in basketball at the Hills and he was admired by a lot of bigger boys for the fact that he could pop a basketball from anywhere.'

'A casual teacher at the school and a good friend of the family emailed me last night to tell the story of the pink tablets. She said that while she was visiting Bwembya in hospital one time, the nurse came in with a tray of tablets, and it was quite an array of tablets. The centre of attention was a large pink pill, she said. It was so large she wondered how or even if Bwembya could manage to get it down, but he gave her a look that suggested he could. Then the nurse looked away to attend to the chart and he got the pink pill and threw it on the floor. When she looked up again, he was taking the pills and nodding and she said, "Well done, B!" When the nurse left the room Bwembya looked up and pulled out the drawer and she said it was full of pink pills. He rolled back his head in laughter. He was quite a character.'

'One of the lovely things about Bwembya that we really enjoyed at school was B the jester. I have heard many stories involving Bwembya and his sense of humour. He had the most powerful observation skills. He was a nonverbal young man, but he made up for it with his observation skills. He was a quiet observer, and that quiet demeanour masked a very intelligent boy, with a wonderful sense of humour.'

'In the latter days of Bwembya's journey, his physical strength and his ability failed him, but that strong spirit of independence never wavered. He found ingenious ways to maintain as much independence as he possibly could. He courageously embraced the medical supports that were required to preserve and maintain him at school and at home. He was never quite happy about embracing them, but through his deep intellect he knew that was the way it was. And I guess he has taught me to accept it the way it was.'

'He maintained his routine in the spirit of peace and dignity, and we really admire him for that. I guess in education today we talk about teaching and learning: teachers teach, and students learn. But you know, Bwembya broke that model at the Hills because we are quite certain that he taught us far more than we ever taught him. Far more.'

'Bwembya, the standard bearer, is the other aspect of Bwembya that will remain vividly in my mind, and in the minds of the Hills community. For Bwembya has taught us much about the prevailing life. The prevailing life of the overcomer. The patience, the persevering time of restriction and pain, embracing the changes. Embracing them with courage and dignity and an independence of spirit and amazingly with an enduring sense of humour.'

'Last Friday, he got off the bus and I could see that he was short of breath and, of course, immediately I said, "Come and sit down, B". But Bwembya, in his inimitable way, said, *No, I will stand, thank you.* I got pretty upset about that, I ran for the chair, and when I came back and looked around, he was standing there enduring his breathlessness. I went over and just put my cheek on his forehead and I said, *It's going to be alright. You're going to be alright.* I stood back, and I looked, and I am sure he said to me, *Yeah, we'll just get on with it, okay?* He just never gave up that sense of humour.'

'And in these latter days of the journey, Bwembya raised his standard and drew our gaze. This week we have drawn comfort, we've drawn strength and we've drawn faith from his journey. He has been a strong role model.'

'Thank you, Patricia and Mwango. We thank you for your continued witness and unconditional love. Of persevering and your faith in God, that he can take your good heart with his journey. And we thank you for your unshakable faith as a demonstration to all. Bwembya has left us with a great and enduring legacy. Thank you for the privilege of taking the journey. We are richer for it, and we are thankful that Bwembya came and raised that standard. Thank you.'

Something Beautiful

You know when something is beautiful,
It shines like the stars
And when it's around you,
It's all you think about.
Whenever you see it, it makes you smile,
Wider than you ever smiled before.
It gives you this warm feeling
And all your problems melt away.

But yet....
Even when this beautiful thing is in pain,
It doesn't let it show.
It suffers more than you ever imagined.
But it still lives on like the prettiest flower in the world.

It isn't the same as other things.
When it was made,
It came out different to other things of its kind.
But yet besides its differences,
It was still beautiful, not that most people would see it
But if you stayed around long enough to see its beauty,
You would think there was nothing more beautiful.

This beautiful something is a very special person
A person I know really well.

The strongest, most brave, loving, happy person
I've ever known in my whole life.
My brother, my hero, my best friend
Bwembya Kasengele

By Bupe Kasengele 2003

'Something Beautiful' is a tribute to Bwembya as befitting him written by Bupe. To honour her brother, Natasha had a star named after Bwembya.

The service finished and the immediate family stood at the door to greet the guests. Mwango and I were both amazed at the number of people who took the time to come to honour our precious son. There were over 200 people from all areas of our lives. School friends of the girls, school friends of Bwembya's, the girls' friends from outside school, parents of the girls', friends, teachers, staff members, doctors and nurses from the children's hospital, staff from Bear Cottage, staff from Home Care, staff from Community Options, staff from Interaction Community Services, staff from the Hills School, staff from Bwembya's previous two schools, Sunday school teachers from our church in Bexley, staff from the bank where Mwango worked, staff from five different places that I had worked, MPS families and other family and friends too numerous to mention. Family and some close friends proceeded to the crematorium for the Requiem Mass which was kept short and precise. We all went home to have some refreshments and join those who went straight home from the church. That was the dreaded day of my son's funeral. An extraordinary but unassuming day as fitting to send off a child like Bwembya.

✦

Chapter 23

People keep telling me how brave I am. Bwembya was the brave one, not me. He did not walk in anyone's shadow; he walked his own path and took the short way home. He was the one who led and showed me the way. He was the brave one, the person who smiled through his tears. I cried and smiled through my tears as I wrote this book, because I miss my son and because there are so many wonderful things to remember about him.

I look back and memories flood my mind. Memories of early on when he bit into an apple and looked up and his tooth was gone. He had just swallowed it. 'Oh, B,' I would say. Or of when I was getting his school uniform ready for the next day and found that every school shirt had little holes nipped all over the front of them. He did not want to wear the uniform. I had to find a plain blue t-shirt for him to wear. He just grinned at me when I said, 'Oh, B.' There was never a dull moment.

There were the not-so-good 'Oh, B' moments, too, like when he would refuse to get out of the car when I went to the shopping centre to pick up something for dinner and could not leave him in the car. He was not getting out and that was that. And moments like when he pushed the emergency button in one of the rooms at the cardiac unit while waiting for the cardiologist, and a team of people rushed into the room expecting to see a real emergency.

This has been a long yet short difficult journey. I have changed so much from the slim shy quiet young lady who arrived in Australia with several suitcases and a little baby. I have not scaled Mount Everest, sailed the seven seas, won a Nobel Peace Prize or an Oscar, but I have fought many battles that changed the way people and organisations did things, so that my son would have the best quality of life that he could have.

I loved beyond what I thought I could, suffered and grieved greatly. I have not been alone on this journey. I have had the love and support of my wonderful husband Mwango. He made me feel like I had to be taken care of, like I was the only one who lost a child, as if what he felt was not as important as what I felt. We both knew it was, but he treated me with tenderness, as if I might break. I have also been fortunate to be supported by my siblings and my parents; their unconditional love never wavered. And there are my daughters Bupe and Natasha who were on the journey with us. We all bear the scars from the battle that has helped to shape the people we have become.

Despite the difficult journey, I have always known who I was. I have moved forward in my life advancing my education and furthering my career even when I seemed to be taking a step backwards with some of the jobs I took on. I did not abandon myself and get engulfed in my son's illness. I embraced our lives at whatever stage we were at and found small measures of joy and fulfilment where they could be found. I have even acquired a sense of humour over the years; now that is something. Bwembya showed me how to live with courage, dignity, and resilience of spirit beyond all imagination. I have taken my cues from him and will live my life well. Do what I want to do, when I want to do it, if I can.

I live a life full of hope. Hope that tomorrow will be a better day. Hope that I will continue to grasp at the little things in life to make my day better. That someone will smile with me, laugh with me, and maybe even cry with me. That I will have the courage to be brave, to face whatever comes my way and to keep looking for the light in dark places. Letting that light shine to brighten my way. I guess I have come to the end of Bwembya and my journey, not our whole journey but this part of our journey. I am still called Bwembya's mother. I will always be Bwembya's mother.

I woke up early this morning. I had one of those dreams about Bwembya, where he looked at me with that look. In my dream, the schoolbus pulled up next to my car at the traffic lights with the windows open. I opened my window and shouted, 'Hi, B', like I used to whenever the bus drove alongside me on my way to work. He looked at me with a thoughtful look on his face as I drove alongside the bus. I woke up and realised it was all a dream.

I lie in bed quietly missing Bwembya. Thinking that since he has been gone, I have never once looked up and expected him to be there, like I expected I would. When he died, I knew there was no turning back, no illusions. I miss him, but not in that heart-wrenching way I had always thought I would, but in a gentle, loving, thinking of you sort of the way. I have learnt on this part of my journey, that even in the darkest place there is always the possibility of hope. Bwembya is still very much around, in my thoughts and in my heart. My dream was probably saying that my son still looks back through the open window as I drive past, as my life goes on, with that contemplative look, saying Mum, I see you.

Remember Me

Remember me with a smile,
a twinkle always in my eyes,
how full of love my life had been.

Remember me with laughter,
that echoed all around me,
how happiness touched my soul.

Remember me because I was here,
and somewhere along the way,
I touched a part of your soul.
Remember me and smile.

By Patricia Kasengele July 2003

Bwembya 6 months old with Patricia in Canberra

Bwembya 9 months old with Patricia in Edinburgh

Bwembya 10 months old with Mwango in Edinburgh

Bwembya and Patricia Scotland 1986

Bwembya 9 months old and Patricia in Edinburgh

Bwembya 2 years old and Santa 1988

Bwembya 7 years old in Dubbo

Bwembya 7 years old

Bwembya 7 years old with Mwango

Bwembya 8 years old with Patricia in Bexley

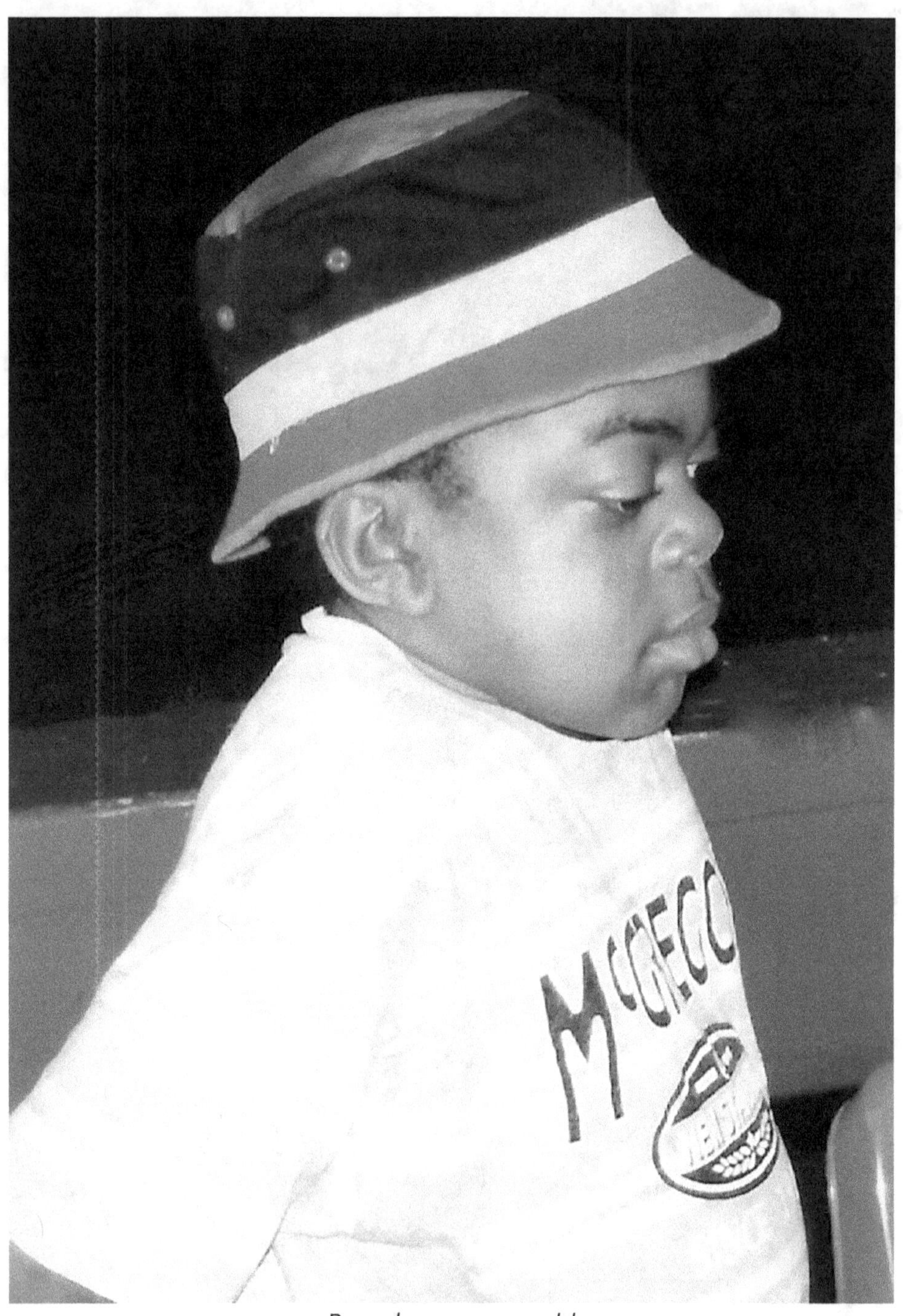

Bwembya 14 years old

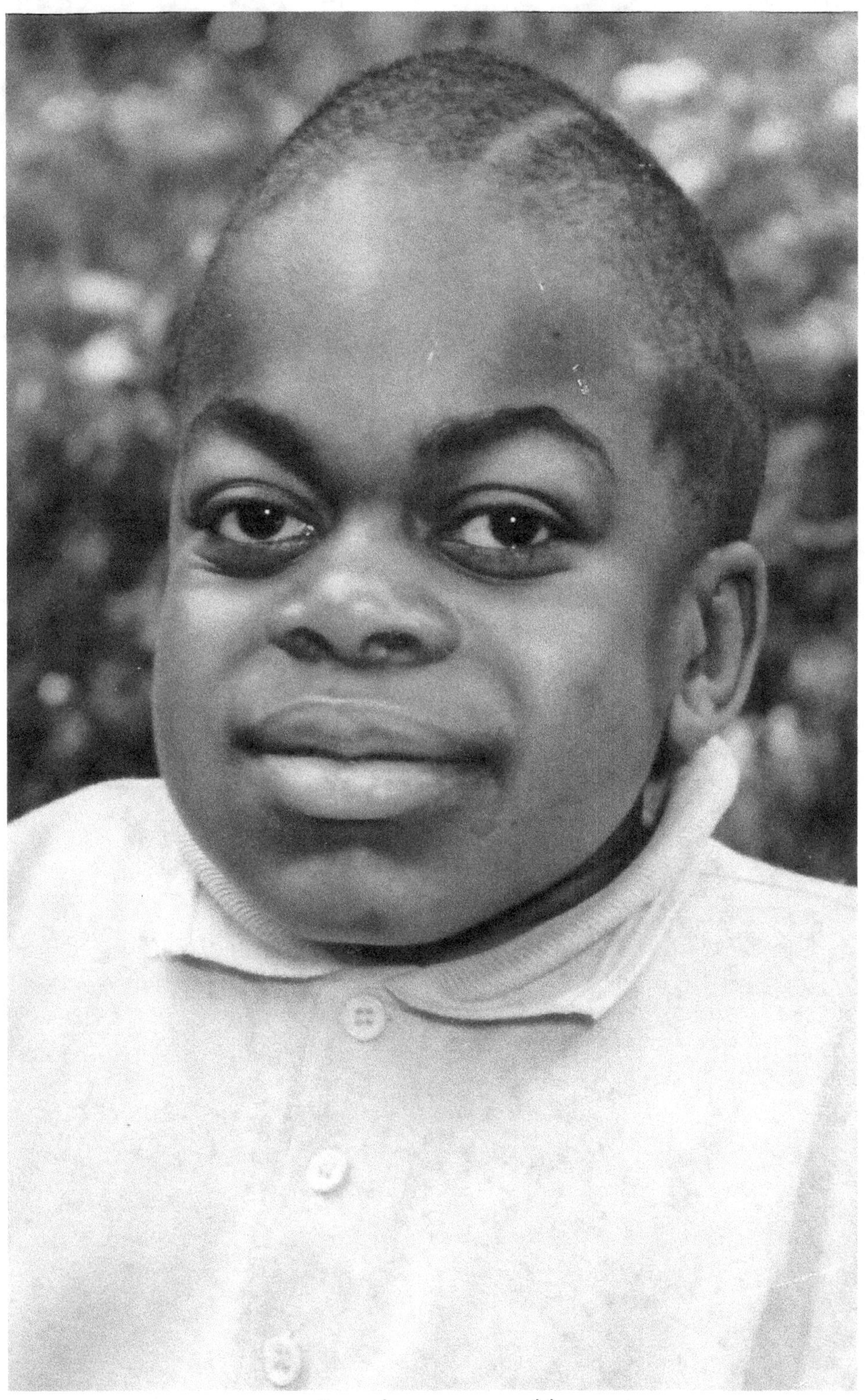

Bwembya 15 years old

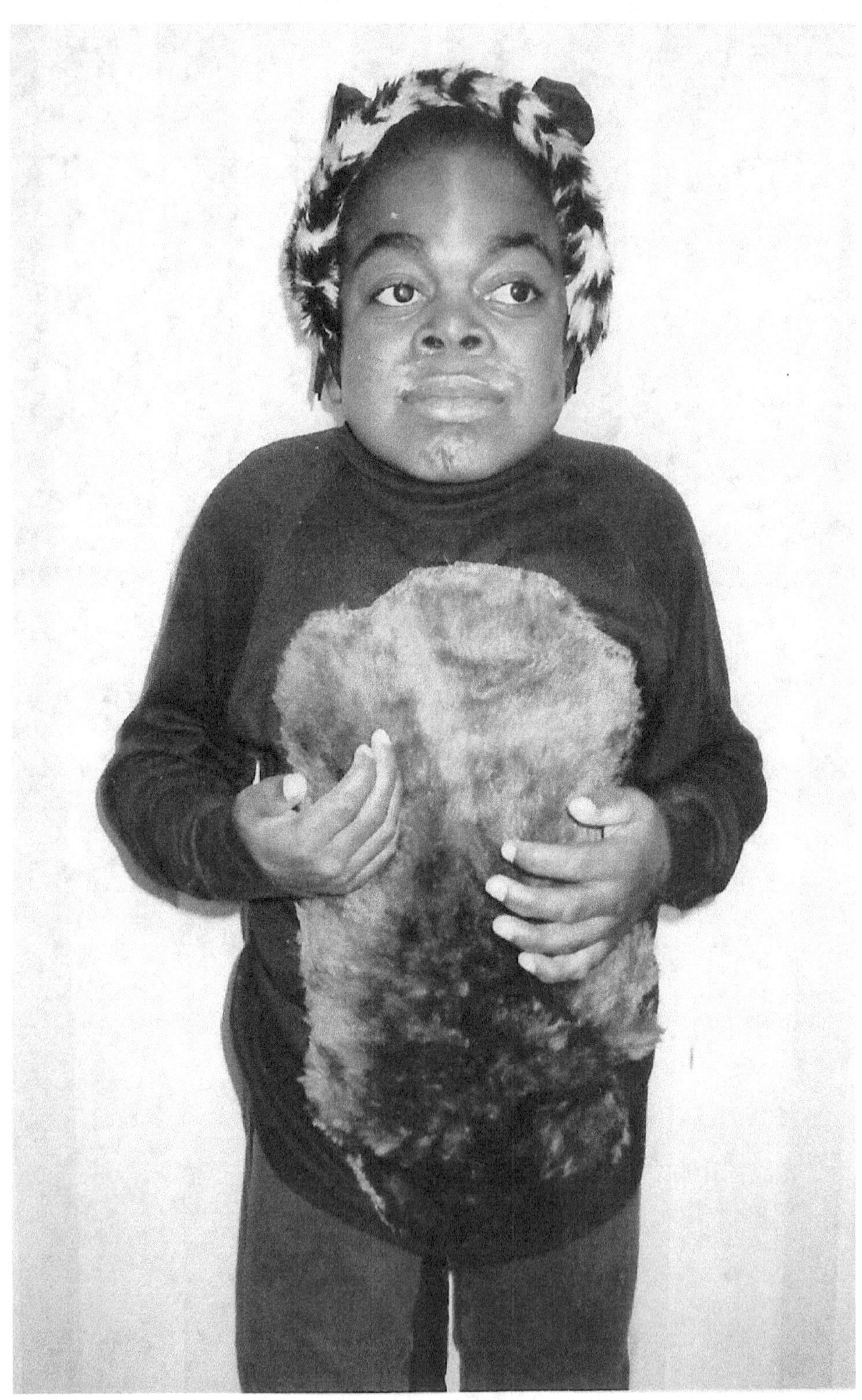

Bwembya in the CATS musical

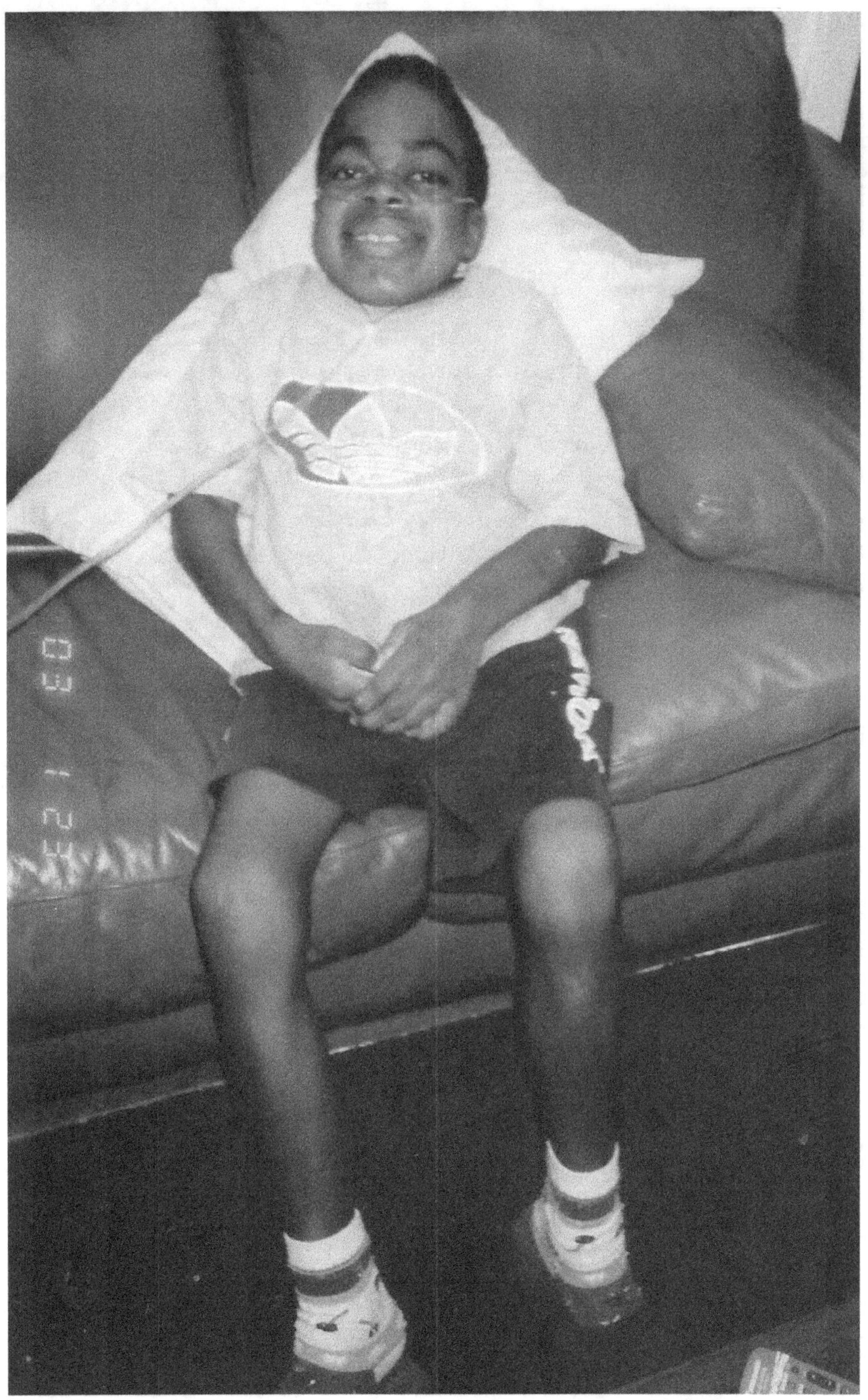

Last picture taken of Bwembya at Bear Cottage January 2003

Patricia 2020

$$\diamond$$

Acknowledgements

I would like to thank my family and friends for believing me when I said I was going to write a book. It only took a little over 20 years.

Thank you to a group of ladies called '11 writers' who have cheered me all the way to the finish line. You encouraged me and had faith in my writing abilities.

A big thank you to Patti Miller who told me not to enroll in her next course but to just go home and write. I went home and finished the book during the COVID 3 month lockdown in 2021.

Thank you to Anthony Reeder for a detailed manuscript appraisal and for his encouragement that this was a book that needed to be published.

Thank you to my friends Peter and Fiona for reading through my drafts. And finally to my friend Yolanda for advise and direction regarding the book cover.